TAKEN

Jennifer Dawson

Praise for Jennifer Dawson & The Undone Series

USA TODAY calls *Crave* a must-read romance

"*Crave* gets the balance between lust filled scenes and a meaningful plot just right. Neither takes from the other and together they just add up to a very satisfying and emotional read." —Between My Lines

"If you love Foster, Kaye and Dawson's *Something New* series you'll love *Crave* and the Undone series." —Caffeinated Book Reviewer.

"Every character in this book (*Sinful*) is amazingly written. " — Bookish Bevil

"You know why I love this author? She takes something absolutely mundane like a "Best Friend's Sister" romance and turns it into a masterpiece." —For the Love of Fictional Worlds

"*Crave* by Jennifer Dawson is a darkly erotic and deeply moving romance."-—Romance Novel News

"Jennifer Dawson's *Sinful* has amazing scenes that get my heart beating and calls for a cold shower, but the love story that is evolving between Leo and Jillian is amazing."—Courting Fiction

Step into *Taken*
An Undone Novel

Brandon Townsend III

Rich, beautiful and entitled, once upon a time he was king of the trust fund babies. He took anything and anyone he wanted, until one day, he walked away without explanation. Now, he's an untouchable mystery, one I'm determined to crack. And I'm not talking about anything mundane like his bed. No, I want something far more valuable.

I want into his head.

Veronica Westwood has blown into my life creating chaos in her wake, and I don't know quite what to do with her. Rich, beautiful and entitled, she represents everything I've sworn off in life, and her being unexpectedly clever doesn't change that. Instincts warn me to stay away, and that's just what I intend to do, no matter her attempts to wear me down. I'm good at saying no, or at least I was until I met her. I don't understand it, but she's like a weakness, and a man like me can't have weakness.

I simply won't allow it.

Want more books? I've got something for everyone.

Something New Series

Small town, contemporary romance with a big city twist.

Take a Chance on Me
The Winner Takes it All
The Name of the Game
As Good as New
She's My Kind of Girl
Head Over Heels

Undone Series

Romantic Erotica that's all about the journey.

Crave
Sinful
Unraveled
Debauched

Dedication

To all you Brandon fans out there…

It's been a long time coming, but we're finally here.

I hope it's worth the wait.

Veronica

"You did what?" My mother's voice is a screech. Well, as much of a screech as a woman of her stature can manage. Despite her distress, she's perfectly coifed, with her tasteful makeup, and razor-sharp, keratin-rich blonde bob. She looks exactly how a wife of old Chicago money should look. Except for the carefully contained rage in her brown eyes.

I understand her shock. In my twenty-seven years, the words most likely to describe me are perfect, accommodating, and gracious. I've never rebelled. I've always done exactly what was expected of me. So it's understandable my mother doesn't know how to handle my sudden departure from the plans laid out for me when I was five, my sister was born, and my parents were told they couldn't have any more children. That was the day my dad's dreams for a son ended, and his plans for his oldest daughter began.

I'd never deviated. I've always towed the company line. Until today. I repress an inappropriate laugh that bubbles in my throat. They don't even know the half of it. Don't understand yet that this story only goes downhill from here.

My mother's knuckles turn white on the wine goblet and she gives my father a pleading glance, as though maybe he can save me from my own insanity.

We're at the Palmer House in what is supposed to be a celebratory dinner in my honor. Things are not going according to their plans, but they are going according to mine for the first time in my life.

I keep my shoulders back, and my chin held high. "I didn't accept the job."

My father, Herald Westwood, leans forward, his eyes narrowed. "Veronica, do you know what I had to go through to secure that position for you?"

"I do." I keep my voice steady. I don't want him to think I'm weak in my decision. That I'm regretting it, because I'm not. Yes, I'm a bit in shock, and I've lived this day a state of eerie, hyper calmness I can't quite articulate, but I've never been so certain of anything in my entire life. I clear my throat. "I'm sorry, but accepting the position is no longer an option."

My younger, twenty-two-year-old sister, Lindsey, a gorgeous, stick-thin blonde with the long limbs of a model, rolls her eyes at me and picks up her phone sitting next to her fork.

"Explain yourself, young lady," my mom hisses.

I would, except I don't know what to say. I'm not sure what happened. Or if I understand it myself.

When I woke up this morning it had started like any other day. I'd taken a shower and gotten dressed, carefully cultivating an image of a budding, powerful businesswoman befitting the high-stakes world of venture capitalism. I'd put on a conservative black business suit that hid my curves, and tucked my thick, long blonde hair into a neat bun, applied a neutral makeup palette, and left my condo to start my mapped-out future.

Despite my father's connections, I had gone through five rounds of grueling interviews and aced them all. I'd been prepared to take the position as a junior partner in the firm my father deemed good enough for his oldest, and most accomplished, daughter. A high-finance job making rich people even richer and utilized my Harvard MBA.

A job befitting of the Westwood name.

I'd done exactly what they expected of me. Exactly what I'd been working for all these years. Exactly what I'd been groomed for. I'd never had one misstep.

My father had to settle for me and I'd made sure never to disappoint him. My entire life I'd focused on being better than everything he'd ever envisioned for a son. Since I'd turned out to be a disaster at sports, that left academic achievement, and I'd excelled.

Until this afternoon.

I'd sat down to sign the contract that would indenture me to the top venture capital firm in Chicago. A position so coveted they'd received a thousand resumes, and the top candidates were so prestigious, they'd interviewed fifteen people the first round. When they called to offer the position I'd experienced a rush of elation. The thrill of beating out my competition, of being granted the seal of approval that I was the best of the best. I'd walked into that room a woman on a mission; ready to prove they had not made a mistake in selecting me.

I picked up the pen, put it right on the dotted line, and I couldn't sign.

In that single moment, sitting there in that boardroom with all its rich mahogany wood and carved moldings, my whole life passed before my very eyes.

I'd work eighty hours a week.

Marry the boy my parents picked out for me and had been dating since high school.

I'd say I was going to keep working, but I wouldn't.

I'd get pregnant and have my requisite three kids.

We'd vacation in Europe.

I'd play tennis at the club.

Lunch with the girls before our afternoon Pilates class.

My husband would have a mistress and screw high-priced escorts.

I'd ignore his indiscretions because I really wouldn't care at that point.

My kids would be entitled little brats who had no perception outside of the world where we belonged.

Eventually, I'd be sixty, my face still smooth and carved by the grace of plastic surgeons and Botox, and all I'd care about was looking perfect for the galas of charities I don't really give a shit about but will put me in the society pages as Chicago royalty.

I could see it all perfectly mapped out and wanted none of it.

For the first time, I'd felt the full weight of my poor, little rich-girl existence. How isolating it was, how lonely and shallow. How it sucks out your soul and leaves you devoid of emotion. Even at twenty-seven, I could see the beginnings of our lifestyle creeping through the women I called friends. Girls I'd known since prep school preschool.

Yes, I live in privilege. I'm lucky. There are people starving who'd kill to be me, but what most people don't understand is this world comes with its own type of prison.

And sitting there at that massive boardroom table, all I wanted was to break out of the cage.

My mom, Betsy, her features honed by the expert surgeon she has on call, shakes her head. Her hair doesn't move. She's very lovely, and she's fond of telling everyone we meet that we pass for sisters. As I study her, I wonder when she last yearned for anything. The last time she burned with passion for something beyond smooth skin and people thinking she's in her twenties.

She frowns at me. "That's it? That's all you have to say?"

Have I ever burned with passion? Would I recognize it if I did?

I leave the esoteric questions behind and steel my spine, preparing myself.

The worst is yet to come.

Despite this display of outrage, my parents don't really care about the job. It's only true function being an accomplishment they can brag about to their friends. I'm only expected to make something of myself until I marry. Once I'm a wife, there's a whole other set of expectations for me, but working is not one of them. My career is merely a check on an endless list. I'd justified this by telling myself I'd be so good, so successful, I'd prove to them I'd be wasted as just a wife.

But today in that boardroom, I'd seen it as a lie.

So I'd apologized to the men sitting around the table, tore up my offer letter, and strolled out of the room as though I didn't have a care in the world. They wouldn't miss me. Someone had probably already called the number-two candidate.

Heart pounding, I'd started walking the streets of downtown Chicago, believing I had no destination until I stood in front of a building and known what I had to do.

Now it was time to drop the next bombshell. I look my mom in the eye. "No, there's something else."

Her knuckles whiten again.

Something in my tone must have caught Lindsey's interest because she looks up from her phone. At twenty-two, she fancies herself a reality star and *everything* bores her except the adoration of her fans. In fairness, she does have a YouTube channel with a million subscribers where she tells people how to curl their hair, do their makeup, and give fashion tips. She's everything you hate about starlets, coltishly gorgeous, vapid, uninterested, and her phone is glued to her hand at all times. My guess is she's waiting for a call from the Kardashians so she can blow out of this hellhole and head to LA where she believes she belongs.

All three of them look at me. Lindsey's expression is placating, but my parents' faces are pinched with stress.

There's only one way to do this, so I take a deep breath and give them the worst of the news. "I broke up with Winston this afternoon."

My sister rolls her eyes and goes back to her texts.

My mom appears as though she might faint.

My dad's face turns beet red.

God, I hope he doesn't have a stroke.

While I wish my father no ill will, I don't respond to his tomato-like pallor. I can't show weakness in my decision. They have to understand this is final.

I have no idea what I'm doing, why I'm doing this, or what's happened to me today to take such drastic measures, but there's no going back now.

From this day on, I'm taking control of my life. I'm going to do things my way. I refuse to turn into someone I hate.

"You did what?" My father's voice is the low tone that used to frighten me when I was a child.

I hated to incur his disapproval.

I keep my own voice strong and resolute. "I broke off my relationship with Winston."

My mom presses her fingers to her lips that now tremble as though she might cry. She won't. It would ruin her makeup. But she can pretend to be close to tears for the sake of dramatics.

"Why?" My dad picks up his glass of brandy and drains the entire glass in one gulp.

I tell him the truth, even though he won't understand. "I don't love him."

"Veronica." My father signals the waiter for another drink. "We are in the middle of a merger with his family's company. What were you thinking?"

I was thinking I didn't love him. A reason good enough for most parents, but one lost on mine. See, in my world, nobody really ever loves anyone. They love what that person can do for them, how they affect their standing in our social set, but real love and attachment is usually not part of the equation.

And Winston Bishop is the man I'm expected to be with. We come from similar families and companies that benefit each other. He has been picked out for me since birth. Oh, sure, they don't call it an arranged marriage anymore, but the expectation was clear. Growing up, I wanted two things out of life—to excel at everything I did and to be approved of. So, of course, at sixteen when Winston finally asked me out, as was expected of him, I didn't think of saying no.

He was my destiny.

Except, I don't actually like him.

He's jealous, overprotective, and shushes me. He wants me for his perfect wife. He doesn't care who I am as a person. He doesn't care about what I want. My dreams. My desires. All he cares about is that I come from the right family, I look good on his arm, and I'm above reproach.

"Veronica," my mother hisses.

My parents are staring at me, waiting for an explanation, but the truth is, no reason I give will ever be good enough. I could admit to them a week ago I walked in on him fucking another girl, but they'd tell me that's to be expected. Boys will be boys and all that. It's unreasonable of me to expect fidelity when we're not engaged.

I could tell them, at least to provide some sort of excuse, but honestly, I hadn't cared much. Maybe that night—when I stood there impassive as he screwed her from behind, against the big glass windows in his apartment and felt nothing but relief I wouldn't have to have sex with him—had been the catalyst.

It doesn't matter, and with no excuse they'd swallow, I deliver my next bombshell. "I'm moving out of the condo."

My mom's eye starts to twitch and she presses a perfectly manicured fingertip to the muscle jumping under the tightly pulled skin.

My sister perks up. "I'll take it."

I give her a droll look. "You can't afford it."

She sticks out her tongue at me. "Can so."

I ignore her. We don't get our trust funds until we're twenty-five, so for now she's dependent on my parents and her YouTube money. Certainly not enough to pay the taxes and live in the luxury to which she's accustom. Although maybe our parents will give it to her anyway. Not that it matters much to me. She can have it.

My mom's brow furrows. "That was a gift for your graduation. Why on earth would you leave it?"

I don't bother answering; they'd be appalled by my explanation. "You can have it back if you want. Give it to Lindsey, or sell it, it's up to you." I wave a hand. "I just don't want it."

Lindsey holds her hands together in prayer. "Oh my god, Daddy, can I please have it? Please, please, please?"

"Not the time," he says, his voice filled with anger.

My mom doesn't even break stride. "And why not? Do you know how many people would kill for that place?"

"I do." It's a massive, four thousand square foot condo in the Gold Coast. I absolutely get what I'm giving up. Fifty-year-old neighbors, two-thousand-dollar-a-month assessment fees, yappy designer dogs, and a state-of-the-art gym.

In return, I'm gaining my freedom. Declaring my independence.

"And?" Her voice raises an octave.

"Veronica, are you on drugs?" My father's face is getting red again.

My mom pats him on the arm. "Herald, your blood pressure."

"I'm not on drugs." I keep my voice completely calm. It's not an act; *I am calm.* I'm blowing up my entire life, and I've never felt so at peace. "I just need something...*different.*"

My sister shakes her head. "Oh my god, you're twenty-seven. Aren't you, like, too young for a crisis?"

"It's not a crisis." I don't care that they don't understand. Not caring about their approval, it's liberating. I want to stand up and scream, *I'm free,* but I'm pretty sure that will raise more suspicions about drug use, so I stay completely composed and reasonable instead.

The waiter brings another drink to the table and my dad takes a large gulp. "You know, I'm still the executor of your trust fund. If I have reason to believe you're mentally incompetent, or a danger to yourself, I can have it frozen."

It's a threat, that's all. He won't go through with it because

8

it will look bad and he'd have to take me to court. The publicity alone would be a nightmare. Besides, he'll lose. There's nothing wrong with me. I'm completely sane.

Saner than I've ever been in my entire life.

I give him a steady look. "Go ahead."

"Are you daring me, young lady?"

"Yes, I am." I don't bother to tell them that once I get a job I'm not going to touch my trust fund. At least until I figure out how to live on my own like regular people, living a regular life.

"Veronica." My mom is staring at me as though she's never seen me before. "What has gotten into you?"

I shrug my shoulder. "I don't know."

All I know is I want to find out what it's like to live a real life. I want to know what it's like to laugh, to have genuine friends, to work, and cry and struggle and strive. I need to understand who I am and what I'm about. I'm not going to live my life as a pawn in a chess game other people have already played out.

I want to be someone different.

Yeah, this is the very definition of first-world problems. And you know what? I don't care. Go ahead and judge me.

It's my problem and I'm not going to sit around whining about it. I'm going to fix it.

Just as soon as I figure out how.

2.

Veronica

"It's him. He's here," Bitsy Stanton says in a mock stage whisper.

I look over my shoulder, taking in the man in question. The man I've been waiting for since I got here two hours ago. My reason for being here tonight, and why I'm willingly subjecting myself to gossip, the topic of discussion behind raised hands. The current theory is I'm on drugs or suffering a nervous breakdown.

I'd love to know what explanation my parents supplied, but they're not speaking to me. Tonight, other than a polite hello they've given me the cold shoulder, as my father is well aware of its past effect on me. I suspect he's growing impatient because I haven't begged for forgiveness yet.

Something I have no intention of doing and he'll figure out sooner or later.

I'm committed. Every day since the day I blew up my life

I've only grown more certain I did the right thing.

I do miss my mom though, and I think she misses me too. Shortly after my bombshell she took me to lunch at her club and tried to talk some sense into me, but when that didn't work, she followed my father's lead.

Tonight I caught her worried expression when she looked at me over her shoulder as my dad dragged her away. For a moment I hoped she'd break away from his viselike grip on her arm and come back to talk with me, but he yanked her to a group of colleagues and that hope had been quickly dashed.

Only Bitsy, my oldest acquaintance and the closest thing I have to a real friend, hasn't shunned me. Up until the man I'd been waiting for showed up, she'd been trying to talk some sense into me. Probing me for information about why I left Winston, telling me if I don't take him back someone else will snap him up. When I'd stated the vultures were welcome to him, she'd looked at me as though I'd grown a second head.

But none of that matters—my parents, the whispered gossip, the darted glances—I don't care about any of it. Because my only reason for being here tonight stands in the doorway.

Brandon Townsend III.

Handsome and untouchable, he's one of Chicago's most illustrious and mysterious playboys. He's tall, probably six-three, lean and lanky, with broad shoulders and a tapered waist that looks custom designed to wear a suit. In our circle, Brandon is legendary. Not only is he the sole heir to one of Chicago's oldest and wealthiest fortunes, he's drop-dead gorgeous, incredibly smart, and everything he touches turns to gold. For the past ten years he's been quietly building a small empire that spans from real estate to upscale nightclubs. If that wasn't enticing enough, he wants nothing to do with our social set.

An extra challenge to people entirely too bored.

That wasn't always the case, once he was the king of our generation, but about ten years ago, something happened and he went into hiding. There were rumors, of course—ranging from mild to the extreme—but no one knew for certain the events that unfolded or where he'd gone. After a year, he'd emerged a new man, with a new business, and no inclination to reclaim his king of the trust fund babies' status. Other than occasionally making an appearance at a charity function, he doesn't associate with any of Chicago's high society.

The mystery and notoriety around him has only grown, and the room takes on a certain kind of buzz whenever he shows up. Tonight's no exception.

From across the room, a beautiful blonde bats her lashes at him and he flashes her a dimpled smile. I'm surprised she doesn't faint right at his feet, or at least drop to her knees. Combined with that dirty-blond hair, cut a touch too long, those intense blue eyes, and killer bone structure I can practically hear panties dropping throughout the ballroom.

Feigning surprise, I say in an absent tone, "I wonder what he's doing here?"

Of course, I'd known he'd be here. He's the only reason I'd come. My plan is risky, and most likely won't work, but I'm going to give it my best shot. He's step one on my path to transforming my life. My first chance to strive.

I haven't made a plan B, and don't intend to unless absolutely necessary. I'm a Westwood. We don't take no for an answer.

I have to try. We have enough in common to make it plausible. At least in my mind we do.

Like me, his family is old money. Also like me, he has a considerable trust fund.

Unlike me, he's managed to break free from the world we grew up in and become his own man, successful, independent of circumstances.

That makes him the most fascinating man in the room.

Bitsy grasps my arm and lets out an excited little gasp. "Oh my god, he is *so* gorgeous."

It's the truth. He might be the most beautiful man I've ever seen. But that doesn't matter to me. Who he is, what he's done, is what I'm interested in.

Other than a greeting of acknowledgment in passing when we're with our parents, I have never talked to him.

That's about to change.

"I wonder what's the occasion." I keep my voice neutral, as though I don't really care, because the last thing I want to do is alert Bitsy to my interest. Bitsy is a talker, and if she catches wind I'm up to something, stories will be circulating through the room and into Brandon's ear before I can make my move.

I want to be a surprise attack.

It's funny; once you start paying attention, information comes to you in the most interesting places. I'd had no idea what to do when I'd turned down the partner job. I'd had no thought but escape. I had options, I mean I have a Harvard MBA, but I wanted something unique. I'd spent hours scouring the Internet to no avail, nothing ever striking me as quite right. Then forty-eight hours later, while I had lunch at the club with my mother where she'd spent the entire time attempting to talk me out of my breakup with Winston, I'd overheard Brandon's name at the bar.

The rumor was he was hunting for a general manager to help him run his business.

Excitement had vibrated through me as the hair on the back of my neck prickled, and I'd known, somehow, someway, I needed to interview for the job.

Nobody really knows much about Brandon or his business. Well, of course they all know who his family is, that he's very connected, and he's successful despite his inherited wealth. The word is anything he decides to invest in turns a profit. So while the men in our circle are wary, they flock to him because he's old money that's somehow managed to adapt and make new money.

Greed and capitalism never go out of style.

And then there are the women.

Unlike the rest of us, who almost exclusively date each other, Brandon Townsend hasn't touched a member of our social group in ages, so details about him are scarce. Of course, there are some rather interesting rumors about him. Namely that he has unusual sexual appetites, but I have no idea if any of those are true, and I'm not sure it matters. Powerful, elusive men of mystery are like shark chum to a group of females that rarely hear the word no. He could be a complete disaster in bed and women would still want him. As a result, every event he shows up at is followed by sacred vows by females that they will be the one he'll fall for.

I mean, we all fancy ourselves Cinderella, don't we?

However, I have no such illusions. No notions he'll fall for me. Or take me to bed and rock my world. My only hope is having no designs on his body will provide me with an advantage when it comes to his company.

Because he has to hire me. I don't know why I'm so certain of this, but I am. Ever since I'd heard about the job, the same instincts that wouldn't let me sign that contract, and forced me to break up with Winston, have pushed me toward him.

I haven't figured out how I plan to get him to interview me, when I'm part of the group of people he seems to despise, but I'll wing it. In business school, and at each of my corporate internships, people always commented on my instincts, my knack for knowing where to look, the right execution, and exactly what to say, when. I didn't beat out all those other candidates by luck, or because of my father. He may have gotten me in the door, but I'd annihilated my competition all on my own.

If I follow my gut, I'll know what to do when I'm in front of Brandon.

Across the room, he shakes hands with his father, and the two of them turn and offer polished smiles for a photographer before he kisses his mother on the cheek.

I tilt my head, studying him.

I wonder how long it took before his father spoke to him again?

Mine shows no sign of letting up.

"How do I look?" Bitsy lets out a little squeal of delight and fluffs her hair. She's a pretty brunette with waist-length hair extensions, full lips, and a gorgeous, gym-toned body highlighted to perfection in a tight, floor-length black gown.

She's supposed to be my best friend.

But I honestly don't feel like I know her. And she certainly doesn't know me. We've done everything together since kindergarten. I know her favorite color, her preferred brand of makeup, how many calories she's consumed that day, and her favorite designers—but I don't know her deepest fears.

Or if she even has fears. If she did, she'd never tell me, just like I'd never tell her mine. I'm not willing to reveal that much. Not to people in this crowd who are always looking for the upper hand as we jockey for position in our small, sheltered world.

"You look fantastic," I assure her, before smiling softly and touching her arm. "But you know that's a foolish dream."

Her dark eyes are hungry on Brandon and she's got a determined set to her jaw that tells me she's going to go after him with a vengeance.

She waves a hand in his direction. "He doesn't have a date tonight."

"True." He usually has a beautiful redhead hanging off his arm. I've noticed he has a preference for redheads.

I sip Champagne as I smooth my blonde hair, contained in a sleek bun at the base of my neck. It is lucky he's unattached tonight. One less person I have to contend with. One less person standing in my way.

"What's the sluttiest act I can offer? Something out of the ordinary to catch his attention?" Bitsy's gaze is still locked on her target.

I don't answer. I'd be willing to bet Brandon Townsend III has been offered every sexual favor known to man.

"What about anal? Do you think that would work?" Her tone is thoughtful as she muses.

"Maybe," I offer, noncommittal. She doesn't have a shot in hell, but I'm not about to tell her that.

She has her plans. With my own plots to hatch, I can't worry about hers.

It wasn't luck that brought us to the same event. Instead, I like to believe it was serendipity. A sign from the gods that I'm on the right path.

After overhearing about him at the club, I'd had a vague recollection of seeing his name on the guest list my mother had sent me when she'd asked me to do a mail merge for her. After all, how else would I use my two hundred grand Harvard education? I'd checked the Excel spreadsheet from my phone at the club and there he sat, like a beacon of hope.

I'm convinced he's my fate.

Now all I have to do is convince him to hire me.

Once you figure out what a person wants, convincing them isn't that hard. But the question is, how do I figure out what *he* wants? A man that's intent on keeping his private life, private.

A man, whom, by all appearances, wants for nothing.

"Are you even listening?"

I jerk my attention away from the sight of him. "I'm sorry?"

She leans forward and her gaze darts around the room. "I've heard stories, you know, about him."

"What stories?" I doubt whatever rumors she's heard will help me, but it never hurts to listen. I drain my glass and watch as he moves around the room, greeting people like he was born to do it.

Which, in fairness, he was.

Her voice lowers even farther. "I've heard he expects girls to do anything for him. That he doesn't take no for an answer."

I laugh. "That's ridiculous. Where would you even hear that?"

"He dated Sharon Manning in high school. She said he was demanding and insatiable. That she couldn't say no, but that it didn't matter because he was so good."

I roll my eyes. "They were in high school."

"But still." Bitsy shrugs. "Even if it's not true, what man can resist a girl that will let them do anything?"

Brandon Townsend III, that's who. I'm not sure why I'm so sure about this, but I am. I'd attempt to dissuade Bitsy from her pointless endeavor, but she won't listen. Plus, if I show too much interest, she'll latch onto him even harder, and I need him unattached. So I encourage her instead. "What do you have to lose?"

"Nothing." Bitsy squares her shoulders. "I'm going to talk to him."

So am I, but I'll keep that to myself. I smile. "Good luck."

"I'll let you know." She pushes her hair back and slinks off toward the man in question.

I lean against the wall and watch. Hoping it will give me some clue as to how to talk him into an interview. My resume is quite impressive, but that doesn't seem like it will be enough. My only real choice is to bide my time.

From across the ballroom Bitsy sidles up to Brandon and beams at him while holding out her hand. He takes it, kisses it, and smiles at her. He's very charming. I've heard he rejects you so smoothly you leave feeling almost flattered.

I'm so intent on Brandon I don't notice my now ex-boyfriend until he's standing right in front of me.

I blink him into focus and straighten. "Winston."

"Veronica." His eyes skim down my body. I wore a white, strapless satin dress tonight with a black sash tied tight around my waist. It's a black-and-white ball.

I nod. "How are you?"

"How do you think I am?" His face flashes with that ugly temper he tries so hard to control but can't quite mask.

I lower my gaze and attempt to look contrite. Sometimes it's best just to take a knee and I have no problem with that if it gets him away from me. "I'm sorry."

"I thought you weren't coming?" His voice is mean, accusatory. Like I've done something wrong.

"I changed my mind." My gaze skirts to my purpose. Brandon is untangling his arm from Bitsy and skirting around her. A couple starts toward him, but he smiles, waves and detours out of the main hall. My heart gives a hard thump and I know it's time to make my move. I nod at Winston. "If you'll excuse me."

He grabs my arm. "We need to talk."

"There's nothing to say." I attempt to shake my arm loose, but he won't release me. "Let me go, Winston."

"She meant nothing to me." His expression shakes with a rage that sends tendrils of fear through me as his fingers tighten on my arm, digging into my skin. "Just let me explain."

Of course he thinks it's about her, when she has nothing to do with it. Yes, I threw the proper fit when I found him screwing the girl up against the glass windows in his bedroom, but I hadn't really felt anything. I can't explain this to him though. He won't understand and when he gets like this he's...unpredictable. All I want is to get away from him, but I have to hold my ground. "Winston, please, there's nothing to explain. It's over."

He doesn't let go as he breathes out a hard, angry puff of air. His hot, gin breath makes my skin coil.

I jerk away, but he's immovable. I give him my most menacing glare and say sharply, "Let go of my arm, or so help me god I will tell every person here you fucked that girl instead of taking the blame like I'm currently doing."

That gets his attention and he drops my arm. The mention of appearances always catches his attention. He straightens and his features twist into that perfect, good-guy mask. "Veronica, if we could sit down and talk, I'm positive we can work this out."

I meet his gaze. "You don't get it, it has nothing to do with her. I don't love you, Winston."

"So?" He shakes his head like I'm too silly for words. "What's love got to do with it? In fact, I think our marriage will work better not loving each other. We can be true partners that way."

Out the corner of my eye I spot Brandon heading down the east hall of the old Chicago historic mansion that's rented out for parties, past the velvet ropes that are supposed to keep us out. I have to follow him. I grit my teeth. "I don't want to be your partner. I don't want to be your anything. Now if you'll excuse me."

Again, rage flashes in the depths of his brown eyes. "This

isn't over, Veronica."

"Yes, it is." I skirt around Winston, holding my breath, and praying he won't follow.

Luckily, he doesn't, and I'm free to chase after Brandon. Maybe it's irrational but he feels like the key that will lead me to the mysterious thing I'm searching for but can't name. And I have no intention of taking no for an answer.

Brandon

"I'll do anything you want, and I do mean anything." A blonde whose name I don't even know, whispers to me in a breathy voice.

I grit my teeth to hide my irritation.

She's plastered her body against mine, tangling her long, lean arms around my waist as she offers up her sexual arsenal. As tall as she is, she can't weigh more than a hundred and twenty pounds, but she's surprisingly strong.

Her trainer must do a good job with her.

I give her my most charming smile, flashing dimples I know drive women crazy, and chuck her gently under the chin. "Now, sweetheart, I know you don't mean that."

"But I do." She beams up at me, her lips overfilled and look hard to the touch, although I'm sure she thinks it's sexy. "I'm double jointed."

Good god, I fucking hate these things. She's the third one tonight, and I've only been here thirty minutes.

I laugh, winking down at her. "I'm sure your yoga teacher is very impressed with you."

She licks her lips, batting lashes so thick I can barely see the blue of her eyes. "Let me impress you."

"That's a lovely offer, darling, but I'm afraid I have to pass." I reach behind and begin the process of untangling her limbs off me.

She rises to her tiptoes to whisper in my ear. "One blowjob, that's all I ask. Let me suck your cock, and if I don't rock your world, I'll never bother you again."

Maybe to most men this would be an offer they couldn't refuse, but I'm not one of those men. I can get a killer blowjob anytime I want, day or night, with one phone call. Not even her easy access persuades me for a second. I do not fuck around with Chicago society women. Ever. And I'm sure as hell not going to break my rule for this woman, whose words are cool, but eyes are desperate.

I touch her cheek, softly. I'm always a gentleman when I reject them. I don't see the point in being cruel about it. In my experience, cruelty just makes them try harder. I chuckle. "That's quite tempting, but I have to pass." I tilt my head. "I have people waiting for me."

She puffs out her bottom lip in a playful pout.

I pat her ass and wink. "Be a good girl and run along."

"Are you sure?" She boldly meets my gaze.

"Sorry, it can't be helped." I jerk my thumb over my shoulder. "Go back to the party and cause a proper riot in that dress."

That perks her up and she nods. "If you change your mind…"

"You'll be the first to know." I watch as she takes her leave, not moving until she's out of my sight to ensure she doesn't get any more ideas and follow me.

When she's gone, I sigh, long and weary.

If I had my choice I'd never see any of these people again, but it's the least I can do for the people who raised me. As part of my truce with my parents, to appease them for the disappointment of their only child, I agree to do one of these events once a quarter.

It makes them happy to pretend to be the perfect family every once in a while. I don't mind much, I even understand it. There was a time I fought hard to stay in this world, that it seemed important to me, but that was a long time ago.

It's not ideal but the contacts never hurt. I'm good at

making money and occasionally someone brings me a deal that's interesting enough for me to take notice. Not often, but it happens.

Now that I'm alone again, I slip down the hallway, past the roped-off part of the house that's closed for renovations and not part of the main event, looking for some air. I open various doors until I find a private balcony and duck out into the Chicago night.

The weather is mild with a soft breeze, a perfect night. I glance at my watch. I'd promised my mother three hours.

My head already hurts.

I'd much rather be off with my real friends, who are all out having dinner together, but I committed and now I'm stuck. I plan on meeting them later and forgetting this life until I'm required to show up again.

For the sake of my parents' wishes I try and play the part, but I won't pretend I don't scorn my peers, and this sheltered world I grew up in. I find them shallow, exhausting and trite. They are completely out of touch with the real world. I used to be just like them. A superficial, entitled, out-of-control brat who would crush anyone that stood in my way.

The best life decision I ever made was walking away. And while I might have more money than I know what to do with, I've made it a point to surround myself with actual people instead of shells.

I'm not sure why I tolerate these things for my parents. Maybe it's because they are the only family I have. I don't need them, but they aren't bad enough to disown either.

Over the years we'd developed an understanding. I go to dinner with them once a month, attend these events every so often, and keep up appearances. In return, they leave me alone and let me live my life without interference.

It's a fair trade.

I sigh. I'll allow myself ten more minutes of peace and then go back in to do my duty.

There's a click and I glance around to see the doors open.

Veronica Westwood, the oldest daughter of the Michigan

Avenue Westwoods, stands in the threshold. The moonlight splashes over her, casting her in an ethereal glow that only enhances her pale beauty. Dressed in a strapless white dress with a black sash, she's long, lean and looks custom designed to stand bookended by elaborate French doors on a stone balcony at night.

I sigh. Not this again. I need a break before the next one. It's exhausting fending off rich-girl advances with a charming smile.

I take in Veronica while she pauses in the doorway, I'm sure for dramatic effect. I might not know her personally, but I know who she is. Old money is a small world, growing smaller by the day as tech geniuses, start-up millionaires and real estate moguls walk around in their ripped jeans and *Star Wars* T-shirts.

Since she's been away at business school, I haven't seen her for a while but she's grown into her long limbs and angular bone structure. She's a stunning woman, but I don't want to talk to her. Don't want to hear whatever she believes she can offer me.

While I appreciate her beauty, I prefer submissive redheads that have nothing to do with the world I grew up in. The day I walked away from this life, I'd crawled out of bed filled with four society girls and a coke hangover, I'd promised myself I'd never again touch one of them.

I hadn't broken my promise and haven't regretted it a day since.

Unfortunately, I also promised my mother I'd be polite so I put on the pleasant expression I reserve for the women at these events. "Veronica, how lovely to see you."

She laughs and flashes me a brilliant smile. "You know, I almost believe that. You're a good actor."

Well, now, this is an interesting surprise. I raise a brow. Most of the girls desperate to get my attention in this crowd aren't so astute. "Apparently not good enough."

"Rest assured, I doubt most people here will notice." She tilts her head and bats her lashes oh so subtly. It's demure, barely perceptible, but it raises the hairs on the back of my neck.

I make it a habit to study people, their motives and desires, the hidden meaning in their words, and I'm very good at it. It's an undervalued and underused skill in both business and in women, a skill I've honed to perfection.

Not only does Veronica Westwood want something, she believes she can outsmart me to get it. She's followed me, sought me out, and now is distinguishing herself from the rest, all while attempting to charm me. Only she can't quite hide the cunning in her expression.

I slide my hand into the pocket of my tux. "Except you?"

"Yes." Her gaze is steady as she smooths a hand over the curve of her hip. "But that's because I believe we have something in common."

"I highly doubt that." My voice is dry and unimpressed.

Veronica knows nothing about me, other than rumors she's heard. She's a few years younger than me, so we didn't go to school together, or belong to the same crowd when I was one of them. All she knows is speculation, which has more to do with them than me.

"You never know, I might surprise you." She walks over to the rail, made of thick stone as was the custom back in the early nineteen hundreds. She looks out to the lakefront and the boats swaying in their docks. She clasps her long fingers and blows out a breath. "I've surprised a lot of people lately."

I experience an unexpected flare of intrigue. Her approach is different from most of the women in this set, who tend to be overt and cloying, telegraphing their intention to bed me from a mile away even when they aren't outright offering. I find myself wondering what Veronica Westwood might define as surprising. "And how have you managed that?"

The wind blows but her hair is pulled back so tight against her head nothing sways in the breeze. By the thickness of the bun resting at the nape of her neck, I'd say that's a real shame. I wonder what her hair looks like down and unrestrained.

She tilts her head. "Do you care?"

I meet her eyes, which I now see are honey brown. They are a pretty, unusual golden color, but that's not what catches my interest. No, it's something else. Something I don't normally see at these events—life. I find myself dropping the feigned politeness. I shrug. "Not particularly."

She smiles. "Bluntness is a rare trait at these parties."

I turn to face her more fully, ready to dismiss her, because there's something about her that's vaguely unsettling, but then my attention snags on her mouth. She doesn't appear to be wearing lipstick, but her lips are full, tinted pink, as though she's been eating raspberries. Instead of sending her away, I say, "Bluntness is easy when you don't care about people's opinion of you."

"There's no stakes. No risk." She rubs a hand over her shoulder and her lashes lift, fluttering slightly. "What's it like to have nothing to lose?"

The question takes me aback. *She* takes me aback. It's such an uncommon occurrence my intrigue grows. Veronica is not an ordinary society girl. I narrow my gaze. "Why do you think I have nothing to lose?"

Our eyes lock and the air shifts between us.

Her tongue darts between her lips. "Do you?"

My cock stirs, surprising me. "We all have something to lose. The only thing that changes is what we place value on."

"And what does a man like you place value on?" There is heat in her words, but not seduction.

Before I can stop myself, I step closer, she smells delicious, like fresh air and freedom.

She straightens but makes no move to back away.

Tension thickens the space separating us.

"What do you have to lose, Veronica?" My voice is low, designed to wrap itself around her and draw her closer.

"Nothing." Her pupils dilate; she scrapes perfect white teeth over her ripe mouth. "I'm ready to risk it all."

There's an intensity in her, in this conversation, that sparks something inside me I haven't experienced in so long I'd thought it was dead. That it wasn't possible anymore.

Challenge. "That is a dangerous proposition to throw out there, little girl."

Her expression flashes and she leans forward, boldly meeting my gaze. "Maybe I'm a dangerous woman."

All my life I've had strong instincts, especially when it comes to women, and they flare to life now. I shake my head. "No, you're not." I dip lower, closer to her, moving to her ear. She sucks in a breath and it pleases me. "But you want to be."

I straighten, and the air stills. There's nothing but silence and the unmistakable pull of tension and chemistry.

Slowly, she nods. "I do."

"What's stopping you?"

She shakes her head. "Nothing."

I smile. "Then you're already on your way."

She glances up at me, her expression searching. "Why do you come to these things if you hate them?"

I study her face, the patrician bone structure, her big honey eyes and full pink lips. "Why do you?"

"Do you ever answer any question about yourself?"

I'm impressed she's noticed my evasion. "You're a smart girl."

A smile flirts over her lips. "You're still avoiding."

I have no idea why I'm entertaining her, and I intend to put a stop to it. Prepared to send her on her way, I look at her, and instead I find myself saying, "I do it to appease my parents."

"Appease them for what?"

Again I answer, although I have no idea why. "It's a small consolation for not being the son they wished for."

"I was always the daughter my parents wanted." Veronica puts her hand on the stone of the balcony. "Or at least I was until a few weeks ago."

"What happened a few weeks ago?" My apathy is gone now. I do care what she has to say.

She swallows and the fine cords of her delicate neck work. "I blew up my life."

"And how did that feel?"

Our gazes lock and heat flares bright. "Like freedom."

Veronica Westwood is no ordinary woman.

I raise my brow. "Is this why you came looking for me?"

She doesn't look away. "Why do you think I came looking for you?"

"Now who's evading?" I lean into her, and her breath hitches. "You want something from me."

Her hand flutters to her throat. "Do I have to want something?"

My attention drifts to her lips and I'm struck with the sudden desire to take her mouth and kiss her the way I'm certain her significant other, Winston Bishop, has never kissed her. He's a weak man. She probably has no idea what it's like to be with a strong one and I want to give her a taste. The desire is…unexpected. And entirely unwelcome. I nod. "Absolutely."

"I do want something." Her voice is soft and holds the barest hint of a tremble.

"And what do you want?"

She rubs a hand over her shoulder as though she's cold. "I think, maybe we can help each other."

I glance down and see faint bruises on her forearm. I frown. I've inflicted my fair share of bruises on willing women, but I never assume marks are voluntary unless they were from my hands. I brush my finger over soft skin and she gasps a little as something akin to an electric current races between us. "What happened?"

She waves a hand. "It's nothing."

Even though I should back away, I step closer, far too close for casual, and crook my finger under her chin, raising her face to me. "Nothing?"

Her pupils dilate. "Nothing."

"Would you tell me if it was something?"

A tiny shake of her head. "Probably not."

I grasp her jaw and search her face, her expression. The look in her eyes, I can't quite put my finger on it, but it feels familiar.

She licks her lips. "What are you looking for?"

"The truth of you," I answer her directly.

"You could ask me." Her voice is breathless, and lurking under everything I feel the pulse of true chemistry, not merely lust or attraction, but kinship, so foreign I almost don't recognize it. The irony of feeling this tension with Veronica Westwood, of all women, isn't lost on me.

"Words deceive." I lean down so our faces are mere inches apart. "But the body, well, the body never lies."

She takes a stuttering little breath. "What does my body say?"

"You're searching for something." I tilt my head in the direction of the party. "Something you can't find there."

"Yes." Her hand comes up to rest on my forearm.

My fingers tighten. "You think I can give it to you."

"I do." Her lashes flicker but her gaze doesn't waver.

It's best to end this interaction, to quell any notion she might have about me. "I can't. Or more importantly, I won't."

She shakes her head. "I promise it's not what you think."

"No?" I release her and step back. She's getting to me. I want her. Even though she belongs to a class of women I determine off limits. Standing here, all I want is to work her dress up her thighs and slip my hand between her legs. With perfect clarity I can imagine pushing her against the stone wall and thrusting into her. I don't like that she makes me want to disregard all my morals for her. "Then I'll ask you one more time, little Veronica. What do you want?"

She straightens her shoulders. "A job."

I blink. Startled at the words. Surely I hadn't heard her right. "A job?"

She nods, and her fingers twist the delicate silver chain at her neck. "I heard through the grapevine you're looking for a general manager. I want a chance to interview for the job."

So while I'd been standing here, thinking about all the terrible things I could do to make her scream, she's been standing here trying to figure out how to ask me for an interview?

Christ. I must be off my game. I straighten and let all traces of intimacy between us evaporate into thin air. I give her my most polite smile and chuck her under the chin. "Sorry, but that's not an option."

She frowns. "All I want is a chance to interview. Give me the chance to convince you."

Not in a million fucking years. I lie. "Sorry, sweetheart, the position was filled last week."

I give her my best charming grin. "Good luck finding employment."

And before she can say anything, I turn and walk away, without a backward glance in her direction. There is no way in hell I am ever interviewing Veronica Westwood. She's dangerous. In one conversation she'd managed to slip past my guard and she'd done it almost effortlessly.

Women do not slip past my guard. Ever.

I make my way through the hallways and step over the red velvet rope, returning to the main ballroom. I check the time on my watch.

Two more hours to go before I can escape.

After I've fulfilled my obligation, I'll meet my friends and forget about what transpired on the balcony. Or maybe I'll call Stephanie, a submissive, redheaded interior designer I fuck on a semi-regular basis, to meet me. I'll take her home and work off all this strange energy.

I spot Veronica slipping back into the crowd. She cranes her neck, searching the crowd until she finds me. Our gazes lock.

A waiter passes, carrying a tray full of flutes. She picks up a glass of Champagne and raises it to me in a toast. Even from across the room her challenge is clear.

I find myself tightening in anticipation. I smirk before turning away.

Yes, Stephanie is definitely in order this evening. I hope she's prepared for quite a ride.

Veronica ~ Sunday

I won't lie the conversation on the balcony with Brandon had given me pause. It had gone nothing like I'd expected.

He'd been nothing like I expected.

There'd been an intensity in our discussion, a recognition or type of knowing I can't quite explain. Everything about him called to me from the flare of heat in his ice-blue eyes, to the way his voice vibrated in my sternum, to our conversation, which had been oddly intimate and revealing.

I'd left shaken.

I'd left excited.

I'd left more certain than ever I needed to pursue this job.

I'd also left with the startling revelation that I wanted him.

Sure, I'd been prepared to deal with some sort of attraction, because I'm human. He's stunning and compelling. And, yes, he's the most beautiful man I've ever seen.

I'd anticipated something akin to a crush. Like a girl might have on her teacher. That's what I prepared for. What I'd gotten was a desire that reached inside me and squeezed.

I wanted to spread my legs for him and bare my soul.

I wanted to tell him my deepest, darkest secrets.

I wanted to do with him all the things I'd always been too scared to think about.

It was disconcerting. After being with Winston so long, I'd determined chemistry a mythical, fictional fantasy. I'm not sure what to do with being wrong.

So, yes, my reaction gave me pause.

I look down at the piece of paper that contains his private email, cell phone number, and address. Information I'd paid a hacker friend of mine who works in cyber intelligence for the CIA a ridiculous sum of money to obtain.

It might have given me pause, but it won't stop me.

I put my hands on the keyboard and begin to type.

Brandon ~ Sunday

In the end, I didn't call Stephanie. Nor did I meet up with my friends as I'd planned.

I'd meant to, but I hadn't.

Instead, I'd come home to my historic Chicago mansion left to me by my grandparents. Long ago I'd promised my grandmother I'd never sell it, or her favorite pieces, and I'd kept my word. It's old, rambling and decorated like a Victorian boudoir crossed with a modern day bachelor pad. Parts of the house are dark, forgotten and cold, while others are well lived in. It's a house from another time, another world that hasn't quite found its place in this one. I equally love and hate it. I could live somewhere else, but choose this place instead.

It fits me.

Last night, instead of the sex I'd promised myself, I'd come home, holed up in my study and watched the first series on Netflix I'd happened upon. But I hadn't paid attention. Instead my mind had been occupied with Veronica and our strange encounter.

An encounter I intend never to repeat.

It's early afternoon and I'm home from playing basketball, showered and sitting down in my office to go through work emails for a couple of hours as is my practice on Sundays. I glance through a contract for a building I'm acquiring, as my computer powers up before opening my email.

Gatorade in hand, I look at my screen and pause, the bottle raised halfway to my lips.

It's an email from Veronica.

How in the hell did she get my private account? An address less than ten people have?

My mouse hovers over the subject line that simply reads, *Resume — Veronica Westwood.*

I don't appreciate the swell of excitement I experience at the sight of her name. Women emailing me, especially one emailing me for a job, does not excite me. Or at least, it shouldn't.

I open the correspondence.

Dear Mr. Townsend,

I appreciate your reluctance to interview me for the position of General Manager, but I'd ask you to reconsider. If you review my resume, you will find I have impeccable education, skills and experience that will benefit your company.

All I ask is you read it and don't judge my qualifications by my lineage. I would also like to point out that you would not have to pay a headhunter fee by hiring me; therefore, I'm already saving you money and increasing your bottom line.

Yes, I understand you will hit reply and say no, but I would like to be clear that I do not intend to take no for an answer.

Sincerely,
Veronica Westwood

31

That I read it twice was bad enough, but that I read it with a huge smile on my face was entirely unacceptable. While I admire her initiative, I have no intention of responding. I will do what I do with all unsolicited email, trash it, and move on with my day.

My mouse hovers over the trash icon. My finger twitches on the button. I veer the cursor at the last second, and hit reply. One response can't hurt.

Dear Ms. Westwood,

No.

Sincerely,
Brandon Townsend III

After I sent, I looked at her resume.
It's...impressive.
Truth be told, it's better than my own.
My email dings.
It's her. There's only one word. *Why?*
I'm not going to answer her.
I'm not. I highlight the message determined to delete and end this.
I hit reply instead.

Veronica ~ Sunday

My heart hammers in my chest when my email dings a minute later.

The position is filled.

Good day, Ms. Westwood.

I bite my lip and contemplate my next move. I know what my business books would say. Just like I know what my teacher at Harvard would say, and what my mentors would advise.

But my instinct says something else. It's a risk. I'm supposed to be professional. Yet, everything urges me not to play that game. So with a held breath, I follow my gut.

> *Dear Mr. Townsend,*
>
> *Lying is unbecoming of a gentleman.*
>
> *Sincerely,*
> *Ms. Westwood*

My email chimes.

> *I have never claimed to be a gentleman.*

Yes, this statement sends an inappropriate shiver down my spine, but I'm choosing to ignore my chemical response to him, to focus on what I want. An interview. The job. His tutelage in this strange new world. That's my goal. Even though my reply is anything but businesslike.

> *You're still lying.*

Conventional wisdom says men like Brandon don't like to be challenged. But maybe, just maybe, it's exactly what he needs and doesn't know it. That my email continues to notify me of his messages makes me even more certain I'm right.

> *And, what makes you so sure I'm lying, Ms. Westwood?*

I blow out a breath. No balls, no babies. My level of Intel will either impress him or deem me a certifiable stalker. I'm banking on the former.

I have it on good authority that, after a series of bad hiring decisions that led to the termination of two previous managers, you have been searching for the perfect candidate for nine months. In that time, you've interviewed a total of twenty-five people and been unsuccessful in finding a good fit for your company. It seems to me, at some point, an intelligent man comes to the conclusion what he's doing isn't working and it's time to try something different.

I am your something different.

Brandon ~ Sunday

I stare at the email for approximately five minutes, debating if I should be horrified or impressed. Right now, I'll admit I'm leaning more toward impressed. Veronica Westwood is managing to surprise me, and that's unusual. I keep telling myself I should stop engaging with her, that I should put a firm end to whatever game we're playing.

But I don't. Engaging her is giving me far too much enjoyment.

Well, well, well, someone's been a busy girl. I suppose this explains how you obtained my email address. How much did your invasion of privacy cost you?

I send the message and lean back in the large, leather executive chair, swiveling ever so slightly, my eyes on the screen.

I'm hard. Which is completely ridiculous, but true. I'm getting more of a rush exchanging mildly charged emails with Veronica than the last time I had sex with Stephanie. This alone is reason to cease, but I'm caught up in it now. The anticipation of matching wits with Veronica is intoxicating, the thrill racing through my blood.

Her name pops up in bold black on the screen.

You're evading.

I have a carnal image of stripping her of everything but a skirt, and doing all sorts of depraved things to her on this chair.

You're pushing your luck.

I'm not interviewing her, regardless of her credentials.

I open her latest email and blink in horror. Across my screen runs a screeching, bawking chicken.

I can't help it. I laugh.

Veronica ~ Monday

I'd made progress, but he still hadn't caved. After the chicken gif I'd sent he hadn't responded. Maybe it was too much. But somehow I didn't think so.

Instinct told me I was getting to him. He's getting to me too, but that's beside the point.

Bright this morning, I email him again.

Dear Mr. Townsend,

Did you think I'd give up? Before you continue to refuse me, please consider my tenaciousness and how that trait will benefit you and your company. All this energy I'm putting into obtaining an interview can be used to your advantage. I never take no for an answer.

Maybe you deem me frivolous and didn't think to read my resume. Let me outline a few of my qualifications that will benefit your organization:

- *I graduated from the Harvard MBA program #9 in*

JENNIFER DAWSON

my class.

- *I recently turned down a mid-six-figure salary from the top venture capital firm in Chicago.*
- *I have letters of recommendations from three professors and four CEOs of fortune 100 companies. All of which were obtained through working directly for them, and not through my family connections. (Although, I'm sure they didn't hurt. And yes, I should get points for honesty.)*
- *I literally have nothing better to do than stalk you.*

I will call you at eleven thirty to discuss why you need to interview me.

Sincerely,

Veronica Westwood

I contemplate the folly of the last line I want to write, but decide to go for it. Polite is not going to wear him down.

P.S. Don't pretend you didn't laugh at my gif. You totally did.

I send it off and hold my breath, for ten seconds before blowing it out in a whoosh. I stare intently at my email inbox, willing it to ding.
Waiting.
Watching.
Praying.
He doesn't reply.

Brandon ~ Monday

The amount of willpower I've expended on not replying to

Veronica is troublesome. Since the day I decided to stop being an entitled, privileged brat I have always prided myself on my discipline and self-control.

Discipline and self-control are the cornerstones of my life and permeates all facets of my existence. My relationship with women, included. I believed them engrained because they've been easy for me for a very long time.

That Veronica is testing my resolve is one more reason in a long list of reasons not to interview her.

That I'm more attracted to her than any other woman I've encountered, is another.

For the sake of argument, even if I wanted to hire her, I couldn't. I have a strict, no fraternizing with direct reports policy. A policy I've fired people for violating. A policy I'm not arrogant enough to believe I won't breach if I see her every day. I cannot continue to engage her and allow her to wear me down.

I read her email again before closing it and returning to the spreadsheet I'd been working on. But I can't concentrate. She's already distracted me. I narrow my eyes at the calendar app on my computer. Slowly, almost as if I can't help myself, I open it.

I glance through my schedule. I'm in a meeting from eleven to twelve. I haven't responded to her last two emails, so I'm assuming she'll take that as a firm no and not call.

I stare at my blue bar, indicating the meeting I'm in, swirling the mouse in a mindless motion so the cursor makes random, erratic circles on my screen.

I grit my teeth and move my meeting.

Veronica ~ Monday

His lack of response doesn't deter me. It's a test. And I always ace my tests.

At eleven twenty-nine I call his private cell phone number, not willing to take any chances he'll rebuff me through an administrative assistant. He already knows I have all his information, so I don't see the point of going through proper channels.

My heart is in my throat, my pulse throbbing as I wait. On the third ring, he answers, and my heart immediately doubles in speed at the sound of his low, smooth voice. "I want the name of your hacker. They do impressive work."

My stomach jumps and I smile. "How did you know it was me?"

There's a beat over the line. "Twelve people have this number and they are all in my contact list. Considering this call is coming in at eleven thirty sharp, I used my powers of deductive reasoning."

I weigh the folly of my response and plunge headfirst into the deep end. "You answered."

"Only to inform you my decision is final," he says, his tone so casual I'm positive he's faking.

I ignore the statement. "Have you read my resume?"

"I have, and I don't intend on changing my mind, Veronica."

Brain spinning, I quickly compile my options. He's talking a good game, but he answered my call. He'd been prepared for me. If he weren't thinking about it, about me, he wouldn't have taken my call. So I go with my instincts. "Since I don't intend to stop until I'm sitting in front of you, we can do this the hard way, or we can do this the easy way."

He laughs. It sounds rich and genuine, and I find myself wondering when the last time he laughed like that. "Oh, little Veronica, you have no idea who you're dealing with."

"On the contrary, Mr. Townsend, I think I know exactly who I'm dealing with." I smile and add. "Which is why it's working."

Brandon ~ Monday

She's right. It is working.

But I'm still not interviewing her. Now that I've heard her voice, the same smooth cadence that glided over my skin the night of the gala, the smart move is to end this phone call, but I find I'm not ready to do that. I swivel in my chair. "And why do you think that?"

There's a pause over the line and I can practically hear her thinking. Using that cunning mind of hers to compose her argument. "I think a man like you is perfectly capable of avoiding me if that was your wish. The fact that you don't, leads me to believe you're interested in your mind being changed."

Of course, she's correct. There are a million ways I can avoid contact with her. What she doesn't understand is that while she's beyond smart, and truthfully, so overqualified she's blown every candidate I've met out of the water, every interaction I have with her solidifies my instinct not to hire her.

Not because she wouldn't be good for my company. Because I'm positive she would be. If this were about my company, Veronica Westwood is the best thing I could do for it. I'm confident under her command every part of my operations would improve.

But this isn't about my company. It's not even about her being part of the world I've closed myself off from.

This is about one thing, and one thing only. I want her. My desire for her is so strong I don't want to take a final, definitive stand and end this interaction between us.

And that means she's not an option.

I toy with bluntness. Of informing her of my rather crude and carnal thoughts about her, but then an image of her significant other, Winston Bishop, fills my head and I discard the idea.

My eyes narrow on the computer screen in front of me. "I took your call to make myself clear. You're not a good fit for my organization, but I do admire your tenacity."

She doesn't even pause. "So you're saying a highly intelligent, ambitious, and connected general manager won't

JENNIFER DAWSON

help your business?"

"Do you even know what my business is?"

There's a fraction of a second where I'm almost positive she sucks in a breath before she soldiers on. "You own The Lair and the office building attached to the club."

That's a small portion of what I own. I'm a dabbler. Not the best business plan, but I'm easily bored, and don't need the money. Besides, I have a sixth sense about what to invest in and after ten years, my net earnings have exceeded my considerable trust fund. Of course, my company is private and only a privileged few know the extent of my reach.

Part of me had wondered if Veronica's hacker uncovered the extent of my dealings, and that was why she was so intent on the position, but that doesn't appear to be the case. Her intel seems to be limited to my contact information.

I shift forward in my chair, putting my elbows on my desk. "And you don't think your Harvard MBA is wasted as a glorified bar manager and landlord?"

"It's not about the position." Her voice takes on an impassioned tone.

"Then what is it about? Because that's the position available."

For the first time a question seems to throw her because there's silence over the line. Finally, she clears her throat. "It's about what it represents."

"And what does it represent, Veronica?" The dominance that is such a part of my nature seeps into my words.

"Freedom to be my own person. To figure out who I am and what I want to be. To learn how to be like you." Her tone is soft, almost reflective.

It shifts the conversation from business to intimate. Just like that night on the balcony. I opt for a version of honesty. "I'm not sure working for me will teach you that."

"I disagree."

"Doing the books, hashing out tenant problems, taking inventory and talking to food and liquor vendors won't fulfill you."

40

"It's a start." She breathes deep into the phone. "All I want is a chance. I don't want to work in an office. I don't want to spend my life making rich people richer. I want to do something that makes me feel alive, and as strange as it sounds, all my instincts point me to you."

I understand just what she means. There's a pull between Veronica and me. Something intangible and indefinable. She feels it as strongly as I do, but unlike her, I don't think working together is the answer. I contemplate my options. She's not going to give up. She's a woman on a mission. There's something dangerous about her. Something that threatens my carefully constructed life, and while I don't like it, I'm not ready to be done with her.

I toy with a pen on my desk and ask a question that would give my HR person a heart attack. "Veronica, what does your fiancé have to say about this?"

"Winston is not my fiancé, he's not my anything. I broke up with him the same day I tore up my contract to work as a venture capitalist."

I don't appreciate the relief that relaxes my abdomen. Neither is this any of my business, but it doesn't stop me. "Why did you end your relationship?"

"Why does that matter? It's not relevant."

"Because I want to know." That hard command fills my voice. Wrong and inappropriate, but I can't seem to help myself.

She's silent for a moment before she asks, "Do you want the truth? Or the nice pat answer I gave everyone else?"

"What do you think?"

"The truth?"

"Correct."

"One night I walked into his place to find him having sex with another woman." She lets out a long sigh. "And I wasn't upset. I was relieved. He's the man I'm supposed to marry, to bind our families together, but I can't. I don't want to. I don't love him. I've never loved him."

I sense there's more and press. "Go on."

"I don't want to live my life that way. I don't want to be that person."

"And how do you want to live your life?" This conversation is long past appropriate, and in this time and space, with the telephone line connecting us, it's just her and me.

"I want to have real friends. I want to talk about more than shopping, diets, and Botox. I want to know what it's like to love for real, deeply and irrevocably. I want to use my brain. Be challenged. I don't want to be clocking time until I become a trophy wife. I want to know what it's like to work. To struggle and strive and fight for something." She laughs a little, high and nervous to cover her vulnerability. "Does that sound crazy?"

It doesn't. I understand exactly what she means. It's similar to my own crisis that morning so long ago when I woke up from a fitful moment of unconsciousness, still coked up, and untangled myself from the bed of bodies I'd lain in. I understand her all too well. And I understand what draws her to me. Slowly, I say, "No, it doesn't sound crazy."

"I can't help feeling you can help me. That you understand what nobody else does."

At the yearning in her voice, at the plea, I make a snap decision. "Veronica."

"Yes, Brandon." Hope lightens her tone, and I smile, because she knows she's got me.

"I'm not making any promises, but meet me at The Lair, Thursday at seven o'clock, I'm going to take you to dinner." I'm committed now, and I have an impending sense that there's no turning back.

"I will be there." Her giddiness is plain and undisguised.

Needless to say, I don't want her to think she has too much of an upper hand, so I say sternly, "See that you are."

"Wild horses couldn't keep me away."

I smile. "Goodbye, Veronica."

I hang up before she can get in the last word.

Veronica

I'm in love.

Excitement thrums through my blood, rushing in my ears and making my heart pound. This is it. I'm doing it. I'm changing my life. After a tense phone call, where my mom insisted they weren't taking the Gold Coast condo back, I signed with a real estate agent to sell the ridiculous place, and for the first time in my twenty-seven years I've gone condo shopping. So far, we've toured five places, and this last one is it. I can feel it.

It's mine.

I'm standing in the middle of a one-bedroom loft apartment with wide plank floors the color of driftwood, exposed brick and woodwork staring out the window at the lakefront. It's exactly what I envisioned when I'd decided to take this bold move.

The complete opposite of my current home that is so glossy it's almost untouchable.

In the heart of Lincoln Park, the place is small, barely eight hundred square feet, but I adore everything about it. On the streets below, the sidewalks are littered with people going in and out of shops and restaurants. It's a bright, sunny day, and walkers, runners and bikers fill the lakefront. The neighborhood is alive and vibrant. Exactly what I hoped for.

I turn to the agent, Nora Becker, a young, pretty brunette I'd researched on the Internet and has zero connections to my family. She's just starting out, eager and hungry, and I loved the uncontained joy on her face when I offered her the apartment. Everyone I know is too concerned with cool dismissal to show happiness.

I smile at her. "I love it."

Her expression lights up. "You do?"

"I do. It's perfect. Exactly what I'm looking for."

She kind of does a contained little dance that's adorable. "Yay! I had a feeling when I pulled the listing you would."

I can already envision how I'm going to decorate it. On a budget, of course, because I'm determined to try and live on a salary. Well, once I have a salary. Maybe it's silly. Or crazy. Which is what everyone in my life thinks, but I don't care. I understand there are people starving and living in poverty. I'm not dismissing my good fortune.

I'll use my trust fund for good, and break free on my own terms. This is the first step in many.

Nora tucks a lock of smooth dark hair behind her ear, and clears her throat. "No pressure, we can look for as long as you'd like, but this place hasn't hit the websites yet, and at this price, for this location, it will go fast. I wouldn't be surprised if it has multiple offers by the end of the day."

"I'll take it," I say, without even the slightest hint of hesitation.

Her brow furrows. "Are you sure? I don't want you to feel rushed and this is your first day looking."

I shake my head. I'd known the second I stepped foot in the place this would be home. "I'm sure. Offer full asking price with zero contingency and immediate occupancy."

Her eyes widen and her lips quiver with excitement. "I'll call the agent right away and tell them we are preparing an offer."

I glance back outside. I can't wait to walk those streets. I'm not willing to risk it with my newfound frugality. "You have my permission to go five percent above any other offer made on the property."

She laughs. "All right then, we'll get it done."

"Great. Tell them it's a cash offer and I want to close as soon as possible."

"I will." She touches my arm. "Thank you, Veronica. For choosing me to handle this for you. I know you had other options."

"It's my pleasure." And it is. I honestly don't know if she'll be able to sell the Gold Coast condo. At that price point you need certain connections and clients that I'm positive she doesn't have. But I'm willing to give her the chance. I hadn't selected her for that. I'd selected her for the place we're standing in right now. Because no real estate agent I know would bring me here. They'd show me places my parents had pre-approved, and I couldn't allow that.

I hope I'm wrong though. I hope she's able to sell the condo; I want her to have that commission. I can't change everyone's life, but I can provide opportunity where I can.

By midnight I'm the proud owner of the first place I can truly call home.

Next on the list to conquer, Brandon Townsend III.

The ringing of my phone jars me from sleep and I blink into the darkness before glancing at my clock on the nightstand. It's two a.m. I squint at the caller ID lighting up my screen before flopping down on the pillow.

It's Winston. After one more ring, the screen goes dark and I sigh in relief.

I haven't seen him since that night of the benefit, but he's been texting and calling me daily. First they were his meager attempts to be cute. Sending me pictures of the two of us together, or smiley faces (his form of seduction). When I hadn't answered he'd graduated to a list of things he had of mine I'd left at his place. Since he had nothing of mine that I placed value on, I'd continued to ignore him. Next he informed me of the things he wanted back from me, including any jewelry he'd given me over the years. He probably believed this would spur me into some sort of panic at the threat of our relationship being over. But, he's underestimated my desire to be rid of him.

My only response was to pack everything in a box and hire a messenger service to hand deliver it to him.

The phone rings again and I reach over and silence the call. He has to be drunk. It's the only reason he'd be calling me this late.

And Winston is not a happy drunk.

As I've ignored him, he's grown increasingly perturbed. Demanding I talk to him.

The phone rings again and I decline.

Immediately, it chimes.

I bite my lower lip. I'm already up and it will be hard for me to go to sleep. Maybe if I answer once, reiterate that our relationship is not open to negotiation, he'll stop this.

When my phone lights up again, I sigh and pick up the phone. "What do you want, Winston?"

"It's about fucking time." His voice is slurred, confirming my suspicions.

I want to tell him that I owe him nothing, but that will just lead us down a path I'm not willing to go, so I restate my question. "What can I do for you?"

"I want to talk to you." He's agitated, on edge, and sounds slightly strung out. Like he's been up for days.

"There's nothing to discuss." The best thing I can do is be calm and rational.

"I dedicated the prime of my life to you, and this is how

you repay me?" His words are full of belligerence.

I want to snap that he's screwed practically all of Chicago, but what's the point? "Winston, our relationship is over. You're twenty-eight, you have plenty of women standing in line for you, so go forth and be merry."

There's dead silence over the phone before he says, "I don't want them, I want you."

I tell him the truth. "The only reason you want me is because I'm the first person that's ever said no to you. When you had me, you couldn't have cared less."

"Veronica, baby." His voice softens. "Please, meet me for a drink and we can talk."

"There's nothing to talk about. We are done. Our relationship is over. There's no reason we can't be civil about this."

"It's not over. We just need to talk."

"No, stop calling me. Stop texting."

"Wait." His voice takes on an urgent tone.

"Goodbye, Winston." I hang up and turn off my phone. Hopefully that's the end of it.

Brandon

My preference for redheads is well established, but as I sit across from Stephanie I find my mind filled with a certain cool blonde. When I'd called the lovely interior decorator and asked her to come over my intention had been to put her through a long, hard session in hopes it would clear Veronica from my thoughts.

I hadn't thought it wise to go into dinner on edge.

Stephanie had been the logical choice. A beautiful, submissive girl with auburn hair I'd been sleeping with casually for the last nine months, she is always up for whatever wringer I dream up for her. In my head, she'd been just what I needed. As odd as it sounds, dominating a woman is good stress relief, and it had been a month since I'd had sex. Not long for some, but an eternity for me.

We are in my parlor, and she's restlessly crossing and uncrossing her legs with a petulant pout on her face she's just praying I'll wipe off. As we've sat there across from each other, sipping cognac, she's getting anxious. I keep meaning to start, to tell her to stand, strip naked, and get on her knees in front of me, but every time I open my mouth I take another drink instead.

She flutters her lashes, glancing around the room where I entertain my guests before taking them down into my basement and the real torture begins. She puffs her lower lip. "I can redecorate this room for you."

"That won't be necessary." We'd met when I hired her to design the club, and I'd had her in my bed before the ink was dry on the contract.

"It could use a makeover." She crosses her legs, hiking up her black skirt dangerously high on her thighs. She's wearing four-inch heels and her legs, kept golden by spray tan, gleam with whatever lotion she's put on. Her legs are endless. Long and supple, and flexible. Very, very flexible.

"It could, but I like the room the way it is." It's a room from another century, with antiqued brocade couches, winged-back chairs, and a wall filled with leather-bound books reaching so high a built-in ladder slides across the floor to reach the top shelves.

Her pout deepens. "I promise not to go over budget this time."

She's opening the bidding, playing her hand because she's tired of waiting for me to exact my power over her. It's a little game of ours. She overspends and I spank her for her infraction. It's play dominance and submission. Not serious. Or meaningful.

She's expecting me to say something commanding here. Something like—*See that you don't, girl.* She'll shiver. I'll beckon. She'll come. And before we know it she'll be tied to my bed in the basement, screaming for a mercy I won't deliver.

She needs it. It's written in the tension of her jaw and set of shoulders. In the way she squirms in her seat and the press of her thighs. Her nipples are visible through her silk blouse; the swell of her breasts a heavy rise and fall while she waits.

She needs it. And the truth is, I need it too. It's been too long and my skin is tight. I need the meditative nature of dominating her to soothe my brain.

Only, I don't want it from Stephanie.

No, I want it from a pale blonde whose skin glows in the moonlight. I want to see Veronica's hair spread out, caressing the curve of her spine. I find myself preoccupied, wondering what her hair looks like down, how long it is, what it might feel like under my fingers. I want to see her naked before me, on the floor between my splayed knees. And I want to sit there, staring at her, watching the expressions play across her face as she comes to the realization about my intentions toward her.

I shouldn't want those things. Not from her. I don't like that she feels like an addiction. That since we last spoke, I've looked at my emails and been disappointed not to see her name. That when my phone has rung, I'm unhappy it's not her. I'm not comfortable with how, in her quest for a new life, Veronica has somehow thrown mine into chaos.

My friend Jillian Santoro, wife to one of my best friends, Leo, always asks me how I can be so unrelenting in my dominance. So cool and collected and in control, never expressing any emotions or attachment. Her only experience is with Leo, and the two of them are so in love, the power exchange in their relationship only heightens and deepens their connection. She can't understand how I remain so detached.

What she doesn't understand, and what I won't explain, is it's because I have no emotion. Of course, I feel fondly toward them. I like them. I never take advantage of their submission. I treat them with the utmost respect and appreciation. When I'm with a woman I ensure an experience she'll never forget.

But I can't remember the last woman I slept with where I cared if she walked away.

Of course, they never do. Because of my nature, I attract

submissive women to whom cool, casual dismissal is like crack. Stephanie is like that. Sitting here, having to bear my silence is making her impossibly wet. She's practically melting with desire. The longer I sit here, taking no action, the more lust thrums through her. My lack of attention on her, my casual disregard to her growing petulance and restlessness, is more effective than any foreplay I could dream up.

She shifts again in her chair, sucking a breath as her thighs probably press against her bare cunt. Other than a brush of my lips on her cheek, I haven't laid a finger on her, but I know she doesn't have panties on because she's forbidden to be in my presence with them on. That's the rule. If she knows she's going to see me, they are to be taken off as soon as the plans are solidified. If I show up unexpected, she is to remove them the second she sees me.

If I take her, use her body as my own personal playground, some of my agitation will abate. To me, dominating women is calming. If I fuck Stephanie, I will go into my dinner with Veronica tomorrow night with a clear head.

It's the only rational action. And rational is the only approach I take with women.

I meet Stephanie's glazed eyes and, without breaking contact, lift my glass to take a drink before slowly putting the snifter down on the table. She leans forward, ready for me, anticipating what I will do next.

I open my lips to issue her forward, but those aren't the words that come. "Stephanie, I'm afraid we need to talk."

Veronica

With my hand on the handle that will lead me into The Lair, I take a deep breath, mentally trying to prepare myself for my dinner with Brandon. I haven't seen him since the night of the benefit and I can't help wondering if I'll experience the same pull I had that night out on the balcony.

I hadn't known what this dinner would entail. Was it business? An interview? Something else entirely? I've had days to think about him. And I'd spent most of that time fending off messages from Winston, packing up the few belongings I want to take with me into my new life, and researching Brandon. For a modern man, he's conspicuously absent from the online world. Yes, there are plenty of pictures of him, plenty of speculation in society rags. But he's not on any social media. Even his club, one of the hottest spots in town, is mysterious. He has a website, but it isn't typical. It's basically a landing page with a picture of an opulent bar that's a cross between a French boudoir and clubhouse. There's only one sentence: *The only way to know is to experience it yourself.* Other than the address that's the only information.

So I have no idea what to expect when I open this door, but it feels a little like I'm Alice about to tumble through the looking glass. The uncertainty regarding the nature of our dinner had made choosing an outfit difficult. In the end, I'd worn my hair down and sleek, curving over my shoulders, and a black dress with a squared neck and three-quarter sleeves that comes to my knees.

It's a dress right for almost any occasion.

I take a deep breath to calm my racing heart and enter.

The picture didn't do the place justice. It's like nothing I'd quite seen before. It's all deep reds, and rich woods. It's the type of place I'd envision for a nineteenth-century drawing room. It's huge, but with the low lights, and buttery leather furniture combined into separate chat areas, it's oddly intimate.

Brandon's club is a visual representation of the man himself. Deep, rich, otherworldly and sophisticated. There's a beautiful woman with raven hair standing at a small podium wearing a silky midnight-blue dress that drips off her.

She offers me a welcoming smile. "I'm afraid we're invitation only tonight. May I help you?"

It's a genius marketing move, making the club so exclusive, but somehow I doubt that Brandon planned it that way. If I had to guess, he does it because it's what he wants, the success of the tactic, merely a byproduct.

"I have an—" I stumble a tiny bit over my word choice. "Appointment with Brandon Townsend."

Expression clearing, she nods. "Ah, one moment, please."

I stand there, waiting, taking in my surroundings and letting them wrap around me. I become so caught up in the details I don't even see him approach until he's in front of me.

I blink, and I can't lie, my heart rolls over before falling into a rapid beat. I didn't think it would be possible for him to look better than he did in a tux, but I was wrong. Blond men aren't supposed to be dangerous looking, that's a trait I'd always reserved for dark hair and brooding eyes, but Brandon appears to be the exception. He's dressed in all black, wearing a form-fitting black knit shirt that clings to his broad chest and even broader shoulders. His pants are so well crafted, such a perfect cut on his slim hips, they could only be custom made for him.

I don't know if it's because of the conversations I've had with him, or that he's spent so much time occupying my thoughts, but he's even more stunning than when I last saw him.

He smiles, flashing his dimples, and it dazzles me. "Hello, Veronica."

Heart a frantic beat I nod. "Brandon. It's a pleasure to see you again."

He glances at a thick-banded watch on his wrist. "You're early."

I tilt my chin. "Did you think I'd work this hard and show up late?"

"No, I didn't." He steps close to me, close enough to suck in the subtle scent of his aftershave, something spicy and mysterious. "Come on, I'll show you around."

My lashes flutter, ever so slightly. "I'd like that."

Instead of moving, our gazes lock, and the air thickens between us. We stand, not saying anything, but the silence feels like a thousand unspoken words. His eyes skim over my face, lingering on my mouth, down the curve of my neck, before traveling back up.

"Are you ready?" His voice is like a caress over my skin.

I shake my head and my words are a bit too husky. "Not really."

The corners of his lips tilt up. "And why's that?"

I'm well aware I shouldn't desire him. That if I want a job I need to keep things professional and businesslike, but that seems impossible right now. There's something between us. Something that burns hot and fierce. Something about him calls to that secret part of me I've kept hidden for so long I no longer have a name for it. It's like he knows me and I know him. Like we are different sides of the same coin. At least to myself, I've stopped pretending that this is about the position.

Now it feels like something more.

I swallow hard. "When I walked in I thought I felt a little like Alice tumbling down the looking glass."

He leans impossibly closer, his body warming me without a single touch. "Tumble away, Alice."

"I will." I square my shoulders. "I'm not backing down."

"I never expected anything less." He stands to the side to allow me to move in front of him. When I step forward, he puts his palm on the base of my spine, and it about sears me through my dress. "I have a few things to take care of before we leave."

"Not a problem." The imprint of his hand feels like a brand. We walk through the room, he steers me through the clusters of tables and I can't help commenting. "This place is spectacular."

His palm drops away, leaving a cold spot in his wake. "Thank you. I wanted to do something different."

I stare up at the ceiling, it's intricate with wood and decorated tiles. "You've succeeded. The ceiling alone is a work of art."

He stops and points upward, giving me a chance to soak it all in. "I imported the wood and tiles from a church in France that was in disrepair. I've always loved old, beautiful things."

I glance at him. "Me too. Everything is so sterile now, don't you think?"

"Yes, that's exactly it." He meets my gaze. "Maybe it's because of how we grew up, surrounded by all that old money and history."

"I'm sure you're right." I smile. "My grandparents live in a historic mansion in Lake Forest and it's always been my favorite place."

Something flashes in his expression. "I live in a historic home left to me by my grandparents. A lot of it is original work."

I bite my lower lip and he tracks the movement, his blue eyes darkening. "I'm sure it's beautiful."

"It is. It's old and rambling, but it's my favorite place."

"It's your home, it should be."

His gaze flickers and he tilts his head toward the back. "My friends are in the corner."

I glance over his shoulder and see three couples, all with various shades of dark hair, all beautiful, and all staring at me with curious faces. I look back at Brandon. "They're watching us."

He laughs. "Indeed they are."

I get an impulse and don't ignore it. "Do they check out all your prospective employees?"

"I'm sure they're not above it." He touches my arm. "I'll take you to meet them."

"If they hate me, will you refuse to hire me?"

His gaze narrows. "They won't hate you, but they have no bearing on my business decisions."

"Does that mean I have a chance?" I have to know. He's throwing me off, everything about our interactions screams intimacy, chemistry and attraction. I have to orientate this night in my head, so I can act appropriately.

He looks down at me. "I don't know quite what to do with you yet, Veronica."

That gives me no answers, but I'm smart enough not to press at this point in time. "Fair enough."

"Come. You'll like them, I promise." He turns, and walks in front of me toward the couples sitting in the corner.

I follow, my stomach doing a little dance. I have no idea who these people are, other than they are friends of Brandon's, and I've never seen them before. They are most certainly not part of my world. Which is an exciting prospect to me. Further solidifying my irrational belief that Brandon holds the key to the life I've been searching for.

When we're in front of the group, Brandon gestures me forward. "This is Veronica Westwood." He offers no explanation of who I am, or why I'm here, leaving me further in the dark about what this dinner date with him might mean.

He points to the couple sitting on the loveseat. "This is my oldest friend, Michael Banks, and his soon-to-be wife, Layla

Hunter. Michael and I were roommates at the University of Pennsylvania."

I'm very practiced at social graces, a skill beaten into me since I was old enough to talk. I offer my most brilliant smile. "It's a pleasure to meet you."

"You too, Veronica." Michael's voice is slightly rough and deep, his unusual hazel eyes direct. He's large, even seated he looks impossibly tall and broad. With his arm over the arm of the loveseat, and his finger casually drifting over his fiancée's skin, he manages to be somehow both gorgeous and scary. The woman to his right is almost hauntingly beautiful, with dark flowing hair and blue eyes. Together, they are the kind of couple you watch as they walk past on the street.

Layla smiles. "And how do you know Brandon?"

"No grilling, girl," Brandon says in an exasperated voice before turning to another couple sitting together on a large chair. The man is dark and looks Italian. The woman next to him is pretty, tall, with full, lush lips, and the same unusual eyes as Michael, signaling some sort of relation. "This is Leo and Jillian Santoro. Leo and Michael are homicide detectives and partners. Jillian is Michael's sister."

My expression widens in pleasure. Real live cops. "It's so nice to meet you, I had the pleasure of meeting Superintendent Fitzgerald a few months ago."

Leo's brow rises. "Oh, really?"

I nod. "Yes, I attended a benefit for the National Law Enforcement Officers Memorial Fund."

"In D.C.?" Michael inquires, his expression interested.

Before I can answer, Brandon interjects. "Veronica's family is very influential and does a lot of charity work both locally and nationally."

Leo looks at me with narrowed eyes. "How interesting."

His wife, Jillian waves her hand. "Ignore them, it's so nice to meet you."

Her expression is warm and friendly, and I feel an instant ease. "Thank you, you too."

Brandon gestures to the remaining couple on a chair. A

clean-cut, good-looking guy and a woman with the coloring of Snow White and wearing a red dress is perched on his knee. "This is Chad Fellows and his new fiancée, Ruby Stiles." He winks at the woman. "The lovely Ruby is going to be singing for us in a few minutes, isn't that right?"

She gives him a little eye roll and shrugs one shoulder. "That's the rumor."

"It's great to meet you both," I say. They are a striking couple, but they don't quite look like they go together. She's got a rocker vibe that's in contrast to Chad's all-American looks.

Chad nods. "You too, Veronica." He gestures to an empty, leather winged-back chair. "You should have a seat."

I glance at Brandon, unsure of what his plans are, but he nods. "I want to hear Ruby sing. I had a sound system installed and this is a practice run to see how the acoustics are."

"Great." I sink into the chair and cross my legs demurely before smiling at Ruby. "What's it like to be a singer?"

She shakes her head. "I'm only one in my spare time. I'm a graphic designer by trade."

"I'd love to be able to at least carry a tune, but I'm afraid I'm hopeless," I say.

A pretty blonde girl that appears to be in her early twenties walks up to Brandon. She gives him a fluttery glance before biting her lower lip. "Reggie is looking for you, Sir."

"Very well." He shifts his attention to me. "Can I trust you to stay out of trouble until I get back?"

Something about his words warms my skin, so I shrug. "Does that mean hacking into your computer system is a no go?"

His expression flashes as the couples laugh. He raises his brow. "With your hacker, most certainly."

There's something about him that makes it impossible for me to resist bantering with him. I snap my fingers. "And I have him on standby, too bad."

He puts his hands into his pockets. "Which reminds me, I still need his name. You never know when those skills can be put to good use."

I smile sweetly. "You'll have to pry his name from my cold, dead fingers. I'm sworn to secrecy."

He laughs. "I have plenty of ways to extract information that doesn't include murder."

It feels like a warning. Like a promise. And by the scowl that forms on the waitress's face, I'm certain it's not in my imagination. "I'll shore up my defenses."

"See that you do." Brandon shifts his attention to his friends. "Don't let her wander off."

Without a backward glance, he swivels and walks off with the girl, leaving me alone with these six people that all know him better than anyone else. These are the people he's taken into his private world, and I want to know them. Impress them. Learn from them.

I put my hands on the arms of the chair, cock a grin and say, "Would it be safer if you tied my hands to the chair?"

Just like I wanted them to, they all laugh before passing each other sly glances I don't understand.

Chad curves his hand over his fiancée's hip. "That could be arranged."

Ruby's lips quiver before blinking innocently back at me.

Leo scrubs a hand over his jaw. "Hmmm... Do you think Brandon has any rope lying around?"

This causes a chorus of hearty laughter.

Jillian's expression goes wide. "I don't know. What on earth would Brandon do with rope? He'd never."

In this brief exchange I learn a few things: one, their closeness is obvious. As is their ease. They have a warmth about them I've never experienced with my group of so-called friends and it makes me envious. They have what I'm looking for. And two, they are all sharing a secret I'm not a part of, that eludes me.

Layla clears her throat and smiles. "But seriously, how do you know Brandon?"

I decide on the barest details. "My family and Brandon's family are old acquaintances. We ran into each other at a benefit about a week ago."

Jillian nods. "And now you're going to dinner together?"

I clear my throat. I don't want them thinking this is a date when it's not. "It's a business dinner. That's all."

Jillian glances at her husband who winks at her. She turns her attention back to me. "I see."

I'm not sure what to say because they are clearly speculating. The best way to get people to open up is to be forthcoming, so I lean forward as though I'm about to reveal important information. "I want him to hire me for his general manager position." I glance behind Michael and Layla to where Brandon disappeared down a hall. "He's…reluctant."

Jillian leans closer to me and mock whispers, "Something tells me you're winning."

"Oh, I am." My tone is sly and conspiratorial.

She sits back to settle against Leo. "I like you."

Leo puts his hand on her thigh and grips her bare leg. "That's dangerous."

"Indeed," she says, sweetly.

He moves up her thigh, and she lets out a little gasp. Leo zeros in on me and he's so direct I try not to fidget. "My wife likes danger."

"Lucky you."

He laughs. "Very much so."

I shift my attention to Layla. "Brandon said, soon-to-be wife, are you getting married soon?"

Layla's expression opens with excitement. "Yes, in a few months."

"How lovely. Where are you getting married?" In my experience, brides are always up for discussing their upcoming nuptials.

"Salvage One," Layla says, naming one of the hottest wedding spots in all of Chicago.

"I love that place," I say, falling into my place in the conversation. "Are you going outdoors or in?"

She wrinkles her nose. "In. That time of year is too risky."

"Well, you can't go wrong, that place is to die for. I'm sure it will exceed your expectations." I make a mental note to call and talk with the owner, and to send the happy couple something special on their day. My rule is I can use my trust fund only for good, and I'm positive this counts.

I turn to Ruby and Chad. "And you're getting married as well?"

Ruby grins down at her fiancé. "Yeah, but we're just getting started. We're recently engaged."

"Congratulations. How exciting." I hold out my hand. "Can I see the ring?"

She doesn't even let me finish the sentence before she's thrusting it out for me to admire. I have to admit, it's quite a ring. At least two carats, it's a clear emerald cut with a simple band. It suits her perfectly. "It's beautiful."

"Thank you." She holds up her hand and tilts her head to look at it. "I'm still not used to it."

I smile at Chad. "You have good taste in rings."

He laughs. "And women."

"I can see that." I shift back to Ruby. "So no date set?"

"Nope. I want to elope." She waves a hand at the group. "But they won't let me."

"Well, you're the bride," I say, my tone light.

Layla scoffs. "She only wants to elope because she hates attention. That's not a good reason."

Ruby rolls her eyes. "I don't see why we need to make a big deal about it. It's a wedding. Marriage is the important part."

Chad squeezes her. "Sorry, little girl, you're outnumbered. No eloping. I agreed to small."

Ruby's brow furrows. "But between your family, mine and friends that's over a hundred people."

"That's small," he says, gazing at her with such love and affection I can't help but be a little jealous.

I've never had a man look at me like that. I've never had a man look at me the way any of these guys look at their women. There's something in the air between them. Like a subtle tension pulling them all tight. Not a bad tension, but it's something, and it pulses through the air.

"It is not small! Your mom emailed me a list of two hundred people she wants to invite."

He laughs. "It's her first wedding. She'll calm down."

Ruby rubs her temples. "Just thinking about all those doctors from your side mixing with the religious, small town group from mine is making me tense."

He grips her chin and forces her face to his before looking deep into her eyes. "Hey. None of that. This is about you and me. Nobody but us matters."

She nods and he releases her. She puffs out her lower lip. "But I want to elope."

"No you don't. You're just overwhelmed at the attention and details," he says.

She curls into him, and he wraps his arm around her, kissing her temple. "Don't worry, it will be perfect."

She nods. "Okay."

"That's settled." Layla claps her hands. "Now we need to go shopping for a dress."

Ruby chuckles and shakes her head. "Not until after your wedding. Besides my mom wants to come. And my sister. And niece." She sighs. "And Chad's mom."

"And me," Jillian says, "Don't forget me."

Layla snaps her fingers. "And Ashley, since she's now dating your future brother-in-law."

Ruby straightens and shakes her head. "How did this happen?"

My they are an intricate, close-knit group, obviously all connected in a tangled web of interconnected relationships.

Jillian winks at me. "What about you, Veronica? Do you want to go dress shopping with Ruby too?"

I laugh; knowing they are kidding, but appreciate she's trying to include me. "Only if you promise to let me call the manager at Belle Vie Bridal Couture to get you a special appointment."

I'm name dropping. I admit it. I'm not ashamed.

Layla's and Jillian's mouths drop open. "No. Way."

Ruby's expression crinkles in confusion. "What's that?"

Layla gives her friend an exasperated glare. "Only *the* place to get your dress."

"Is it expensive?" Ruby asks.

"Of course," Jillian says.

Ruby shakes her head. "Pass."

I smile. "Well, let me know, even if you don't get your dress from them you really should go there at least once. They'll make you feel like a princess."

From the corner of my eye I see Brandon walking toward us, and my heart speeds up at the sight of him. Our eyes lock, and the conversation around me dims, growing fainter and fainter the closer he approaches.

When he reaches the group, he says, "You didn't run her off yet, I see."

The room blares back into focus.

Jillian cranes her neck to peer at Brandon. "Hardly, in fact, we've decided to keep her."

This fills me with such glee I can barely contain myself.

Brandon sighs. "Why am I not surprised?"

I quirk a grin in his direction. "Because your friends are an excellent judge of character?"

His brow rises. "Or you're a con-artist."

"I prefer persuasive and tenacious, thank you." I keep my voice light, and proper.

Jillian straightens her shoulders. "I demand you hire her."

Brandon gives her a look of affection before turning to Leo. "Your woman is getting bossy."

"Looks that way," Leo says.

"Do you intend to rectify that?" Brandon crosses his arms over his chest.

"Why, do you want to help?" Leo shoots back, before smirking at me.

It's like they are all having a type of veiled conversation. Brandon is clearly in on their secrets. I bide my time, awaiting his response.

He shrugs. "If you're unable to handle the job."

Leo laughs.

Brandon shifts his attention to Ruby. "Are you ready, darling?"

Ruby stands and straightens her skirt. "Ready."

Chad encircles her wrist with his long fingers and pulls her down before covering her mouth with his. In my circles, public affection is frowned upon, especially in company. Most deliver chaste kisses to cheeks, or brief brushes over lips.

But that's not what I experience now.

Chad devours Ruby's mouth, curling his free hand around her leg and pushing her skirt up in his path. Ruby, who'd given me every impression of a woman not intent on wanting to attract attention, sinks into the kiss, seeming unconcerned with her audience.

They slowly pull apart and I watch as his fingers flex on her wrist before he says, "Sing pretty."

"I will." She gives him an intimate, killer smile and he releases her. She turns to Brandon. "Any requests?"

He glances at me, his expression unreadable. "Whatever you desire."

His blue eyes seem to hypnotize me, and by the time I manage to pull away, Ruby is already onstage, talking to band members that have appeared. After a few minutes of discussion, she takes center stage and the lights dim, casting her in spotlight.

I can't help looking at her fiancé, wondering if he's nervous for her.

Up there in front of everyone, she seems to transform into something exotic and mysterious. I have no idea what to expect as she starts to sing, but from the second she belts out the first cords to, *Be My Husband*, by Nina Simone I'm kind of stunned by her voice. It's deep, raspy and soulful, and the whole room sort of stills to listen to her.

Chad doesn't take his eyes off her as she sings and I'm transfixed by his expression until I feel the tug of Brandon's gaze on me, pulling me to him.

Our eyes meet, and even in the darkness, the intensity of his stare is unmistakable. My throat goes dry, and I'm unable to glance away. A thousand words pass between us and in that moment I know this isn't about business. It's about us. Him and me. The chemistry and that spark I've been trying to shove down, roars to greedy, demanding life.

My heart starts to beat a frantic rhythm, and as Ruby sings in her rich, soulful voice accompanied only by the beat of a drum, I have a sudden bold desire to rise and go to him, push him down on one of these lush, leather chairs and straddle him. I want to press my mouth against his while her fevered song wraps around me.

And suddenly, it's over. The spell breaks as the music ends and I'm left wondering if it was in my imagination. Brandon stands and walks over to the stage, and I watch as he talks to Ruby and the other musicians. Another man, a tall, broad, handsome black man, with a close cropped dark hair and chiseled features joins them and they all start gesturing around, obviously discussing the acoustics.

It's a lot of activity, but Brandon is who captures my attention. He's fascinating to watch. The tilt of his head when he listens. The set of his jaw. The flex of his muscles moving under his shirt as he motions.

The more I watch him, the more captivated I become, until I'm so riveted I'm forced to tear my gaze away and look straight into the eyes of Jillian Santoro. I'm caught red-handed.

And before I can stop it, a flush spreads over my cheeks.

She smiles.

I smile back, shrugging.

Her lips widen into a grin. "Do you need to use the restroom, Veronica? I have to go, and I thought maybe you'd need to as well before you leave."

The hair on the back of my neck rises as my instincts go on high alert. Instincts I know aren't wrong when her husband casts her a sideways glance, a smirk on his face.

I debate, but in the end curiosity gets the best of me and I nod. "Sure, thanks."

I stand, and only when Jillian stands do I realize how tall she is. Even at five-seven I feel practically tiny next to her. I follow, and out the corner of my eye, I spot Brandon turning to watch me.

I don't know exactly what possesses me, but I raise my hand and waggle my fingers before disappearing down the hall.

Brandon

I'm standing next to my friends, staring down the corridor where Veronica and Jillian disappeared, wondering what they are possibly up to, when Michael's voice rips me from my thoughts.

"Christ. He's smitten," he says, amusement clear in his tone.

I frown, jerking my attention back to my surroundings. I know he's talking about me, but I'm not about to admit it. I shove my hands into my pockets. "I'd hope so, Chad is marrying the girl."

Chad chuckles. "He's not talking about me."

I raise a brow. "You're not smitten with the lovely, Ruby?"

Leo rolls his eyes. "Dude, you are fucked."

"I'm afraid you've lost me." I am putting on a very good show, my voice maintaining its normal coolness, but deep down I know they aren't buying it.

That's the problem with real friends. They know you. And these guys know me better than anyone else. I can't fool them. Instinctively, they've looked at Veronica and myself interact, and know there's something between us. Something that isn't typical for me.

Layla straightens, her blue eyes dancing. "I like her."

"It's just business, darling girl, but I'm glad you approve." I can't help glancing down the hall where the women disappeared. They'd made quite a sight. Jillian leading the way like an amazon warrior, her shoulders back, spine straight, all that lush hair streaming down her back. With Jillian's larger-than-life presence one would think Veronica would disappear, but instead she made a startling contrast. All that refined, cool beauty hiding all that fiery passion. It's her eyes that betray her. She can't mask her hunger.

It's the hunger that reaches inside me and twists.

The desire I'd experienced on the balcony pales in comparison to the lust that's taken hold of me since she walked through that door. I finally have the answer to what her hair looks like down, it's smooth and silky, cascading to the middle of her back.

I want to drag my fingers through it. I want to mess it up.

If only it were chemistry, but there's something else. It practically burns up the air when our eyes meet. I have no idea how to make it through dinner without touching her.

I see the women appear, and my eyes lock on Veronica in her sleek black dress. She moves like a rich girl, all glide and grace, and it shouldn't call to me, but does. I get a flash of pushing her against a wall, raising the hem of her dress, sliding my fingers into her panties.

I shake it off, but I'm sure I'm not hiding the intensity of my expression because she falters a little before tilting her chin with that hint of defiance. When she's standing in front of me, her spine straightens and her shoulders square, as though she's preparing for battle.

And I suppose that isn't far from the truth.

My fingers twitch with the desire to wrap them around her wrist, but I smile, my gaze flickering over her features. "Did you have fun?"

Her honey eyes spark. "I did."

"Are you ready to go?"

"Yes." Her voice betrays her; it's a bit too husky for casual.

"Where are you going to dinner?" Jillian asks, her tone innocent. Too innocent.

I tear my gaze away from Veronica. "None of your business."

She plants her hands on her hips. "Maybe we should come since you've been having such a hard time finding someone on your own. We can help." She smirks at me. "Besides, I already know Veronica is *the one*."

"I don't think we're invited, girl." Leo's voice is filled with amusement.

Jillian puffs out her lower lip in a pout. "I think it would be fun."

"No." The word firm, and absolute. I turn to Veronica, grasp her elbow, ignoring the current that races along my skin and her almost imperceptible shudder. "It's time to leave, Veronica."

Her pink tongue flicks over her lips and she nods, before waving, "It's nice to meet you all."

"You too," Jillian says, beaming. "Don't forget to call me."

Inwardly, I groan. This is just like Jillian.

"I won't," Veronica says.

"Come to brunch with us, Sunday," Layla says, quickly jumping on the Veronica bandwagon.

"Yes, come," Ruby follows, before pressing her hands together in prayer. "Pretty please. Just us girls."

God help me.

Veronica's entire face lights up as though she's just been given the keys to the Forbidden City. "I'd love to."

"It's a date," Jillian says, waving. "Go. We'll talk."

I shake my head.

Leo curls his hand around his wife's thigh and smirks. "So fucked."

I look down at Veronica, and to my horror, my heart actually skips a beat.

He's right. I'm fucked.

6.

Veronica

We are sitting at an intimate table for two in GT Prime, a steak place filled with dark gray woods, plush chairs and low lighting. Brandon ordered wine, and we'd decided on the bone marrow for an appetizer.

He'd had a car service take us, and the ride over was filled with tension that has made me hum with excitement. Now that the orders have been taken, there's nothing to distract from the space between us where everything lays unspoken.

The restaurant still gives me no answers. It's both the kind of place you'd take someone for a business dinner, and seductive. All the warmth, the rich woods, and candlelight wraps around me, almost cocooning us.

He folds his hands on the table. "And what have you been doing with yourself since you blew up your life, Veronica?"

It's not the question I expect, but I answer honestly. "I bought a small one-bedroom condo with a view of the lake."

He nods. "How did that make you feel?"

I bite my lower lip. "Free."

"It's a good feeling, isn't it?" The corners of his mouth tilt, but he doesn't deepen into the smile enough to flash those dimples of his.

I answer with a question of my own. "You can relate?"

"I can." He doesn't elaborate.

I decide my current strategy is working and go for bold. "Have you ever told anyone why you left our life?"

His gaze flickers. "No, I have not."

I lean forward. "Will you tell me?"

His eyes narrow, and he shrugs. "I'm afraid it's not much of a story."

"I'm not looking for a story." I bring my wine to my lips and take a sip. "I'm just looking to understand you."

"And why do you want to understand me?" He tracks my movements, like he's a predator, and I can't quite repress the shudder. "Do you attempt to understand all your prospective employers?"

I shake my head.

"So it's personal?"

I square my shoulders. "Isn't it?"

He leans back in his chair and studies me for a long time before he speaks. "Honestly, I'm not quite sure what to make of you, Veronica."

My heart starts a frantic gallop. "What are your choices?"

He takes a drink of his wine before tilting his head. "I think your talents are wasted on the position I have available."

"Maybe. I don't really know." I'm not going to pretend I'm not overqualified. I have impressive skills, and despite throwing away the chance of a lifetime, I would have no problem finding a job. "But your position gives me something others don't."

"What's that?"

"Exposure to life outside our little bubble."

"What if you find you need the bubble? That the world isn't what you anticipated?"

"I don't think that's possible." I answer with my most

direct stare. Unwavering.

His expression flickers. "I can see it burning in your eyes. I recognize it."

"So you know I'm not bluffing. That this isn't some socialite game I'm playing."

"I do."

I lean forward, putting my elbows on the table. "What do you have to lose by giving me a chance? Can you honestly tell me I'm not better than anyone else you've seen?"

He shakes his head. "No I can't, but that's not the problem."

"Then what is the problem?" I ask the question, but I think I already know. It's the unnamed chemistry lacing all our interactions. My only curiosity is if he'll admit it.

He continues to study me with that intense gaze of his until I shift in my chair and drink more wine to distract myself. He sighs. "I have strict rules for my organization. There's not many, but they are absolute. I have those rules in place because they serve a purpose. You will violate my rule."

My throat goes dry and I lick my lips. "What is your rule? I'm sure I will abide by it."

I'm not sure at all, but I want to be.

He smirks. "No fucking your subordinates. Ever."

I blink, unprepared for such directness. "Oh."

His gaze darkens. "And I'm afraid, I very much want to fuck you, Veronica."

I can't help it, my cheeks flush and I find myself unable to speak.

He laces his fingers over his flat stomach. "That wouldn't be a problem in itself, except for one important fact."

"What's that?" The words kind of stumble out of me. I'm used to Winston, he's the only man I've ever been with, and he'd always been proper with me. He saved his depravity for the girls he took to bed on the side.

"I believe the feeling is mutual."

I pull myself together and say coolly, "Is that not a bit presumptuous?"

"No, I don't believe it is." His expression is intent, purposeful. There's not even a hint of shyness, or chagrin at so blatantly discussing the attraction between us. He tilts his head in the direction of the bathrooms. "I think if I walked you down that hall, and laid my mouth on you, there's very little you wouldn't do for me. I'd push up your dress, slide my fingers into your panties, and nothing could stop me from making you come. And you would come, Veronica. I would make sure of it."

Hot all over, I swallow hard. I have no idea how to respond to this so I make an attempt to keep it on business. "Are you saying I'm incapable of being professional?"

He laughs. "No, I'm saying I am."

"Oh."

"Indeed."

I swipe a lock of my hair behind my ear, suddenly deflated. "Does that mean you're not going to hire me?"

The waiter chooses that minute to deliver the appetizer. He sets it down and without even looking at him, Brandon says, "Please give us a minute."

He nods and takes his leave.

"I've been thinking about this, and here's the thing, I want to help you." Brandon pours us both more wine before placing the bottle back on the table. "You and I, I think, somehow, we are the same."

My chest swells with hope because I can't deny it. I want it all. I want him and the position. "How so?"

"You mean you don't know?" His voice is light, almost amused.

"I do." I smooth my hand over the tablecloth. "It's hard to articulate."

"It is." His gaze meets mine. "I can give you what you desire. I've already started."

I'm not quite sure I understand what he means and my brow furrows.

He smiles. "Did you not like my friends?"

"I did, very much so."

"Did they not ask you to go to brunch?"

I nod.

His smile widens and his dimples do flash now. "Did you and Jillian not have an interesting talk in the bathroom?"

My mind turns to Jillian and me talking. Her giddy excitement over me. How she kept telling me how interesting all this was. "Yes."

"Are you going to tell me what you discussed?"

I shake my head. Not in a million years. Not that we'd talked about anything too telling. But I like that he wants to know.

"I figured as much." He chuckles. "Let me ask you, you have a sharp mind, what do you think I should do?"

"I think you should give me a chance to prove myself." I answer without hesitation. It's also the truth. I want what he can give me. Want to do something besides work in a corporate office. But I can help him too. I'm good, very good. I can make his business life easier if he gives me the opportunity.

"I think so too." He picks up a fork. "Here's the thing, Veronica. I understand, that thing you're searching for. But I don't really think the position I have is it. I think you're meant for something you haven't quite found yet."

"I don't know, but experience is the only way I know of to figure it out."

"I agree. So here's what I propose, if you're interested. I will hire you as a contractor, for a minimum of six months."

My whole body releases its tension. In six months I can make myself indispensable. Make it so he can't live without me. "Thank you."

"You start on Monday. Nine o'clock sharp."

"I promise I won't let you down, Brandon. You won't be sorry."

He tilts his head. "We'll see, won't we?"

Brandon

I let her bask in her excitement for a bit, and I can't deny she's a pleasure to watch. She can't quite hide the thrill of victory in her eyes, and I let her have it. Because in this battle, she's won. She wore me down, and I've conceded.

But what she doesn't understand is that this is only the first battle, and I let her win because it suits me. Or at least that's what I'm telling myself. Simply put, I want her and I'm not ready to be done with her yet. I also firmly believe in what I've said, she's meant for something else, but I do think allowing her to walk this path will help her find it. And I do want her to find what she's searching for.

It's a compromise. I'm not hiring her outright. It buys us time. I have unwavering self-control; I'm sure I can resist her for six months.

I take a bite of the bone marrow and it melts in my mouth before I ask, "What do you think your parents will say about this?"

She shrugs, her face still shining with pleasure. "I don't care. Since they aren't talking to me, I won't even tell them." Her brows knit. "Did your parents not talk to you when you abandoned them?"

I nod. "We didn't speak for eighteen months."

"That's a long time."

"It is." I'm not sure why I entertain her question, or why I want to provide her with additional information, but I find myself adding, "In fairness, I spent a year in Europe with no cell phone."

Her expression widens in surprise. "So that's where you went when you disappeared?"

"Yes, that's where I went." I laugh. "It's all rather cliché, isn't it? Rich boy jets off to Europe to find himself."

She tilts her head. "I suppose that depends."

"On what?"

"On if he found himself."

My mind flashes back to that time in my life where I roamed aimlessly, checking in only periodically at some Internet café. "I did."

She scoops up a forkful of our appetizer and her fork disappears between her lips before slowly sliding it back out. She moans, her eyes close, and I imagine this is what she looks like on the verge of orgasm. Only messier. Much, much messier. I shift in my chair.

Her lashes flutter open. "That's divine."

It is. "Have you never been here before?"

She shakes her head. "No. I haven't had the pleasure."

I wonder what else she hasn't had the pleasure of. I'm guessing quite a bit. I pick up my wine. "I'm glad."

Her gaze flickers. "What did you do, out there in Europe?"

I think about not answering her, of evading, but decide against it. "I did it the old-fashioned way. I took twenty thousand dollars out of my trust fund before I left and gave myself that to live. I backpacked, lived in hostels, took trains. I completely disconnected. I saw all the sites, sat in silence on the top of mountains, communed with nature."

She blinks, and I know she's surprised. "I'm having a hard time picturing you that way."

"I can imagine."

"Why'd you do it?"

"For a couple of reasons."

"Do you wish to share them?" She smiles, softly, and it curves over her mouth I want to taste.

I realize I can't remember the last time I had a real conversation with a woman. Can't remember the last time I engaged in learning another person or having them learn me. I find I want to tell her things, if only for her to understand that I can relate to her as few people can. "Well, at the most basic level, I wanted to dry out."

"Oh?" I love the way her brow knits when she's concentrating. It's so intent. She glances at my wine. "From what?"

"Coke and sex."

She straightens. "I see. Did it work?"

I laugh. "I haven't touched drugs since the morning I left. I made it almost the year without sex."

The barest hint of a flush highlights her cheekbones. "Who changed your mind?"

"A very pretty Parisian girl I met in Prague."

She laughs, shaking her head. "It's always those French girls, isn't it?"

"Indeed."

She dabs her lips with a napkin. "What was it about her that changed your mind?"

I consider the question. It was so long ago, I hadn't thought of Mona in quite some time. I answer Veronica honestly, if only to see what she will do with the information. "She was the first woman I ran across that I wanted to fuck for passion and not sport."

Other than a flash of emotion I can't decipher, her expression gives nothing away. "Did you fancy yourself in love with her?"

I shake my head. "No, I fancied myself in deep lust with her. I've never been in love."

I don't think I'm capable, but that's a different story.

Veronica's gaze meets mine and the tension ebbing and flowing between us tightens back up again. "I've never been in love either."

The air thickens, hot and tangible, reaching across the table.

She glances away and her next words send a shiver of shock through me. "Do you ever wonder if, for people like us, it's not possible?"

I don't ask her what she means, because I know what she means. There's something detached about the world we grew up in. Something that doesn't lend itself to deep connection. "Yes, I have wondered."

"And what do you think?"

I shrug. "I honestly don't know."

She fiddles with her fork. "I can't remember the last time my parents told me they loved me. I was probably a child."

"And Winston?"

She shakes her head. "We only said it once or twice, back in the day, and we didn't mean it."

"Is he the only man you've ever been with?" This is an inappropriate question to ask the woman I've just offered employment, temporary as it might be.

When she speaks the word is soft. "Yes."

"Not even when you were away at Harvard?"

"No, I was too busy proving myself to be distracted by men." She frowns before looking at me. "Do you think that's strange?"

"No." I let a smile play over my lips. "All it means is you haven't met your Parisian yet."

Her spine straightens and I can almost see her gathering her courage. "Do you think you're him?"

The directness surprises me, I raise a brow. "Do you think I'm him?"

Her eyes flicker. "I don't know how to answer that, considering you have rules and just offered me a job."

"I think you should answer it truthfully and see where it takes you."

Her chin tilts. "Yes, I think you might be."

"I think you're correct. It's what to do about it that remains the question." I take a sip of my wine. "For now, we will put you to work, and leave the question off the table."

Her shoulders square and she leans back, placing distance between us. "Yes, that's probably prudent."

I do my best not to smile at her disappointment.

7.

Brandon

I can't believe I'm considering what I'm considering. It's entirely out of character for me, but I can't get it out of my mind. Friday, with the chaos of work, I'd managed to put it out of my mind, but today it's lingered. Nagging at me. Impossible to ignore.

Tonight my friends and I are going to a new, upscale pool hall that opened a couple of weeks ago. I'd called the owner and we'd agreed on a trade, ensuring VIP seating for the night. Originally, I'd intended to bring Stephanie, but now that we've severed our relationship, that's not possible. I'd toyed with the idea of bringing one of my other playmates because that's what I should do.

Only, I don't want to, because I want Veronica.

I want to see her. On Thursday I'd thought it would be easy to stay away from her, knowing I'd be working with her come Monday, but I see now that nothing with her is going to be easy.

Truth be told, she's distracting me.

It's an uncomfortable feeling. Women do not distract me. I distract them. But I can't get her out of my head. I could call and invite her, but I'm not willing to do that. The option I'm considering is telling, and unlike me, but I can't dissuade myself from the notion.

I've ignored it all morning, but find I can't ignore it any longer.

With a sigh, I pick up the phone and call Leo.

He answers on the second ring. "Hey, what's up?"

I close my eyes and shake my head. I cannot believe I'm lowering myself this way. I sigh. "Not one word."

He laughs. "This should be good."

I grit my teeth. "I need a favor."

"Sure." His tone is casual, unconcerned.

I want to be like that. I *am* like that. Only, I'm not right now. But I can play it as cool as possible. Not that it will fool Leo. Fucking cops. "I want Jillian to call Veronica and invite her to come with us tonight."

Silence. Complete and utter silence.

I clear my throat.

Finally, he says, "Oh, really?"

Luckily, I've thought about this way too much and have an excuse prepared. "Yes, I've hired her on a temporary basis, but she has no idea about the sex part of my business. With the club's latex party next Thursday, she'll be unable to avoid it and I want her to get somewhat familiar with some of the dynamics before then."

"I see," Leo says, his tone amused. "So why not ask her yourself?"

That is a very good question. One I have a lame response for. "As her boss, if I ask, she'll feel obligated. Jillian asking her gives her an excuse if she has other plans."

More silence falls over the line before he laughs. "You don't think I'm actually buying this, do you?"

In my coolest, most dismissive voice I say, "There's nothing to buy."

"Come on, this is me you're talking to, you don't think I know how hot you are for her?"

"I am not hot for her. I'm her boss. She's my employee. I want to expose her responsibly."

"You know we can't be overt with her there." He's right, outright exposing your kinks to non-consenting parties is frowned upon.

"I'm not suggesting you be overt. Just hint at it enough to make her wonder."

"Because you want to see if she responds."

"Because she's going to be exposed to it quite aggressively on Thursday," I shoot back. Yes, I have my underground sex club where depravity rages Thursday through Saturday night, but The Lair is a mainstream club that hosts private parties once a month for those willing to pay my prices. It's a safe place for the more upscale BDSM community to publicly express their preferences.

The story I'm telling Leo is one hundred percent true. Veronica will be exposed, and I want her to see what it looks like between actual couples before she witnesses some of the more extreme practices that can be quite frightening to a newcomer.

"Bullshit. You're testing her."

He's right. I am.

I evade. "Are you going to have Jillian ask her or not?"

"I'll have Jillian ask her, not because I owe you either, but because I can't wait to see you sweat."

"Don't be ridiculous." The more defensive I feel, the more my upbringing comes out, and my inflection could rival royalty at the moment.

Not that it fools Leo. He's intuitive and knows me way too fucking well. Leo and I might have met through Michael, who I met in college, but we've long ago developed a friendship outside of Michael. Mainly because we share certain perversities Michael has never been much into.

Of course, I've seen Layla, Ruby and Jillian in all matters of situations. I've seen all three of them on their knees. I've seen all three of them glassy-eyed with desire. I've seen all of them come. Maybe not directly, but certainly in my presence.

We're all good friends after all.

But with Jillian I have taken a more active role. Leo's wife, and the woman I now consider one of my best friends, has quite an exhibitionist streak in her and I'm the only one Leo trusts. Once upon a time, before he was married, we routinely mutually tortured some poor girl. Leo and I have always been good at silent communication and working in tandem. Sometimes we take that out on his wife. It's all in good fun.

But it makes him know me better than Michael or Chad.

Of course, I could have asked Michael or Chad for the favor, but Jillian is the one that took her number.

"I'll have Jillian make the call," Leo says.

My shoulders relax. "Thank you."

"This is going to be fun." Leo chuckles and I want to punch him.

"It's all for the good of her education."

He outright laughs now. "Such bullshit, but consider it done."

I hang up, not commenting any further less I give him more ammunition.

I narrow my eyes, staring at the row of bookshelves lining my office, trying not to think too much how I hope she'll be there tonight. Fifteen minutes goes by when my phone beeps, signaling an incoming message. It's Leo. *She'll be there.*

Good. Now I can relax and get on with my day.

Veronica

Jillian's call asking if I wanted to join them tonight at a new club was an unexpected surprise. When I talked to her, I didn't ask if Brandon was going to be there because I didn't want to reveal my interest. But all my instincts have told me he would be, and I'd dressed accordingly.

I understand I'm not supposed to want to seduce him with my appearance since I'll be working with him come Monday, but I can't seem to help myself. While we are going to a pool hall, which sounds casual, it's actually an upscale establishment, lending itself to the cocktail dress I'm wearing. With my hair loose and wavy, I chose a silky plum-colored dress with long sleeves that rides high on my thighs and a scooped neck. On the surface it's pretty and looks good on me, but it's the back that's the real show. It's a plunging deep V that ends right before the curve of my hips.

It's something he won't see until I'm facing away from him.

It makes me feel sexy. Daring. Alive somehow.

I want him to see me in it. The hope and excitement that he might be there flows hot in my blood, and now I get to find out if my instincts are correct.

I walk past the long line outside to give my name to the doorman. He nods and points to a man on the top of the steps. "He'll show you to the VIP area."

My certainty that Brandon will be there grows and heat spreads out on my cheeks in anticipation. I walk up the steps to a man in a dark suit. "Right this way."

I follow, walking through the crowded main room before reaching a set of steps that leads to a group of about six pool tables. I spot Brandon immediately.

As though he's scented me on the air, he glances up the steps, and our gazes lock.

My heart begins a fast, frantic beat as my throat goes dry. He's the most beautiful man in the room, although in fairness, I don't notice anyone else is even alive. He's standing there, his hand on a pool stick, wearing all black, which he seems to favor. But it's his expression that rivets me. It's dark, dangerous and intent. A series of goose bumps race across my skin.

I walk down the steps, my eyes never leaving his, so when Jillian steps into my view it startles me away from the hypnotic trance he's put me under.

Beaming, she pulls me into a hug. "You made it."

We break apart and I smile at her. "Thank you so much for inviting me."

She laughs, and it's full and throaty. "Believe me, the pleasure is all mine."

She's wearing a red dress, and looks stunning. Grabbing my hand, she pulls me over to the rest of the group. As I take in Leo, Michael and Layla, and Chad and Ruby I can't help marveling at how beautiful they all are. And I don't mean looks, in my circle, almost everyone is beautiful and glamorous. Made that way by wealth and privilege and the help of plastic surgeons. Beauty is a dime a dozen, so I'm not talking about that.

There's something alive about them. Something compelling and captivating. Maybe because they all have that indefinable *thing* I'm searching for. I wave at everyone and say politely, "Thanks for inviting me."

They all say hello, and when my gaze meets Brandon's, it flitters away, because there's a very distinct tension between us. A persistent awkwardness as we feign a casual greeting I don't think either of us feels.

Michael, who I've only seen sitting down, looms over me. He's tall, like really tall and even in my heels I have to crane up to look at him. He holds out a stick to me. "Do you play?"

I nod, taking it from his hands. "I do."

"Excellent." He cocks an evil grin in Brandon's direction. "You're with him."

My pulse practically pounds out of my neck. "All right."

Leo winks at me. "What can we get you to drink?"

"I'll take a Manhattan, thank you," I say, my tone polite.

"Interesting choice." Leo glances around the small room, spots a waitress and signals her over.

Layla and Ruby take turns hugging me and there's a flurry of activity and chitchat before they turn their attention back to the game.

Chad, runs a palm over Ruby's hip, encased in an electric-blue dress that makes her look even more like Snow White. Her lips are red, enhanced by gloss, but I can't help but wonder if that's why her parents named her Ruby. It matches her so well.

Chad nods down at her. "You're up, little girl."

She rolls her eyes but her face practically glows as she looks at him. She takes her stick and bends over the table. But she's not lined up properly, her stance is off, and she takes the shot way too fast. The white ball hits a stripe, and bounces off the table.

Chad laughs and shakes his head. "Oh my god, you suck. I need a new partner."

She straightens and frowns, glaring at him before planting her hands on her hips. "I told you how bad I was, but you wouldn't listen."

"I thought you were being modest," he says with a grin.

"Well, I'm not."

Layla takes a sip of her drink. "Don't worry, Ruby, I suck too."

Ruby tilts her chin. "Thanks, Laylay."

Like Michael, Layla is in black. He's sitting on a stool, legs spread, and she's leaning against his broad chest. His hand is pressed to her stomach, and he runs his hand over the silk of her dress, traveling up to brush the underside of one breast, and my breath catches in my throat. It's not overt, but there's something very sexy about it, and quite simply, they are stunning to look at.

They almost look like one of those film noir-inspired fashion shoots you see in art magazines. All gritty, raw and powerful.

Michael presses his lips to her neck and says, "We'll have to swap partners around then, won't we?"

Layla peers back at him, shrugging one shoulder. "Jillian sucks too, so you should all even out."

Michael shifts his attention to me, pinning me to the spot. "What about you, Veronica? Do you suck?"

The directness of his gaze makes me shift on my high heels, but I smile. "No, I'm afraid I don't." I grew up with rich kids, and playing pool was a common Saturday night when we were growing up.

"Lucky, Brandon." He smirks, and again his hand travels slowly, and sensuously, over his soon-to-be wife.

I tear my eyes away, thankful to see the waitress returning with her tray of drinks.

I've been avoiding looking at Brandon, afraid my excitement and anticipation at seeing him will be way too obvious. He's leaning against the table where the drinks are being placed, and I have no other choice but to confront him.

I smile, hoping I look casual. "Hi."

His gaze flickers over me. "You came."

I square my shoulders. "Yes."

Again he roams over my body before nodding. "Good."

The others appear to be watching us, and I wonder if the tension is as obvious to them as it is to me. My lashes flutter. "So I'm with you?"

"You are." A brow rises. "Do you have a problem with that?"

I shake my head. "Not at all."

It doesn't escape my notice that we are all paired up. I take a sip of my drink and let it burn down my throat.

Leo says, "You guys can play the winner."

"Sounds fair," I say.

"Jilly, you're up," Leo tells his wife.

She takes the stick.

Drink in hand, I turn to watch her play.

Behind me, there's a shifting. I crane my neck to peer over my shoulder.

Brandon's gaze is on my back. His jaw tightens.

I attempt to tap down my delight and return my attention to the game.

I can't pay attention though, because my mind is spinning with Brandon. Wondering what he's thinking. Wondering what this night will bring. Wondering what might happen between us. Because something will happen.

There's too much attraction. Too much chemistry scorching the air. The tension will have to reach a tipping point.

The only real question is when.

Brandon

Veronica is stunning at pool. Maybe even better than I am. After the last game, the rest of the couples decided that we needed to play head to head. Right now, she's at the top of the table, pool stick in hand, bent over, concentrating on breaking.

With smooth, fluid movements, she draws back and sends the balls flying across the table, she straightens, flashing me a grin. "Good luck."

I step up and survey the results. I'm going to need it. If I had any blood in my brain, I'd have a better shot, but she's distracting me. I want to focus on her and not the game in front of me. I walk to where she is, coming to stand next to her. My attention drifts to her mouth. "Where did you learn to play pool?"

She shrugs. "Where'd you?"

"Point taken." Of course she'd know how to play pool, it was a pastime growing up, although they called it billiards in our circles.

"Do you think you can beat me?" She's confident now, full of sass and power.

I'm almost struck dumb by a visual image of putting her on the table, lifting her skirt, and smacking her ass until it melts right out of her. I smirk. "Shall we wager?"

Her honey eyes flash with interest. "That will make things more interesting."

I'd say the things that are interesting between Veronica and me are growing by the second. It's quite clear that there's something between us. Something that isn't willing to be denied. I shift my stance, turning to face her more directly. We're a touch too close, edging into a dangerous territory.

Her chin tilts.

"It would." I travel the length of her, pausing on her hard nipples, visible under the fabric. With her backless dress that almost gave me a coronary the second she turned around, she's not wearing a bra and I want nothing more than to ask her how her breasts feel abrading the silk.

Calling attention to the sensation would have a ripple effect. One she'd dismiss at first with a laugh and maybe a roll of her eyes. It would float out of her head, but before long it would boomerang. She'd move and become hyperaware of her nipples rubbing against the fabric. She'd try and ignore it, but before long it would be all she could think about.

I frown. Or at least that's how it works with submissive girls. I peer into her eyes, trying to discover the truth of her, but all I can read is hunger.

Her brow creases. "Why are you frowning?"

I shake my head. "Nothing."

It's disconcerting I have no idea how to handle my attraction to her. What's worse is I have no idea how to broach a subject that's not been on the table, nor should it be. I'm quite sure Veronica has never come close to experiencing sex the way I need it. And I do need it. Dominance is not optional for me. It just is, and has been for a long time. I have no experience with a woman never exposed to submission.

Once, both Jillian and Ruby were novices, having no

knowledge or understanding of their nature. Ruby went as far as outright disgust at any hint of power exchange. Only, with them, it was easier somehow. I'd known from the second I laid eyes on them they were submissive. While I'd seen Layla at my club, and met her when she was already well involved with Michael, she still would have been obvious to me.

It's always been like a homing device. But that normal skill eludes me with Veronica. She's like a mystery. But she doesn't instinctively lower her gaze, even when I give her my most intent, most focused expression. A habit even the most defiant submissive girls seem to have when in the presence of a strong dominant.

Veronica doesn't even flicker. She just stares right back at me. Unwavering. Like a dare. Challenging me.

I don't know what to make of her. All I know is that attraction and chemistry burns between us, and she's not giving me any of the normal signs I've come to expect.

Her tongue flicks over her lower lip. "Why are you looking at me like that?"

If I didn't have an audience, I'm not sure I would be able to keep myself from grasping her chin tight in my hand, but I'm well aware my friends are looking on with interest. I tilt my head. "I'm looking for the same thing I was looking for that night on the balcony."

Her expression widens with recognition. "Any luck?"

"Nope."

Our gazes become tangled and interwoven. An entire unspoken conversation passes between us.

She finally breaks, and while she doesn't look away she does gesture toward the table. "Our wager?"

"Any suggestions?" My voice is low, far too seductive.

Her hand flutters to the silver chain at her neck. "If I win, I want you to buy me a drink."

A smile touches the corner of my lips. "Have you paid for a drink all night?"

Her attention shifts to my friends pretending to be engrossed in conversation when I know they are hanging on my every interaction with Veronica. She shakes her head. "Alone. After we leave."

She's bold. I'll give her that. I glance down at her mouth. "And if I win?"

She smiles. "What do you want?"

"You don't know?"

She shrugs one shoulder. "I do, and I don't. Name your price."

"If I win, I have a business lunch Saturday afternoon. You'll go with me." The delight that fills her features makes me laugh. "We have a deal?"

Her chin tilts. "I'll go with you even if you lose."

"I know." Because of course she will. Just like we'll end up going for a drink if she does.

"So game on?"

I nod. "Game on."

What follows is a vicious battle where we are neck and neck, until the final ball.

She lines up, her stance rock solid. Her muscles flex as she draws back the stick.

The crack of balls. I watch as the eight ball rolls smoothly into the left corner pocket.

I've lost.

She beams at me. "I win."

"I can't believe it," Jillian says, pointing at me. "She beat you."

Veronica laughs.

I raise a brow. "We'll have to rematch soon."

I'm not surprised she's beaten me. Not only is she skilled, I have a distinct disadvantage in that I'm completely distracted by her. If I'm being honest, I don't like it. I don't like it one fucking bit.

Veronica Westwood is dangerous.

I should end this, but I already know I'm not going to do that. She's too addictive. And I haven't come close to satisfying my appetite for her.

I can take the loss since it will leave me alone with her,

which is exactly where I want to be.

Veronica

Brandon had a car come and take everyone home. I'm sitting next to him, vibrating with tension, practically insane with the anticipation licking a path along my skin. The other couples are laughing and joking, but Brandon and I have remained mostly silent.

While he's not touching me, our thighs are pressed together, and the fabric of his pants rubs against my bare leg like the worst kind of tease. I can't even process how I feel. Because it's not anything I've ever felt before.

I had no idea want like this existed. Or what to do with it. All I really know is that the second we are alone something is going to happen.

It's the most alive I've ever felt. Validating my every instinct I've had about him. Just not in the way I'd envisioned. Come Monday I'll discover if my career ambitions will come to fruition, but tonight, tonight this is about me. Becoming.

We've already dropped off Ruby and Chad, and as Layla and Michael climb out the car, it leaves plenty of room for Brandon to move over and give me space. I'm not remotely surprised when he doesn't. He stays right where he is, the heat of his muscle and bone searing along my nerve endings.

Across from us, Leo and Jillian sit. Jillian is smiling, curled next to her husband. He glances at Brandon, who gives a subtle nod I don't understand. Leo puts his hand on Jillian's thigh, looks at me, and says, "Uncross your legs, girl."

His gaze is so direct on mine, for a split second I think he's talking to me, but when Jillian goes from lazy and relaxed, to alert in a flash of an instant, I know it was in my imagination.

Her gaze darts to me, then to Brandon. Leo squeezes her leg and she complies, uncrossing her legs but leaving them closed. Leo's fingers curl around her thigh, inching high on her leg.

The air stirs and I shift restlessly, unsure what's going on. Brandon's leg presses more firmly against mine.

Leo pushes Jillian's thighs apart, not far, just a little nudge, and begins tracing circles along the inner space above her knee. Slow. So very slow.

Jillian lets out a tiny gasp.

I try my hardest to avert my eyes, but I can't seem to stop watching as he inches higher. It's not obscene, but there's no question that it's sexual. It's not even the most sexual thing I've ever witnessed. I grew up in a world of excess. Where we all had no boundaries, and access to anything we could possibly want. I've seen people have sex before and this is nothing like that.

I never responded then, but I'm certainly responding now.

I bite my lip.

Leo leans over and whispers something in Jillian's ear that makes her lashes droop. I want to know what he's saying.

Leo smirks at me. "Are you enjoying yourself, Veronica?"

My cheeks flame and I clear my throat. "Yes, thank you for inviting me."

His fingers continue their crawl over Jillian's skin. "The pleasure is ours."

I smile and force my attention off them to the street. It's Saturday night and the neighborhood bustles with activity. Next to me, Brandon's leg shifts, abrading against now hyperaware flesh.

I don't quite understand how the tension has amped up, filling the car, but it's all I can think about.

"Do you want to come to brunch tomorrow?" Jillian asks, her voice breathless.

I jerk my focus back inside the car. Leo's hand is even higher up her thigh. I swallow hard. "That would be great. Thanks."

For the first time, Brandon speaks. "Jillian, do you think you'd be able to take Veronica shopping for the private party next Thursday?"

Jillian's expression widens with what looks like excitement. "I'd love to. We could go after brunch."

My brow creases and I risk a glance at Brandon. "Party?"

He nods. "Once a month The Lair hosts a private party for a very select group of clientele. Each month there is a theme. As part of your job, you'll be required to attend, and you'll need to dress appropriately."

Jillian grins at me. "Don't be scared."

Leo laughs.

"Scared?" Why would I be scared of a party?

Brandon shrugs. "It can be a bit overwhelming for a newcomer."

I bite my lower lip. "What's the theme?"

Brandon meets my gaze, and his focus is direct and intent on mine. "Latex."

The answer confuses me even more. "I don't understand."

"It's a fetish party, Veronica." His attention shifts to my mouth and the words get jumbled in my brain.

"Oh." I have no response to this information.

Jillian offers another bright smile. "Don't worry, we'll all be there to make sure you're okay. We'll help you sort it all out."

Leo squeezes her thigh. "Tell Veronica about your first party."

She laughs. "It was…not fun."

Leo glances at her and cocks a brow. "All those orgasms you had begs to differ."

My lashes flutter with this information. Does that mean? All of them? I risk a peek at Brandon. Him?

Her expression turns chagrin. "Those don't count."

"Why don't they count?" Leo asks. "Since I allowed them, this is new information to consider."

My brows furrow. Allowed them?

Jillian straightens. "Umm…"

He grins at her. "Careful, you're about to talk yourself into hot water." He reaches over and strokes a thumb over her jaw. "I can see it in your eyes."

I can't help leaning forward. Wondering where on earth this

is going. But the car comes to a halt and Leo pulls back, and winks at me. "This is us."

Jillian scrambles to get her purse and other belongings before turning to me. "We usually go around eleven. I'll text you with the details."

"Sounds good." Nerves slither along my spine. Once they leave this car I'll be alone with Brandon. And I have…questions.

From outside, Jillian leans down and says, "We'll talk tomorrow. I promise."

Then the door closes. And I'm alone.

With Brandon.

I eye him, shifting into the corner away from him. His blue eyes are intent on mine. His expression one I can't decipher.

He smiles. "I owe you a drink."

I nod, tilting my chin. "You do."

The driver looks in his rear-view mirror. "Headed home, Mr. Townsend?"

He's silent for a moment, looking at me as though he's trying to peer inside me. Finally he says, "What would you think about having that drink at my house?"

My throat goes dry but I manage to say, "I think that would be fine."

"Good." He glances to the driver. "Yes, home, Gerald."

Then he slowly raises the glass and we're alone.

He glances down my body before meeting my eyes. "I'm not sleeping with you."

"All right." My stomach jumps at the mere mention of it.

"We're going to have a drink or two, and talk. That's all."

I don't know what makes me say it, but the words are out of my mouth before I can stop them. "Are you trying to convince me? Or you?"

He laughs, shaking his head. "Maybe both of us." He rests his arm on the seat in back of me. "It's been quite some time since I've been attracted to a woman that's as much of a handful as you are."

My shoulders square. "That seems unfortunate."

"Indeed. But I can't forget our working relationship, Veronica. I won't."

"Understood." The disappointment seeps through me like air hissing out of a balloon.

His dimples flash. "I'll admit, taking you home doesn't seem the smartest move."

"Yet, you're still taking me home."

"Yes." He nods, as though to give further confirmation. "It will be a challenge to keep my hands off you." His gaze darkens. "Especially when I can feel your arousal. Your want."

My pulse takes up a throbbing rhythm in my neck. In this moment, it occurs to me, when I blew up my life, I didn't just change my circumstances. I changed myself as well. In this short time, I've stopped being the woman that wants to play things safe. Stopped being the woman that wants to do nothing but hold her standing in society and make up for the fact that I was born female instead of male. I did more than change my profession.

I changed my perception.

The woman I've become, who I want to be, takes risks. Even if they are scary. Even if they lead me to places I don't understand. So I throw caution to the wind and state what I want. I swallow hard. "What if I don't want you to keep your hands off me?"

He raises a brow. "What are you saying, explicitly?"

I grow bolder. "I want you to touch me."

He tilts his head, assessing. "I think it's best if we keep things professional."

"Because you're afraid."

His expression flashes. "Because you're about to work for me. You need to see what that looks like first. To experience it without my influence clouding you."

"There's more." I don't know how I know, but I do.

His fingers tighten on the seat, flexing into the leather, and I wonder if he's restraining himself from reaching for me. If it's as much of a struggle for him as it is for me. His jaw hardens. "There's a lot you don't know about me. About the

94

things I need."

Unwilling to shy away from the subject, I lick my lower lip. "Like the fetish party?"

"To start with." He leans closer, close enough for his body to warm mine. "But there's much, much more."

"Will you tell me?" My voice comes out in a thready whisper, like I'm not sure I want to know.

"Yes. I don't have a choice in the matter."

"Because you want me?"

"That, and because the longer you work for me, the more unavoidable it will become." He juts his chin toward the window. "We're here."

The door opens and I stare at the historic mansion that Brandon calls home. I have no idea what waits for me inside, but I want to find out. I'm not backing away.

We climb out and walk up the steps where he unlocks the heavy wood door. I enter a grand foyer with sweeping ceilings and rich woodwork. It is out of another time, yet something about it is distinctly Brandon.

Not many men would look at home here, but he does. He wears the opulence and the age well. He peers over his shoulder. "Come with me."

I follow, glancing into a parlor lined with bookshelves and antiqued, brocade furniture, past an office with a huge desk. We walk down a hall and he pushes open double doors to a living room with leather couches, a big screen television, and a bar along one wall. Instinctively I guess this is where he spends most of his time.

He points to the couch. "Sit down."

I slide off my shawl, dropping it and my purse on the chair before sinking into the couch. "It's lovely. Your house."

"Thank you." He walks over to the bar. "Is brandy okay?"

"Yes." I watch as he picks up the decanter, the muscles moving under his shirt, captivating me.

When he returns he puts a snifter in my hand before sitting down in the opposite corner. I decide to make myself at home and kick off my killer heels before tucking my legs under me.

He tracks the movements, his expression dark, and hungry. Or at least that's what I want to believe. I take a drink, letting the liquid burn down my throat and settle in my stomach.

He also takes a drink, hissing a bit before he says, "I want you to know something."

"What's that?"

"I don't invite women into this room."

Surprise sneaks through me. I frown. "I find that hard to believe."

He smiles. "I'm not saying I've never had a woman here, I'm saying this isn't where I take her."

I push my hair off my shoulder. "Do I want to know?"

He laughs. "I usually keep them in the parlor, and in the basement."

I blink at his word choice, and stumble for something to say. "I see."

Those dimples flash. "Let's talk about the party on Thursday."

I straighten a little in my seat. So he's going to keep it to business after all. I nod. "All right."

"Once a month I hold a private party for my upscale BDSM clients."

Of course, I know what BDSM is, or at least what it looks like. I clear my throat. "Oh?"

"As you learned earlier, they are themed. Thursday's theme is latex. You'll need to look the part. And you'll need to be comfortable dealing with things you're probably not used to seeing."

"I can assure you I've seen all matter of things. I don't think it will be a problem." My voice is ultra sure, ultra confident. I believe me. Kind of.

He nods. "I'm hoping that's true, but some of the people who attend will surprise you. I want you to be prepared."

"How do you suggest I do that?"

"The girls tomorrow will help. And I'll give you research. We'll talk. Hopefully you'll have enough time to fake your way through it."

I run my fingers through my hair again. "You know how we grew up, surely it won't be that bad."

"It depends. Some nights are more outrageous than others. It's hard to tell how each event will go."

My brow furrows as a million questions stream through my head and I try to sort through them all. I settle on the least confusing one. "The Lair is so successful, why do you do it? It doesn't seem necessary."

"There's the million-dollar question." He takes another sip of his drink before continuing. "Quite simply. I do it because I want to. Because I remember the frustration of not having a safe outlet for my perversities. I wanted to give those people like me a place to express themselves without judgment."

I can't stop the flush from creeping over my chest. His words can only mean one thing and I fumble over the question. "So does that mean…" I trail off, unable to complete the thought.

"Yes, it does."

"But…" I frown. "So, what are you saying? You like to dress up in latex?" My mind flashes to images of people in head-to-toe rubber and I can't help but shudder. Some of my desire cools. I'm not sure if that's a deal breaker.

He laughs, a hearty genuine sound that has my lust kicking back up again. Okay, maybe I can learn to live with it. He shakes his head. "No. I do not. But some do, and that's why I have themes for the month, to allow people to indulge in their kinks. Even if they are not ones I share."

My stomach relaxes and I smile. "Is it wrong to say I'm relieved?"

He shakes his head, then gives me that intent stare he's been blasting at me all night. "That's not one of my depravities. But I have many others."

My heart pounds in my throat. "Such as?"

He doesn't even hesitate and his words send my heart thundering in my ears. "I dominate women. I'm a bit sadistic. A bit cruel. And I'm afraid it's a non-negotiable for me."

Veronica

I'm not even sure what to make of that statement. I blink at him. "Oh."

He shrugs, as if it's no big deal. "You'll see a lot of that on Thursday night, so I wanted you to be prepared."

I swallow hard. "And that's the only reason?"

"For now." He meets my gaze. "I did think it was something you should know. It might change your attraction to me."

"And…" I clear my throat. "If it's not okay with me? What then?"

"I'm not sure what you'd like me to say here." His words are slow and deliberate. Measured. Like he's guarding his secrets, and perhaps, maybe he is. "This isn't a situation I expected to find myself in."

"What situation is that?"

"You have a number of strikes against you."

"And those are?" It's like we're negotiating, but I'm not

sure what we're negotiating about. This situation is tangled and complicated.

"You come from a world I want no part of. I don't mix business and pleasure. I only date submissive women." He leans forward and puts his glass on the table before turning to face me. "And I find myself in the odd predicament of not wanting to say no to you."

I suck in a stuttery breath; it catches in my lungs and makes it hard to get air. "I'm not sure what to say."

"You don't have to say anything. I only want to expose you, to introduce you. Partly because it's part of the job I have, and partly so you can make up your mind about it and see how you feel. I'm not going to sway you by using our sexual attraction against you." He meets my gaze and that look is back. "But understand, this is how I am. There's no changing it for me. If we ever sleep together, if I ever touch you, I will dominate you. I will crave hurting you. I already do."

My cheeks flame what I'm sure is bright red. "Hurt me?"

He nods. "I understand this is a difficult notion for you to take in. It's why I'm staying far away from you for the present. Regardless of what I wanted to do to you in the back of that car."

Despite the strangeness of his words, a burning desires licks through me. "What did you want to do to me?"

The air thickens and his expression takes on a type of feral heat. A possession that steals the air from my lungs. "I wanted to kiss you, certainly. When Leo slid his hand up Jillian's skirt, I wanted to do the same. I wanted to dig my fingers into your flesh and listen to your helpless gasps. I wanted to tear your dress from your body. Bite your neck. Wrap my hand around your throat. I wanted to mark you. I wanted to turn you over my knee, shove your dress past your hips and spank you."

I might hyperventilate. I might have a heart attack, right here on this couch. I don't even dare breathe let alone interrupt.

He continues, relentless in his description of what could have happened in the car on the way to his home. "I wanted to shove my fingers between your legs and make you come. And then I wanted to fuck you in the way only I can. In a way that will surely ruin you. Because, Veronica, that's what I really want. I want to ruin you. I want to ruin your perfect hair and flawless skin. I want your mouth swollen and wrecked. I want to put red marks down your back merely because you've taunted me with it all night. I want to bruise your inner thighs. I want you to lie in bed and feel my teeth in your flesh. I want to see those pretty eyes filled with tears and begging. I want to systematically and ruthlessly destroy you until there's nothing left but aching need for me."

I might melt. Just liquefy into heat and longing. I have never even had the imagination to dream a man could think such things, let alone say them. A shudder passes through me, leaving behind goose bumps. I press my thighs together.

His attention dips to my lips. "That's what I want to do to you."

"I see." I can't think of one intelligent thing to say.

He laughs. "So you can understand why I'm restraining myself."

I nod.

"It's something for you to think about."

"I will."

"Are you ready to go home?" He tilts his head toward the door. "I have Gerald waiting."

I don't know what I'm ready to do, but I do need time to think. To process. Because I understand now. Sex with Brandon will not be just sex. It will be life altering. I want life altering. But I need—I don't know—to prepare for it. I drain the rest of my drink and put it on the table next to me. "Maybe that would be best."

"I believe you're right." Brandon stands, picks up his phone and texts. "Gerald will meet us outside."

In silence we walk through the house, the sounds of my heels clicking across the marble foyer laid in an intricate design. He opens the door and the car is already waiting. We walk down the steps, and when I get to the door, I turn to him. My smile wobbles, but I can still manage it. A question pops into my head, and I don't resist the urge to ask it. "Did you arrange for me to join you tonight?"

His expression flickers. "Yes."

"Why?"

"I could pretend it was for your education, but it's not the truth." He puts his hands into his pockets. "I didn't want to wait until Monday to see you."

"Why didn't you ask me yourself?"

"Because I wanted you to feel like you could say no."

"Oh." I go and try to leave, but find myself returning to him. "Thank you, for tonight. For everything."

"You're welcome." His gaze roams my features, sliding over my cheeks and lips and neck like a caress. "I'll see you Monday. It's a big day."

I can't make my feet move. It's like they are cemented in concrete. "I don't think I want to leave."

He steps closer to me. "I don't think I want you to leave."

I clear my throat. "So Monday?"

He nods. "Monday."

When I don't move, he comes even closer and it's like all my cells come alive. "Go, Veronica."

"I'm going." I don't even twitch.

"I'm not going to kiss you. No matter how much your body is begging me."

"All right."

One hand slides out of his pocket, lifts, and curls around my neck.

My heart quickens.

His fingers trace along my shoulder and slide down my spine. My knees actually tremble. Down my back he goes, his touch hot. I gasp as his palm comes to rest on the curve of my spine.

"Your skin is soft." His voice is gruff.

I nod.

"You're shaking."

"Yes." Not from fear, but because I want him that much.

"I'm not going to kiss you." He leans closer, close enough to see the shards of electric white in his eyes, lit like bolts of lightning. "But I can bite you."

My lips part on an intake of breath.

He takes full advantage, swooping down and capturing my lower lip with his teeth. His tongue flickers over the damp flesh and I feel it everywhere. From the top of my head to the tips of my toes.

Back and forth his tongue strokes.

I clutch at his arm as my knees go weak.

He releases me and when I sway, he clasps my waist and holds me steady. He lifts his head. "Good night, Veronica."

"Good night, Brandon." My tone is practically panting, revealing my desperateness.

He squeezes my waist, his fingers shift through strands of my hair, and then he steps away. He opens the car door. "Go."

I climb in, and he closes the door, patting the top of the car to signal the driver.

The tips of my fingers brush over my mouth, the feel of his teeth lingering.

Like a brand.

Brandon

Veronica texts me at three in the morning and I'm not even surprised. Not surprised to find she's still awake, unable to sleep. Because I have been lying here, staring at my ceiling for hours. Not even jerking off alleviated the ache. The lust.

I don't know the last time that happened. Maybe never. At least not with any woman I can actually recall. And I'm pretty sure I will remember standing at the bottom of my stairs, my arm wrapped around her, listening to her panting, needy breaths for the rest of my life.

It worries me. My reaction to her worries me. Her reaction to me worries me.

Even though I should, I can't stop from answering her. I read her text. *I can't sleep.*

Tell me why. I answer her as a dominant, too tired to rein it in.

My phone chimes. *I can't stop thinking about the things you said to me.*

Good. Because it is good. I want her to think about them. Want her to be distracted by the things I want to do to her.

That's not helpful.

I can't help but smile into the darkness because her response fills me with a hope I have no right to, or want any part of. It's a girl's response. That's the only way I can describe it. *What would you like me to do about it?*

Her response is almost immediate. *Make it stop.*

I am walking a very dangerous line here. I war with what's right and my more base desires. *Have you touched yourself?*

No!!!!!

I laugh. Such a girl. *Touch yourself until you come. That will help.*

Thirty seconds goes by before she responds. *I can't.*

Why?

Because I'm afraid.

My cock stirs, and I slide my hand to grasp my shaft. *What are you afraid of?*

That it will make it worse.

I groan. God she is driving me out of my fucking mind. The amount of willpower I've expended over the course of the evening is more than I've required in an entire year. It wasn't too long ago a naked, writhing girl lying on the floor, begging me, didn't make me think twice about resisting her.

Unlike tonight, when I have never worked so hard not to kiss someone. Because it was work. And sadly, it was that, that stopped me. Because I didn't think I could stop. I blow out a breath and type out, *It will make it worse. But it will also make it better.*

Okay. That one little word says everything.

I resisted laying my mouth on her—well, kind of—but I don't resist the impulse that comes over me. *And, Veronica, when I see you Monday morning, the first thing I'm going to think is that you came for me.*

A full minute passes before her text. *Why did I even text you?*

That's easy.

Why?

Because you couldn't help yourself.

Good night, Brandon!

Good night, Veronica.

Grinning, I put the phone on the nightstand and I can't deny, right or wrong, I'm feeling much better.

10.

I'm at brunch with Brandon's friends' significant others, and I can only sit back and watch them, marveling at their easy manner. I've never had friends like this, and I'm fascinated. They are all sunshine and laughter and support. Their affection toward each other obvious.

I want to be part of them. To understand what it feels like to view women as confidants versus competition. There's talk of weddings and brides and flowers as we sip mimosas. Even if nothing happens with Brandon, I'm thankful to have been given the chance to be a part of something I've been craving for as long as I can remember.

My phone goes off and I look down, my heart surging that it might be Brandon, only to see a text from Winston. *I need to talk to you.*

With a frown, I darken my cell and return to the table. He's getting more insistent and once again I contemplate if I should talk to him in hopes he'll stop.

"Is everything okay?" Jillian's voice has my head lifting.

I put a bright smile on my face. "Yes, thanks, everything's great."

"You sure?" Her head tilts. Her hair is in a ponytail this morning and the dark mass swings.

I wave a hand. "Yes, I'm sure."

"Good." Jillian nods before her expression turns sly and she looks at Ruby and Layla. "So, girls, what do you think we should get Veronica to wear for the party Thursday?"

Layla grins and looks me up and down. "Hmmm... Everything will look good on her."

I laugh. "Thanks, not true, but thank you."

Ruby shakes her head. "Let's round her out with the rest of us."

"Ohhh." Jillian nods. "I like that idea."

The inclusion warms me. I can't help it, my grin widens. "I have no idea what I'm in store for, so I have no choice but to leave it in your hands."

Jillian picks up her flute and takes a sip. "Brandon said to have Monique put it on his account, so money is no object."

Surprise has me straightening in my chair. "Oh, that's not necessary."

"But it is." Jillian winks at me. "It's for work after all."

I decide not to fight her on it. I'll just pay when I get there. Instead I say, "We'll see."

Layla says, "I'm wearing pink, Jilly you're in red, and Ruby is in black, of course. So that leaves white."

Ruby looks me up and down. "White would be perfect."

"But we have to make it heart stopping," Jillian says. "Because Brandon needs to sweat."

My cheeks heat and I hold up my hands. "You've misunderstood, there's nothing between Brandon and me."

All three of them laugh.

I feel exposed, and I deny too vehemently. "I swear. It's business. I'm his employee. Nothing more. Nothing less." Last night speeds through my head as though in fast forward, ending with his teeth sinking into my lower lip, and then later, much later, when I'd stupidly texted him before slipping my fingers between my legs.

Layla pats my arm. "Veronica, we've all known Brandon a long time, and trust us, we know only business when we see it."

Ruby squirms a little in her chair. "He's smitten."

"And we're all really excited about it," Jillian adds.

It's such a preposterous word to describe him my mouth falls open. "He is *not*."

"But he is." Layla leans over the table and mock whispers, "He couldn't take his eyes off you. I've never seen him look at anyone like that before."

I can't help it, a type of girlish excitement I've never experienced before rushes over me, heating me all over. Because I want to be different. I don't want to be someone he's merely attracted to, but something unusual. I want to change him. Like he's changing me. "I'm sure you're exaggerating."

Jillian shakes her head. "I can assure you, we're not."

Ruby shrugs one shoulder. "So it's our job to make sure he suffers."

I cover my face with my hands and a little laugh escapes. "I want to be professional."

"Honey," Layla says, patting my back. "You're going to a fetish party. There's nothing professional about it."

I raise my head. "I don't even know what a fetish party is."

Jillian raises her glass like she's toasting me. "That's what we're here for. To teach you all about it."

Ruby gives me a soft smile. "And don't worry, I've only been to a couple, we can be newbies together."

"So what are your questions?" Jillian asks.

I blow out a hard breath. "I don't even know where to begin."

"We'll help you sort it out." Layla circles her hand around the table. "To start with, always remember you don't have to participate. You can just watch. Only try not to judge what you see, even if it surprises you."

"Okay." That sounds like an easy enough start.

"And if you see something that worries you, tell one of Brandon's people and let them take care of it." Ruby laughs. "I once made the mistake of thinking something was wrong, but the girl just really wanted to be beaten."

I blanch. "Beaten?"

Ruby grimaces right along with me. "I had to turn away, but Chad and Brandon assured me it was all consensual."

I can't help but ask the question. "So, does this mean, all of you?"

They all nod.

Well, isn't this a strange new world I've entered. I clear my throat, hoping to practice my cool. "Are you the dominant one or the submissive one?"

This makes them all howl with laughter. Belatedly, after meeting their men, the notion that those males might be the submissive ones is ridiculous.

Jillian waves a finger around the three friends. "We're all submissive."

Layla grins at her future sister-in-law. "You should try and order Leo around a little and see what happens."

This causes a fresh batch of hysterics. Jillian wipes under her lashes. "I'm going to try it and tell him it was your idea."

Layla huffs. "And have Michael take it out on me, no way!"

I wrinkle my nose, really tying together their familial relationship. "Isn't that awkward? Considering you're siblings?"

Jillian and Layla shrug at each other, before shaking their heads.

Jillian speaks first. "It was at first, but we got used to it. The rules are we are open about it, but if we're together, anything sexual happens in separate corners."

"How does that work?" This is fascinating, and they are all so free, it's hard not to appease my curiosity.

Layla laughs. "It means we get into trouble frequently, but that beyond the basics, we are dealt with separately."

Ruby huffs. "Which really gives them an unfair advantage. I can get dealt with anywhere, anytime. It's so annoying."

I swallow. "Dealt with?"

Jillian gives me a once over, her hazel eyes sparkling with mischief. "You'll see. I mean, it's not like we'll go a whole night without someone getting punished."

They all giggle like they've got some sort of plan.

"Punished?" The word kind of sticks in my throat.

Ruby leans forward. "It's much better than it sounds. It's hard to explain. To be honest, I was a very reluctant submissive."

"Very reluctant." Jillian rolls her eyes. "That's putting it mildly. She was deep into it and still kicking and screaming the whole way."

I don't understand any of this, but I understand to some extent they are all clueing me into an aspect of Brandon's life I have no understanding of, and by sharing their experiences they are giving me knowledge without making me have to ask the direct question. So, I might as well take advantage. I shift my attention to Ruby. "Why did you do it then?"

Ruby wrinkles her nose. "Well, I liked it. I just didn't want to admit I liked it. You make these discoveries about yourself, and they are uncomfortable."

Jillian grins at me. "But orgasmic."

Layla winks. "If you're allowed to come, that is."

My head practically spins and I have so many questions I don't even know where to start. "It's hard to understand."

"True, but I have a feeling you'll find out soon enough." Jillian touches my arm. "Just remember, on Thursday it's okay if you're uncomfortable. It sounds weird, but it's kind of the point."

I decide to focus on that, and not on her presumption about Brandon and me. They are confirming what Brandon said last night, and I'm not even close to being able to wrap my head around it. Instead, I focus on the party, which looms on the horizon like a big unknown. "I don't understand."

"Pushing your boundaries, embracing what scares you is part of why we do it in the first place. But don't feel obligated. It's certainly not for everyone. Brandon will want to make sure you're comfortable enough not to react negatively when you see something extreme. Which you're bound to see at a fetish party where everyone is out there to be seen." Jillian laughs. "And honestly, compared to a lot of people we're kind of tame."

"I suppose that's some sort of reassurance."

Ruby tucks a lock of hair behind her ear. "The most important thing to remember is that it's consensual, something that I remind myself on the regular."

Layla nods. "Yes, but if you see something that doesn't feel right to you, make sure you let one of the monitors know so they can check it out and assess the situation."

"Monitors?" I ask.

"Brandon has people who are watching to make sure everyone is safe," Jillian says.

"That's good to know." Although it brings me no sense of relief. In fact, the more they talk, the more nervous I become about what I'm getting into. Not that I'm about to let that stop me.

Ruby picks up her flute and downs the rest of her drink. "I wish this wasn't the first party. Next month is a schoolgirl theme, which is a lot more fun and playful than the latex scene. I still have a hard time when I see people covered in head-to-toe rubber and zipper masks."

My eyes go wide in shock.

Jillian laughs and wiggles her finger in a circle. "I think this is the reaction he's trying to avoid."

I cover my face with my hands and hang my head. "Oh god, I'm sorry!"

"Don't be! It's totally normal." She snaps her fingers. "Here's what you do, when you get home Google latex fetish and look at all the images for an hour. That should give you a good idea what to expect and help relax you and get you used to what you'll see."

"I will." Knowledge is power.

Layla smiles at me. "The gist is there's as many flavors to BDSM as there are ice cream, but when there's a party everyone is a bit more out there."

"Good to know."

Ruby holds out her glass to the waitress for a refill. "As a fellow newcomer, the best advice I can give you is to go with the flow, relax and have fun. Pay attention to what you like and what you hate and save it for further analysis when you're not working." She crumples up her napkin.

They all nod in unison.

I finger the neckline of my top, a camel-colored, silky spaghetti-strapped number I'd paired with jeans. "I've never been to a fetish party before, thanks for helping me figure out what to expect."

"We've all been there, not too long ago." Jillian waves at Layla. "Except for Layla, she's been a slut forever."

"Hey!" Layla hits Jillian on the arm before winking at me. "Although it's true. I was introduced to it back in college by my first fiancé."

My brows furrow. First? I don't know her well enough to ask for an elaboration but she must read the confusion on my face because her expression dims a touch before she smiles softly. "I was engaged to my college boyfriend, but he died shortly before our wedding."

My heart instantly squeezes for her. "I'm so sorry. That must have been terrible."

"It was." She shrugs. "It almost killed me, but it led me to Michael instead."

Ruby squeezes her friend's hand. "And we are grateful for that."

Layla peers off in the distance before her vision comes back into focus. "Anyway, regardless, we were all new at one time. Since you will be working in some official capacity, I think the important thing for you is to act very casual about whatever you see."

Ruby nods enthusiastically. "That's what I do, even if I'm shocked, I make no mention of it and tuck it away to ask Chad about later."

"That makes sense," I say.

Jillian interjects. "Take your lead from Brandon."

All three of them glance at each other mischievously then giggle, leaving me out of the joke.

Ruby looks back me. "Sorry! We'll be good. We can't help it. We've been waiting for this forever, so we're a little overexcited."

Might as well practice my coolness again. "I'm afraid you've lost me."

Jillian takes a corner of the sweet bread on the table. "Brandon is *very* dominant. He expects to lead; it's how he's most comfortable. We are all just relishing his demise."

My cheeks heat. "I'm sure I won't be his demise."

Jillian shakes her head. "I'm not so sure about that, but it's sure going to be fun to watch."

Before I'm forced to respond, Ruby's phone beeps and she picks it up from the table. After a few swipes of her finger, she looks up. "Seems we're being summoned to my house for an afternoon of debauchery."

I try not to feel too disappointed. I smile. "I'm sure you'll have a great time. Thanks so much for inviting me to brunch."

Ruby shakes her head. "Oh, you're not getting off that easy. Chad specifically mentioned you were to come."

I blink as my heart beats faster. "Oh?"

She grins. "Brandon is already there."

Jillian bounces in her chair and claps her hands. "This is going to be so fun."

I duck my head, hoping to hide my grin. Fun indeed.

Life is getting very interesting.

Brandon

As I sit on Chad and Ruby's rooftop deck, I let the conversation swirl around me as I contemplate the folly of once again merging my professional and personal life. Veronica hasn't even started working for me and I'm already walking a fine line.

It's not the smartest thing I've ever done, but when the opportunity presented itself, I didn't pass it up. Today I hadn't orchestrated the events, hadn't arranged for this get-together, but I hadn't dissuaded it either. Hadn't objected when Chad asked if he should tell Ruby to bring her.

After the text had been sent, they'd all smirked at me, but I'd ignored it.

I have no good reason for why I want to see her, despite my better judgment. And wasn't that the problem with her? My lust for her went beyond common sense.

The door to the rooftop opens and the girls come tumbling out of the narrow walkway in single file. I don't even register the other women as I wait for Veronica to emerge. And when she does, my heart skips a fucking beat and my cock gets instantly hard.

Her hair is down again, loose and carefree with a slight bendy wave. Her coloring is only enhanced in her slip of a top and skinny jeans. I shift in my chair, not remotely paying attention to anyone as our eyes lock.

She sucks in a breath, just the slightest of hitches as she nods at me.

"So, this is fun," Jillian says, pulling my attention away from this woman that is fast becoming a fixation.

Leo hooks his fingers through her belt loop and tugs until she sits down on his lap. "Are we looking for trouble today?"

Veronica bites her lower lip and darts a glance at me before quickly looking away.

Jillian smiles down at her husband. "Would I look for trouble?"

He grins at her. "Absolutely."

Ruby walks over to the table where Chad has set up drinks and snacks, and surveys the spread, before turning to Chad. "You're a much better host than me."

He laughs. "It's why we make a good team." He crooks his finger and beckons her close. She tosses her glossy black hair and practically saunters over to him, a far cry from the woman that looked like she might expire if anyone looked at her the wrong way.

Chad's eyes hood as he looks her up and down, and when she's standing in front of him he curls his hand around her leg, made bare by a short frayed skirt, and slides up her thigh. Ruby stiffens, her eyes riveted on him. He taps her inner thigh. "Open."

She squares her shoulders. "No preamble?"

"Nope." He squeezes. "Do it."

I glance at Veronica, curious for her reaction. Since Veronica is not involved with any of our kinkiness, everyone here will be mindful of exposing her, but that doesn't mean they won't engage a little. They want to see her squirm as much as I do. Even more, they want to see how we bounce off each other, considering the unusualness of this circumstance. I'm *always* with a woman that knows she might be forced to strip at a moment's notice. Why, it wasn't too long ago when we sat in this very spot and I made Stephanie act as my coffee table. Threatening dire consequences if she spilled my drink. Which, of course, she did.

There won't be anything like that today. And I'm disconcerted to find I'm disappointed.

My eyes meet Veronica's. The color on her cheeks is high and she's working that lower lip again. She shifts on her high-heeled sandals, telling me she's nervous and unsure what to expect.

Good. I'd hate to be the only one.

I tilt my head toward the empty chair next to me.

Her chin rises, but she can't quite hide the smile that quivers at the corners of her mouth. She shrugs one shoulder and walks to take the spot next to me.

I smirk at her. "Did you finally get that sleep you were searching for?"

Her throat works as she swallows. "Yes."

"Good." I let the word linger, letting my silence speak for itself. Making her aware, in the space between us, that I'm well aware she slid her fingers down her stomach last night and came thinking about my teeth sinking into her flesh. When she twists her fine gold necklace at her throat, I turn back to Chad and Ruby.

My point is scored.

While I observe the couple, my attention is intent on Veronica. In the tautness of her muscles, and not quite even breathing. I'm hyper focused on this woman that appears to have invaded my life, crawling into some dormant place inside me.

Chad's hand has disappeared beneath Ruby's skirt, his actions are concealed from the rest of us, but the air is thick, ripe with anticipation.

Next to me, Veronica crosses her legs, restless in her seat.

I turn the conversation to something safe, leaving Chad to exact his will on Ruby. I glance at Veronica. "Did you have a nice brunch?"

She jerks her head, her attention swinging toward me. "Yes."

I lean forward, putting my elbows on my knees and craning my neck to look at her. "Did you learn anything interesting?"

Her shoulders ease a little. "I did."

"Such as?"

"They gave me an idea of what to expect at the party on Thursday, and how to prepare myself for it." She shrugs. "Some rules to follow. What to avoid."

I nod. Good. That's exactly what I was hoping for. "Did you get a dress?"

"I did."

"Do you want to tell me about it?"

She shakes her head. "Nope."

I laugh. "All right then, I do like surprises."

Our gazes meet and hold, and tension seeps between us.

We sit like that, suspended, unable to sever the contact and unable to speak.

Finally I break the silence. "I shouldn't have had you come today."

She swallows hard. "Why?"

"Because I want to fuck you." The words are blunt, as harsh sounding as I feel at the moment.

She sucks in a breath. "I see."

I raise a brow. "Did you have a good orgasm last night?"

Her lashes flutter, as though she's fighting the urge to back away from our too intense connection.

I can't say I blame her.

I'm impressed when she doesn't shy away. Other than the fingering of her necklace she appears completely composed. "Yes."

My gaze dips briefly to her mouth. "Did it help?"

"No."

"Good."

Her brow furrows and I smile. "I like a girl needy."

Color splashes across her high cheekbones. "Oh."

The rational part of my brain that refuses to mix business with pleasure is warning me to get back to safe ground, but that dominant part of me wants her so badly it overrules. I tilt my head. "If you were mine, I'd make you ask even to touch, and if I decided to let you—and, Veronica, that's a big if—I'd make you beg me before I even considered letting you come."

Her thighs flex, tightening in response to my words, and my lust flairs out of control.

"What…" She stumbles over the word. "What does that mean?"

My voice grows low, dark and menacing. "It means I'd own your cunt and would decide exactly what I let you do with it."

Her honeyed eyes grow wide, dilating at my bluntness, but she stays silent, not asking any of the questions I'd expect from someone experimenting with submission for the first time. Doesn't fluster. Or nervously laugh. She doesn't even move.

Instead we just stare at each other, locked in some silent war, which is only increasing the tension and desire that sits between us.

"Hey! Hey!" Jillian's voice rips me away from her.

I frown and snap, "What, Jillian?"

She gives me that sassy smile of hers and waves. Everyone

has moved to the table while Veronica and I were in our own little world. "We're going to play poker."

"What kind of poker?" I ask.

"The fun kind."

I sigh and straighten. "All right."

I stand, and look down at Veronica. "I'm assuming you know how to play."

"Of course."

I shake my head. "What was I thinking?"

We walk over and Veronica and I slide into seats next to each other. My leg brushes hers and stays pressed against her.

Leo grins at me. "How are you doing over there?"

"Fuck off," I respond, picking up the two cards they'd already dealt to us.

Michael laughs and eyes Veronica. "You, girl, can come around whenever you want."

"Why thank you." Veronica studies her own cards and smiles. "I accept."

I shake my head. Jesus Christ, what the fuck am I doing?

Veronica

I'm standing in the bathroom letting cool water pour over my hands as I stare at my fevered eyes in the mirror. I'm burning up. Like I'm being licked with fire. I had no idea want like this even existed. Brandon is making me crazy. The tension is thick and hot and aching.

What's most scary is, other than the press of his thigh against mine, we haven't touched. But everything he'd said to me sat between us. Growing and expanding until I couldn't concentrate on the game we played with the other couples.

I don't understand what he said, or why it started a heated pool of lust low in my stomach, but with every second that passes the ache becomes more insistent and demanding until I can think of nothing else.

I have little knowledge at what he hinted at, but I find myself obsessed with the thought. How it would feel? I might not comprehend the dynamic that exists in this group, but I can't deny it pulses with an energy I've never experienced before.

Everything about what he'd said to me, the day, watching the other couples, has put me on high alert. Hyperaware of a possibility that lies just out of my reach.

Right now, after hours of obsessing about it, it's all I want.

I blow out a breath and finally turn off the faucet, wiping my hands on the guest towel hanging next to the sink. Reasonably under control, I open the bathroom door.

And find Brandon leaning against the wall, arms crossed. He's all lean and lanky in a tight black shirt and jeans. I stop short, freezing at the look in his eyes.

He doesn't say anything, just swiftly and suddenly advances on me.

I gasp, bracing myself as his hands slide on my hips and he pushes me back, enclosing me in the small powder room. He kicks the door shut, and keeps walking me backward until I slam up against the wall.

"This is a bad idea," he says in a dark voice.

But before I can respond, his mouth is on mine and madness takes over.

Our lips fuse, our tongues instantly tangle. All the lust and desire we've been keeping at bay spills over.

His mouth is a brand. Possessive and demanding.

My hands tangle around his neck, dragging him closer as I press into him, practically climbing up him in an effort to seep into him. To somehow, someway, show him how much I want him.

His hands clutch at my waist. Yanking me up as we practically fight through this kiss neither us is sure should be happening but has taken on a life of its own. Consuming us.

And it is consuming.

Our breathing turns to hot, angry pants as our mouths part and meet again, an almost angry clash. The air thickens, turning humid as our bodies mold together.

Closer. Closer. God, closer.

I need it. Need something from him I can't explain. But it storms over me as all rational thought leaves my mind and my body takes over.

His hips press into mine.

I rise to my tiptoes, fitting my body against his and lifting my leg so he slides between my thighs. His grip on my hip tightens.

He thrusts.

I rock up, gasping as he hits the perfect spot.

He lifts me and I wrap my legs around him.

His mouth is like a drug and I'm helpless against it.

His cock is hard against me, driving me out of my mind, as demanding as his lips and tongue and teeth. He growls, low in his throat, slams me harder against the wall.

My head hits the surface, and I arch up.

God, I had no idea things could be like this. My passions have always been contained, unlike now when they are raging out of control.

His mouth rips away and he curses. "God damn you." Before claiming my mouth again, with a type of fevered brutality.

It goes on and on.

The heat of his mouth searing into the very center of me.

Letting me know everything I've ever heard about him is a lie. They were wrong. He's so much worse. So much better.

I want. God, how I want.

I want his cock inside me, pounding away, taking me. Claiming me. Changing me until I no longer remember life before him.

He hits a spot and I groan, clutching at his shoulders.

Suddenly, he rips away, and in a harsh tone, he says, "We have to stop."

He grips my legs and untangles them from his waist, stepping back.

I sag against the wall, my knees wobbling as the loss of him cools my blood.

My mouth feels too full. Swollen. I touch my lips and his eyes darken.

He shakes his head, dragging his hand through his hair.

"That was a mistake."

"No." The word is a whisper.

"Yes." He pinches the bridge of his nose. "I should not be touching you."

"I want you to touch me." I'm not going to pretend otherwise. I refuse.

He sighs before stepping farther away. "Veronica, in a few short hours we are going to be working together very closely. I have rules set in place for my employees, and I will not violate them for you. I can't."

My chin tilts. "You mean you won't."

His blue eyes narrow, turning razor sharp. "I already have."

I take a deep breath, attempting to steady myself. "There's something between us."

"Be that as it may, this is non-negotiable." His tone is stiff, as though he hadn't devoured me moments before. "It won't happen again."

I bite my lip, and his gaze darkens. I want to argue, but to what purpose? He's right. We absolutely need to keep things professional. How can I demonstrate my value to his company blinded by my passion for him? So he's right, but it's also a lie. Chemistry like this is impossible to contain. But it seems prudent to agree with him. I nod.

"Good." He frowns and again runs his hand through his hair. "I shouldn't have said those things to you earlier. I wanted to give you a taste of what you'd witness on Thursday and went overboard. I apologize."

"I understand." I touch my swollen lips. I want more. I want him. "Do you honestly think we can keep this professional?"

He steps close to me, despite his insistence he is to stay away. "You'll learn soon enough Veronica, my will is iron clad."

"Not when it comes to me." I'm not sure where the words come from but they are out there, sitting between us, before I can stop myself.

The spark of challenge lights in the blueness of his eyes.

"We'll just see about that, little girl."

"Yeah, we will." And with that I duck past him and walk out of the bathroom.

Well, I must say, that was satisfying.

He's not getting out of this that easy.

Of course, neither am I, but I'm ready to fall.

Brandon

Teeth gritted, I put my hands on the wall and close my eyes. Every part of me, the good, the bad, and certainly the ugly, wants to go after Veronica.

I want my mouth on hers.

I want my cock buried deep inside that sure to be willing cunt.

I want my hand wrapped around her throat.

I want to fuck with her head until she's a needy mess, willing to do anything for me.

I want to punish her. Push her. Violate her.

Which is why I needed to get the hell away from her.

In that one kiss—a kiss I'd told myself five hundred times I would not give into—I learned everything I needed to know about her.

Veronica Westwood is a dangerous woman.

She has... Even in my thoughts the words struggle to break free. Power.

Over me.

No woman has ever had power over me. I do not like it.

I cannot tolerate it.

Especially when she's going to be fucking working for me.

Which is why I need to contain the situation. Contain her. Limit my exposure to her. This game I'd been playing with her this weekend, toying with her, flirting with the chemistry between us, I see now I miscalculated. Believed I could control it when it's clear now I cannot.

I see the lie I'd told myself about her in order to be around her.

A mistake I won't make again.

The only course of action I have is to build a wall of cold, professional reserve and cut off all interaction outside of the job.

It's the only way.

If I do that, I can control the situation. Control her. Put her in an off-limits box and compartmentalize my lust for her.

This, I know how to do.

I take a deep breath, leave the bathroom and walk back to where they are all waiting. The second I enter the roof deck, my eyes lock on her. Unable to help myself, my attention drifts to her mouth, still swollen and pink.

My mind jerks back to the bathroom. Our tangled tongues. The brutal press of our mouths. Her pussy arching and rubbing along my cock.

As though unable to help herself, she runs the tips of her fingers over her lower lip. All my muscles tense, and I have an inexplicable desire to run, a thought so foreign to me it sends a cold chill down my spine.

I force my legs to move, taking the only open seat next to her.

Leo raises a brow at me. "Everything okay?"

A sharp nod. "Everything is fine."

Veronica shifts, squirming in her chair.

Leo's gaze narrows.

I glance at my watch, it's late in the afternoon and it provides me with an excuse to get the hell out of here. Away from Veronica. "It's time to get home, I have some things to take care of."

Now Michael gives me a look identical to Leo's, reminding me that they have been partners for a long time. But I ignore it. I stand and turn to Veronica. "Tomorrow will be a long day."

Her chin tilts. "I'm ready for it."

"We'll see."

The challenge, the defiance, is written in her beautiful

features. She flashes me a brilliant smile. "Any chance you'd be willing to drop me home?"

She is clearly evil, and fuck is she playing with fire. Everything in me says to refuse her, that being in an enclosed car with her is the worst possible idea, but somehow I'm agreeing, despite myself. I jerk my thumb over my shoulder toward the door. "Let's go."

Veronica stands, and like the perfect society girl she is, nods at Chad and Ruby. "Thank you so much for having me, your home is fantastic."

Ruby grins and tilts her head at her fiancé. "I'm afraid that's all him."

Chad puts his hand on the back of her chair. "Yeah, it is."

Ruby laughs and hits him in the stomach.

Veronica turns to me. "I'm ready to go."

I nod.

Layla wiggles her fingers at us. "You two have fun."

I want to growl, to set them all straight, but I don't acknowledge the comment as we say our goodbyes and are out the door.

Five minutes later after a short, silent walk we are in my car. When the doors slam shut I turn to look at Veronica. "What game do you think you're playing?"

"Game?" she asks, her eyes wide with feigned innocence. "I don't know what you mean."

"You don't fool me, Veronica."

She gives me a slow grin. "I'm barely out of your way, so I didn't see the harm in asking."

"My decision is final." My words sound biting enough to put most women I associate with on high alert.

"It's a ride, Brandon." She shifts, leaning against the door. "You could have said no, I would have understood."

She's trapped me by my own ego. I wonder if she knows it or not. I peer deep into her eyes and see the cunning there. She knows exactly what she's doing.

She throws me off my game and I *do not* like it. I want to show her I'm in charge. That I tilt her, not the other way around.

We stare at each other, waging a battle without a single word. I recount my arguments to her in the bathroom, the imprint of her lips, still fixed on mine. I never lose. Never back down on my word. Girls have begged me. Begged for me to show mercy and I never break. Ever.

Then she raises one brow and a sly smile spreads over her lips.

Before I can process my actions, I lunge at her, capturing her mouth in a startled gasp.

The second our lips touch the fierce desire to possess her storms over me, blocking out any and all rational thought.

Christ I want her.

I eat at her mouth, furious and consuming.

She moans, tangling her fingers in my hair and bringing me closer.

I become more demanding. A brutal, harsh fusing of our hungry mouths.

She meets me head-on, giving as good as she's getting. For the first time since I can remember, my mind does not drift, does not plot on how to twist her. I think of nothing but the way she feels straining under me.

I shift, gripping her hips and yanking her forward, covering her upper body with mine. I growl low in my throat as our tongues entwine. Her head hits the window and I slam my palm against the glass, as I devour her.

I should have never broken the seal. Never.

Because she tastes like something I could be addicted to.

My other hand snakes under her top, sliding across smooth stomach to cup her breast. I stroke my thumb over her peaked nipple and she arches into the touch.

I'm out of control. Since that morning when I woke up, I have never been out of control, but I am now.

I hate it.

I can't stop it.

Her mouth feels like something I need.

In the small space of the car, our breathing is ragged and

panting.

I unclasp her bra, baring her breasts, cupping and squeezing, before I pluck at the hard bud and tug.

Into my mouth she groans, shifting and rolling under me to work my hand for her own pleasure.

I rip away, intending to stop, but then I lick at the skin on her neck before sinking my teeth into her flesh.

Her hands tighten on mine as she sucks in air and whimpers. Arching her neck to give me better access. Into my ear, she whispers, "Fuck me. Please. I can't take it. I want it so bad."

The words send fire through my veins, and in that second I come to grips with the knowledge that I can't resist her. Not with my body demanding I claim her. Possess her.

My tongue plays over her pulse as I roll her nipple between my fingers. I raise my head and capture her mouth with a hard, ruthless press of my lips before saying, "I'm going to own every fucking part of you, do you understand me?"

"Yes," she breathes, before I crush my mouth against hers again.

Everything turns wild and untamed, hot and needy and desperate.

Our bodies are straining because in the bucket seats we're not nearly close enough. Not for what I need to do to her. But I can't pull away from her mouth long enough to move us to a better location.

That's how much I want her.

I curse against her lips before covering them again.

It's the most fucking consuming kiss of my life and I'm completely lost to it. Drowning in her, unable to stop, unable to control the situation or her.

There's a knock at the window.

I jerk, looking up into Leo's smug, amused expression.

"Fuck." The word's almost guttural as I move, sliding my hand from under her top and pulling away.

She shifts in the seat, straightening, and when she looks up at Leo her skin flushes a faint pink. She clears her throat, attempting to calm her breathing as she smooths her hair.

With a smirk, Leo motions for me to lower the window.

I do, unsure if I want to kill him for interrupting me, or be thankful. Thankful, probably, since five more minutes and I would have had her on top of me, impaled.

I still glare at him.

He reaches in and hands Veronica her wallet. "You left this on the table."

She beams at him, like we hadn't just been going at it like a couple of wild animals a few seconds ago. "Thanks. How silly of me."

He winks at her. "You must have been distracted."

She laughs, shrugging. "Must have been."

"Are you done?" My words are sharp.

Leo chuckles. "Oh, I'm done."

I roll up the window, starting the car with a push of the button, and before I can start up where we left off, I pull out onto the street.

I say nothing, and unlike most women who would start talking and trying to gauge what the fuck just happened, Veronica only says, "Do you need my address?"

"No." My grip is tight on the steering wheel. So this is what it's like, huh? To work and use willpower? And to think all this time I thought I was so cool and collected. So in control. When it turns out I haven't cured my impulse-control problems at all. I merely hadn't allowed myself to be put in the path of temptation.

I pull up to her Gold Coast building and unlock the door.

Instead of getting out she turns toward me. "Thanks for giving me a ride home."

"You're welcome." My voice is cool, filled with a dismissal I certainly don't feel.

"So tomorrow, what time do you want me there?"

"Nine is fine."

She nods. "Brandon?"

I raise a brow. "Yes, Veronica?"

She smiles. "Thanks for a lovely and memorable weekend."

And with that she's out the door.
Leaving me straining to go after her.

12.

Brandon

Veronica walks into my office at nine sharp, looking every inch the professional businesswoman. Her suit is gray, cut sharp and fitted against her slim frame, her hair is back, tucked into a neat bun not dissimilar to the one she wore the night I met her.

She should look severe. She does not.

A carnal lust twists in my chest as a vision of tearing her jacket from her body and spreading her on my desk rips through me. I want to shove her skirt up her hips, splay her thighs and lick her cunt until she begs me to show mercy.

Jesus Christ.

I push the image away and gesture her to the chair, sitting back in my own as she takes the seat across from me. Our eyes lock and I remember the imprint of her mouth on mine. The heat. The straining desire.

I rest my arm on the chair. This is it, she's officially working for me, so it's time to stop fucking around. I nod. "Veronica."

She nods back. "Brandon."

I steeple my fingers. "I've arranged for my bar manager, Reggie, to take you on a tour of the building and explain that facet of the business. After, I've had my admin, Marisa, set up individual meetings with all the key staff members, all of whom will be reporting to you and myself until you're acclimated. That will keep you busy for the morning. Marisa will support us both, and she has your schedule for the day waiting."

She smiles, and it dazzles me. "Sounds great."

"I will take you to lunch and you can tell me your first impressions and we'll discuss your main responsibilities." The conversation is purely professional, but the tension between us is thick, filling the space across the desk, threatening to suffocate me.

"I look forward to it," she says, her voice a husky purr that strokes against my skin and makes me hard.

I barely resist an eye roll at my own foolishness. This morning, before I'd seen her, I'd determined action was the best course since my words with her tend to backfire. I'd keep things strictly professional, treating her as I would any employee, but I already find myself wavering. Wanting to call attention to our palpable chemistry. The notion strengthens my resolve.

I need to build a wall between her and me. Something impenetrable. I rise and walk around the desk to stand before her. She gazes up at me, her honey eyes peering right into me. My finger twitches with the desire to reach for her, stroke over the line of her jaw, grip her chin in my hand and squeeze.

That sadistic part of me that wants to break pretty things, wants to hurt her. I am no stranger to my inner sadist, but I've always kept it checked. Cool and controlled, casual. But Veronica calls to that monster, hidden deep inside me.

Her lashes flutter, almost imperceptibly.

I grip the desk to control my base instincts to push her, turn her slightest crack into a crevasse so I can see the very heart of her. Slowly, I say, "Let me show you your office and introduce you to Marisa."

"Very well."

She stands at the same time I straighten and suddenly we're too close. The heat of her sears right through me. I'm on the verge of caving, to reaching for her and claiming that fucking mouth of hers. The temptation she presents is hard to ignore because all my instincts fight to mess her up.

I grit my teeth.

She bites her lower lip.

But she doesn't back down from the intensity of my gaze.

We stand like that, toe to toe, the distance between us too close for professional.

She makes this sound, somewhere between a gasp and a whimper and it's almost my undoing.

Before I give in, I step back and gesture her to the door. "Let's go."

Her brow furrows. "Brandon?"

I swear to god, if she challenges me in any way, I'm going to break. I raise a brow.

The fine muscles in her neck work as she swallows. "Thank you for the opportunity. You won't regret it."

Well, that depends on the type of regret we're talking about here, now doesn't it? I don't doubt Veronica will be good for business, but good for me, now that's a different story. Not that I'm about to tell her that. I nod. "See that I don't."

Veronica

As I follow Brandon out of his office I take in the wide breadth of his shoulders and the easy way he owns a room. This man, who's fast becoming an obsession and is also my boss. I can see by the hard set of his features as he spoke to me from behind his massive desk he's determined to keep me at arm's length. In theory, I agree, this is his business and it's important to be professional. In practice, I want to push him.

I want to see him break.

131

I don't understand why I have this notion, but it persists, and has persisted since he kissed me in the bathroom yesterday. He's susceptible to me, as I am to him. But unlike myself, he hasn't accepted that fact yet.

Unlike me, who wants to fall.

I'm ready. Impatient for something I don't quite understand but burns inside me, waiting to be explored. Brandon is the key to that, but he's not ready. He wants to resist me.

For now, I'll let him. I'll play his game, but it's just a matter of time.

The chemistry burns, fills all the space. It chokes us.

I can be patient. Because he's worth it. What he gives me will be worth it. But more than that, I believe I'm something he needs.

We come to stand in front of a reception desk where a beautiful girl with deep red hair and stunning blue eyes sits. She beams at Brandon. "Good morning, sir."

He nods and issues me forward. "Marisa, this is Veronica Westwood, she'll be the acting General Manager and as we discussed you'll support her as well as myself."

Marisa's gaze flickers across my face, subtly sweeping down my frame, before meeting my eyes. I see the challenge there, lurking in the depths. In five seconds she's deemed me competition and isn't happy about it. Brandon has been crystal clear about his policies, but I'm equally sure Marisa isn't the only female who works for him that fantasizes about him caving, just for her.

I smile, friendly and bright. "It's a pleasure to meet you, Marisa. I'm looking forward to working with you."

"You too, Ms. Westwood."

"Please, call me Veronica." The best way to win over an adversary is to make them feel valuable, and I don't hold back. "I'm sure I'll be depending on your expertise quite extensively as I get acclimated."

Marisa's lashes flutter ever so slightly before she nods. "Whatever you need, I'll be happy to help."

Brandon puts his hands in the pockets of his fitted black pants. Good god, can that man wear black well. It's like the color was designed to highlight his beauty. "Do you have Veronica's schedule?"

Fast like a whip, Marisa picks up a piece of paper and hands it to him. "Of course." She shifts her attention to me. "If you give me your cell phone, I will have IT set up your calendar and email."

"That would be great." I slip my hand into my bag and pull out the device, handing it over to her.

Brandon turns to me. "Do you need anything else before I leave you in Marisa's capable hands?"

I shake my head. "I'll be fine."

Our eyes meet and that ever-present tension kicks up. We linger, a little too long, before he nods.

"I'll leave you to it." Then he turns and walks back to his office.

I turn back to the stunning receptionist, who's staring at me with suspicion written across her features. For a second I think she's going to comment, but she's far too professional for that. Instead, she stands, revealing a figure that could rival a runway model, and gestures to a closed door, "I'll show you your office, and then take you to meet Reggie."

"Thank you," I say before taking a deep breath.

Off into my life I go.

It's Thursday, and I've been working with Brandon for four days. The job is going well. I've met with staff, learned the organization, formulated my plans and come up with ideas for changes.

I'd had the impression that Brandon's dealings were mostly in entertainment, but as it turns out, that's not the case. He has diverse holdings ranging from real estate to stakes in high-tech companies. In business school we learned that this is not a good strategy, but like most things, Brandon appears to defy the odds. That he's known to have a Midas touch is not coincidental. As I've poured over his books, I'm hard pressed to find fault with his pursuits.

His weakness is in operations. Which is where I come in. It's my strength. I thrive on it. We'll make an unstoppable team if he lets me. In the past four days I've compiled a list of projects, ranking them in order of priority and potential impact, presenting them to Brandon at the end of the day as we recap.

All my instincts about Brandon have proven correct. He's a shrewd and cunning businessman. Calculating, exacting and clearly a natural leader. Everyone who works for him admires him, respects him and is thankful for the pleasure of working for him. Of course, every single woman in the place wants him, but he appears to ignore the flattery and bids for attention.

As for us, well, we've effectively ignored the elephant in the room. We discuss business, keep it professional, but there is an undercurrent of tension and brewing lust that is stretched too tight. We stay on topic, but our eyes catch and hold too long to be polite, and when silence falls, our chemistry becomes a live, palpable thing.

I don't know when we'll snap, but it's coming.

Thankfully, I'm currently busy as hell in preparation for tonight's party. The club is full of activity as they change certain aspects of The Lair from upscale nightclub to upscale nightclub hosting a sex party. I'd wanted to gain the confidence of the people working under me, to make sure they knew I was right there with them, so I'd dug in, helping with anything that needed done, even if that included hauling ice buckets and taking out trash.

It was exhausting and rewarding, but best of all it gave me no time to think about the evening to come and what would happen here tonight. And for that I was thankful.

I wiped my hands on the back of my jeans and picked up my clipboard to review the liquor inventory, given to me by the bar manager, Reggie. A tall, handsome black man, with close-cropped dark hair and built like former military, who's become my closest ally. We'd taken an instant liking to each other and he's been my right-hand man as I've worked my way through the inner workings of The Lair and Brandon's underground club, open only a few times a week.

Everything looks in order, and as far as I can tell there are no trouble spots.

"Veronica." Brandon's voice behind me has my shoulders straightening.

I turn to face him. I hadn't seen him all day and the sight of him makes my throat go dry. He's wearing jeans. Brandon in a tux is mouthwatering, in a suit, commanding, and in business casual clothes far too distracting for comfort.

But in jeans Brandon should be outlawed.

My knees actually go a bit weak. He's wearing a heather-gray T-shirt that stretches over his broad shoulders and clings to powerful biceps that were so cut and defined my mouth watered.

Oh sweet Jesus.

Built narrow, his lean hips and flat stomach and long legs are made for—

"Are you quite done?" His voice is wry and amused.

Shit. My gaze snaps to his face and heat crawls up my neck as I realize I've been practically raping him with my eyes. I brush a hand over my ponytail, shrugging.

"I trust you remember Chad." He shifts his attention, and to my horror I realize Ruby's fiancé is standing right next to him.

Chad's blue eyes dance as he grins at me. I'm almost one hundred percent certain he's attempting to repress his laughter. He winks. "I'll try not to be insulted you didn't see me standing here."

My spine straightens and my chin tilts. I refuse to be embarrassed I'd been caught gaping at my boss. It's not like Chad didn't see us interact all weekend. He knows as well as anyone there is something going on with Brandon and me. "Hey, Chad, it's great to see you again."

Brandon smiles at me, his dimples flashing. "Chad stopped by to discuss business I thought you might be able to help us with. We want to go in on a renovation property together and I thought with your connections it would be a good idea for the three of us to sit down next week and discuss what we're looking for."

My family has deep connections in Chicago real estate so this interests me. I nod. "That sounds great."

Chad covertly assesses me. "We've been looking for something for the last nine months but haven't been able to find what we want. Do you think you'll be able to help?"

"I'm sure once we sit down and go over what you're looking for, if it exists, I know people who can find it. If you give me some times, I'll have Marisa set up a meeting." The admin still hadn't warmed up to me because she wants Brandon all to herself. I'm positive she's harboring nightly boss/secretary fantasies.

Brandon's gaze flickers over me but his expression remains impassive. "I thought we could meet Chad for a long lunch on Tuesday."

"Perfect." I shift my attention back to Chad. "I'm looking forward to it."

"Me too," he says.

Brandon raises a brow at me. "Don't forget Ruby is new to the sex party scene as well, so you two will be able to commiserate."

Chad chuckles. "Ruby's excited you'll be here. She's been desperate to meet *anyone* who—as she says—doesn't act like it's totally normal to be spread out on a table in front of a bunch of people."

Brandon outright laughs. "I do love watching her eyes grow wide with horror."

Under my white T-shirt, emblazoned with The Lair's logo, my nipples pull tight. Suddenly his choice of white doesn't strike me as odd since he's clearly a deviant.

Brandon's gaze skims over me, pausing at my breasts but he doesn't speak.

"Me too," Chad says, smiling before turning his devious nature on me. "Make sure you come by at a time that's most embarrassing for her."

Playing it cool, I laugh and shake my head. And to think, he looks so all American.

My gaze catches Brandon's and not for the first time I wonder what tonight will bring, and what exactly I've gotten myself into.

I suppose I'll find out soon enough.

Brandon

Chad and I are back in my office, settled around my seating area before he mentions Veronica.

He cocks a brow. "You two are about five seconds from snapping, you know that, right?"

I play it cool. "She's my employee."

Veronica in a pair of jeans, The Lair's T-shirt, a ponytail, and zero makeup threw me as much as I threw her. I've worked hard this week to build the wall of professionalism between us, but Christ, I want her. I didn't miss her hard nipples at the mention of spread-out girls. Nor did I miss the hungry expression on her face as she practically ate me alive. Chad's right, no matter how hard I try, we are always about five seconds away from disaster.

Chad laughs. "You're smitten."

"I'm not smitten." The words sound ground out, like broken glass.

Smitten is not the word I'd use to describe my desire for her. Smitten is cute. Manageable. Controllable. None of which I feel.

"Oh no?" Chad tilts his head. "Are you sure about that?"

"She's my employee." It bears repeating. If only to remind myself.

Chad's eyes narrow as he studies me. He's a more recent

137

member of our group, but has become so ingrained he's no longer an outsider. In fact, I now count him as one of my closest friends. Out of us, he's the most mellow and understated, with Leo and I being the most brutal, and Michael falling somewhere in the middle.

He says in a smooth voice, "Do you want to talk about it?"

"No." I look away and rub my eyes, shaking my head. The words spill out before I can rein them back in. "I fucking want her."

"Yeah. That's clear." He shrugs. "At least it's mutual."

"I'm not sure that's better." While we've been good about maintaining our distance, we're like a ticking bomb waiting to detonate. I don't know how much longer I can resist her.

"You have a point." He scrubs a hand over his jaw. "It's killing you that you can't control it, huh?"

I snap my head in his direction. "What does that mean?"

He laughs. "I pay attention. I see how you operate. You like to keep your relationship cool and borderline detached. I've never even seen you break a sweat with a girl." He points to the closed door to my office. "That girl makes you sweat and you don't like it."

I frown. He's right. I don't even keep one girl at a time. I'm always honest and upfront about it, but I make it very clear I'm not a one-woman kind of guy. If a woman isn't okay with that, I let her walk away and don't think twice about it. If she agrees, I'm attentive, and I do everything a good dominant should, but I'm always removed somehow. It's like I have a thick layer of ice around me I don't let her penetrate. I watch her respond to me, to what I do to her, at a distance.

In thirty seconds Chad has pinpointed what makes me so on edge about Veronica. I can't say no to her.

The night I met her, I didn't want her on that balcony. She stayed, captivating me so I'd thought of her the next day.

I didn't want to interview her and she wore me down until I did.

I didn't want to hire her, and I hired her anyway.

I told myself not to kiss her, I did.

I haven't touched another woman since I met her.

I don't want to want her and I can't stop.

She's thwarting me at every turn.

Even in my desire for her, she's twisting me up. It's not only that I want to sleep with her. It's that I want to crawl inside her and own her. I want to enslave her. I want to take her until I'm imprinted on her fucking DNA. When she looks at me with that needy, hungry look, practically begging me to handle her, it's taking every ounce of willpower I have not to give in.

I blow out a hard breath and realize Chad is watching me. I grit my teeth, resisting the urge to talk.

The guy should have been a therapist instead of a software developer.

I wave my hand. "It will be fine."

Chad nods. "At least she's submissive."

"I'm not so sure about that." All my normal instincts are clouded by my insatiable lust for her, so much so, I have no idea what to think.

"She might not be your normal type, but she's still got the signs," Chad says, as though it's perfectly clear. "You know every time she sees it, witnesses it as a bystander, her need for you to take control is going to grow."

It's what I want. To the point of distraction. Obsession. I pull out my old standby logic. "So what? I should break my rules for her?"

He shrugs. "Yeah."

"I don't want to talk about it."

He flashes a smile. "I bet she's feisty as hell."

I can't even think about it. "Shut the fuck up."

"I'm banking she's got a bratty side."

Before I can stop myself I ask, "Why do you think that?"

"It would serve you right."

I frown, not wanting to envision breaking her of that particular trait. I've never been attracted to brats, but Veronica's challenging defiance makes me so hard I hurt sometimes. I shake my head. This isn't helpful. I cling to my stubborn rules, the plan I laid out that sure as hell isn't working. "It doesn't matter because it's not going to happen."

He laughs. "I don't even give you a week."

I give him my darkest, meanest look, the one I reserve to make girls shake, but it has no effect on him other than to increase his mirth. I point to the door. "You can leave now."

Later that night the party is underway and I'm talking to my friends when Veronica comes through the door.

I turn to see her.

I lose my breath.

She looks like she's stepped out of the sixties—like she took a picture of Brigitte Bardot at her most sexy—then compounded it by a thousand. Her dress is white—and by the sheen under the lights I know it's latex—with a scooped neck, the dress fits her like a glove before flaring out ridiculously high on her thighs. She completed the outfit with white boots that fasten above her knees. Her hair is full and wild, and I want to tangle it in my fist while her legs wrap around my waist.

Jesus H. Christ.

I am fucked.

The crowd parts as she makes her way through the room and I have to bite back the surge of possession when men, attached and unattached, turn to watch her.

I frown when she stops to talk to Reggie, and he puts a hand on her arm. His dark skin next to her paleness is a striking contrast. They've become fast friends, and it irritates me, although I say nothing. He smiles at her and she beams back.

I shove my hands into the pockets of my black pants because I want to go over there and rip her away from him before saying something completely idiotic like, *Don't fucking touch her again.* A thought so foreign to me I have no idea what to even make of it.

Except for sex, I'm not a man of violence.

She laughs and grins up at him.

I turn away before I do something regrettable and look into the faces of my six closest friends, all grinning at me like satisfied cats.

I should ignore this, and go on with what we were talking about, but I can't remember the subject, and I'm so thrown off balance by how she looks I zero in on Jillian and growl. "You are going to pay for this."

She laughs, before shrugging. "Sorry. I couldn't resist."

I shoot a look at Leo. "And what do you intend to do about this?"

"Sit back and enjoy the show." Leo slides his arm around his wife and kisses her on the temple. "You did good, baby."

I grit my teeth.

Michael gives me a cocky grin I kind of want to punch off his face. "I've been waiting to see this since the day we met in college."

Next to him Layla, looking as gorgeous as ever in a pink dress, presses her lips together, trying to contain her amusement. Her blue eyes sparkle when she says, "We dressed her to match us."

I open my mouth, to say god knows what, but Jillian points. "She's coming this way."

I whip back around, scowling. Veronica's completed her ode to the sixties look with elaborate cat eyes that make their honey-brown color practically glow.

Our gazes lock.

She falters a bit.

I can only imagine my expression but I can't seem to work it into an appropriate mask of passivity.

Per usual, she keeps on coming and her shoulders straighten, pushing back. I recognize that look. The defiance. The—*I don't care how you're looking at me; you're not stopping me*—expression.

It makes me hard. The tension, growing and building

throughout the week, threatens to choke me. My hands clench.

When she's standing in front of me, and I look down at her, a fierce visceral lust running hot and dangerous in my veins.

"Brandon." My name quivers on her lips.

Good. It should.

Because I want to make her hurt until she comes screaming my name like I'm her fucking god.

13.

Veronica

Brandon stands there, glaring at me like I murdered kittens.

He's not happy. But I don't know why, I let Jillian pick out my outfit, and she said it was perfect. It had struck me as having a sixties vibe, so while I got ready I decided to pretend I was going to a Halloween party.

All things considering, I thought I looked good.

I glance around the room. I don't appear out of place, in fact, my outfit is conservative next to the other guests. I study the three women sitting around the lush, leather chat area with their significant others. I don't look like I've made a misstep, although damn, they are all gorgeous.

Since Brandon's said nothing, and is still scowling at me, I decide to ignore him. I smile at the table. "Hi. Are you all having a good time so far?"

Next to me, Brandon's body grows even more rigid.

Jillian, stunning in her little red dress, sitting next to her dangerous-looking husband, glances at Brandon, then back at me. "So far, so good." She waves a hand over me. "And holy shit, girl, you look fantastic."

I smooth my hand down my stomach. I've never worn a latex dress before. I didn't think I'd like it. I was wrong. "Thanks. So do you." I wave at her husband. "Hi, Leo. It's a pleasure to see you again."

Brandon still says nothing, unless you count the anger rolling off him. Luckily I was born into a world where social necessities are second nature to me. I turn toward Chad and Ruby, he's casually running his finger up and down her bare arm. She's wearing a strapless black latex corset, a short skirt and thigh-high tights with black boots. She's striking and, and quite a contrast to Chad's all-American look, but sitting together, so close they may be melded together, they fit. I smile and hold out my hand to her. "You look awesome."

She winks at me. "Thanks."

I smile at her fiancé. "Hey, Chad."

"Veronica." He nods, cups Ruby's shoulder then whispers something in her ear that has a healthy flush rise to her cheekbones.

I look back at Brandon to see if perhaps he's calmed down. He narrows his eyes and his jaw clenches.

I guess not. Unable to help myself, I shoot him a dark glare before plastering a smile on my lips and turning to the last couple. Layla and Michael are a sight to behold. As any other time I've seen them, as a couple they are formidable, with an almost untouchable quality.

And then Layla grins at me, and the otherworldly quality disappears and they look human.

I incline my head. "It's wonderful to see you again."

"You too," Layla says.

Michael stands up. I've forgotten how tall he is. I feel tiny and small next to him. He nods. "Veronica."

I meet his gaze and my lashes flutter a bit. I swallow hard. He's very intimidating. He's studying me, looking for god knows what but his unusual hazel eyes feel like they are burning into my very soul.

144

I bite my lip.

"Oh my god," Jillian says, her voice amused. "You're terrifying her."

His eyes narrow. "No, I'm not, am I, Veronica?"

"Only a little." I smile and it makes him laugh.

He chucks me under the chin. "I just wanted to get a good look at you."

I have no idea what that means.

He sits back down and pulls Layla close, kissing her temple.

She smiles up at me, and tucks a lock of hair behind her ear, flashing her huge engagement ring. When she speaks her voice is full of sass. "Don't let him scare you. He's harmless."

He cocks a brow. "Harmless?"

"Of course." She gives him a smile so filled with cunning it's hard to miss.

I instinctively take a step back, knowing something is about to go down and I'm finally going to get to the crux of this sex party business.

He traces a path over her neck. "Are you looking to get hurt?"

Hurt? My mind stutters over the word.

"Duh," she says, clearly she's unfazed.

Jillian and Ruby laugh.

That strange, addictive heat licks low in my belly.

Michael's looking at Layla with such menace I don't know how she's not shaking.

I take another step back and somehow end up bumping into Brandon. His hand curves over my hip as he steadies me, touching me for the first time in days. His palm is a brand on my skin, sending a shiver down my spine.

Michael's easy movements shift and I gasp as he suddenly takes Layla by the neck, his fingers like a vise around her throat.

Layla's eyes dilate as her chest swells.

"Did we not talk about overplaying your hand, girl?"

She nods.

Michael juts his chin and releases his hold before saying in a

145

low voice, "Get on your knees. Facing me."

They stare at each other for what feels like an eternity before she stands.

Michael opens his legs. She steps between them. He smirks. And back ruler-straight, she falls to her knees between his splayed thighs.

And just like that the air is thick with that indescribable tension.

He lifts her chin and she gazes up at him. His expression flashes dark and hungry. "I'll hurt you when I'm good and ready to do so. Until then, you just sit there like a good girl and think about it."

Her grip tightens on his pant leg. "Yes, Michael."

Brandon's fingers dig into my hip and I find myself shifting, moving against him.

He stiffens and I realize what I'm doing and jerk away.

I turn to look at him.

His expression is angry, his blue eyes hard and cold.

I frown.

What in god's name is wrong with him? The silence grows between us and what's been threatening all week, snaps. "What?"

"I don't like what you're wearing." His voice is filled with a threatening rasp.

The comment is like a slap across the face, the sting a harsh blow. I resist the urge to flinch.

"Brandon!" Jillian yells, her voice breaking the strange hold he has on me.

I want to say something scathing, but I'm so close to losing it, I keep my mouth shut. I shake my head and put on that smile I've worn a thousand times in my life. I turn back to the table and try not to look directly at any of them. "Have a lovely evening. It's time for me to get back to work."

Then I walk off, head held high.

Brandon Townsend III can go fuck himself.

Brandon

God fucking dammit.

I watch Veronica walk away. I don't understand what possessed me to say that.

"What the hell, Brandon?" Jillian's voice whips me from my trance and I jerk my attention back to the table. She points at me. "You need to go apologize."

"Mind your own business, Jillian." The words are a growl.

"You're being a dick." She crosses her arms over her chest.

I'm in a foul temper and in no mood for her interference. Ever since Veronica stepped through the doors some primal, unreasonable part of my brain has taken over. I narrow my eyes at Leo. "Control your woman."

He cocks a brow. "My woman is perfectly under control and none of your fucking concern."

Layla peers over her shoulder and glances up from the floor, her brow furrowed. "Are you all right, Brandon?"

I open my mouth to lash out at her and catch Michael's dark, warning gaze. Layla has gone through severe trauma in her life. Michael does not tolerate even a wayward glance in her direction. It clears my head. What the hell is wrong with me? I'm going to yell at Layla? Because I want a woman I can't have?

I give her a gentle smile. "I'm fine, darling girl."

Michael's expression eases.

I need to get away from them for a second. From everything. To clear my head and pull myself back together again.

I pull my silent phone from my pocket, pretend to read it, and say, "I've got to take this."

And before they can say anything I walk off in the direction of my office.

I open the door and find Veronica sitting on the couch.

Christ. I need to get the fuck away from her and the last thing we need right now is to be alone. I snap. "What, Veronica?"

She stands, stomps over to me, and jabs me in the chest. "If you don't like what I'm wearing, don't look at me."

I bat her hand away. My temper, which I never, ever let get the better of me, starts a rapid boil. "I am not the kind of man you tell what to do."

"Oh really?" Her voice rises. "Too bad. I'm not one of your little girls you can boss around. I'm not going to fall in line for you. So you can just go to hell."

The tension, simmering between us all week, takes over in the form of fury. I yell, "I am your boss, and this is your place of employment. I can't have you walking around like an open fucking invitation."

She rears back. "You made me dress like this."

Any and all rationality clouds my brain. The man I was before Veronica lurks in the corner, smirking and dismissive, shaking his head, but he doesn't rise to the surface. I'm too far gone for that. I wave a hand over her. "I never once told you to wear a dress that barely covers your ass."

She points at the door. "You told me to look a part. I've accomplished that. If you don't like the results, that's too goddamn bad."

"I don't like the results."

She plants her hands on her hips. "You told me to dress for a sex party. You told your friends to make sure I looked a certain way and this is what *they* picked out. I don't look any different than anyone else."

"Yes, you do." I don't want them. I want her and it's driving me right out of my mind.

"How?" she screams. "I saw a woman with her breasts hanging out."

We're both breathing hard.

"That's different!" I answer, completely irrationally.

"You're being ridiculous." She shakes her head at me, then veers around me and puts her hand on the door. "Don't talk to me for the rest of the night. Don't come by me. And definitely don't look at me."

Like lightning I reach out and slam the door shut, and then I'm on her, shoving her against the door and trapping her with my body. I lean down and growl into her ear, "Don't give me orders."

She gasps, and her hands splay on the wood. "Go to hell."

I shove her hips against the door. My hard cock brushes against her ass and she presses back. I groan and kick out her legs.

She struggles against me, and her breath is coming in fast pants. "You're being inappropriate."

"No shit."

"Stop it."

That one word pulls me from my state. Christ. I was two steps away from smacking her on the ass before taking her. She's not my submissive. She's my employee. I've pinned her against the door. I'm acting like a maniac. I release her, step back and run my hand through my hair. "Leave."

She straightens, tugs on her skirt. "Fine."

A second later she slams out the door.

Jaw clenched, I can only stare at it as frustration gnaws at me.

I hate everything about the way she makes me feel. Everything. And for the first time in a long time, I have no fucking idea what to do about it.

Veronica

I'm hiding in the bathroom, attempting to compose myself.

I'm shaking. With rage and lust, both unexpressed and unrelenting.

Nothing about us feels under control. He pushed me. I pushed back. Something needs to break between us. We can't go on like this.

I take a deep breath and look at myself in the mirror, trying to figure out what it is about my appearance that set him off so.

But I can't see it.

The door opens and Jillian walks in, her brow furrowed.

I smile, but I fear it wobbles at the corners. "Hey. Having fun?"

She walks over to me, and puts her hand on my arm. "You know it's not you."

The one thing I've noticed about this group is everyone cuts to the chase. I'm not used to it. Where I come from no one says what they think. I shrug. "Isn't it *exactly* me?"

"Well, yes, that's true." She smiles softly. "I don't know what to tell you. Honestly, I've never seen Brandon fuck up with a woman before, so I'm not sure what action you should take."

I tilt my head. "What do you mean?"

She sighs. "He's one of my best friends. I love him—well, not quite like a brother considering the things he's seen me do—but close. I've known him for almost two years and in that time I've seen him with a lot of women. He always says and does exactly the right thing. Always. He's never thrown off his game. Never breaks a sweat. Never makes a mistake. He's always perfect. Always in complete control. And then you came along."

My throat tightens. "I don't know what he wants from me."

"I think that's kind of the problem. He doesn't know." She smiles again. "But trust me, he likes you in that dress."

I laugh, feeling a bit better. "Oh yeah, I can tell."

"Honey, you don't understand. He was having to use willpower not to slam you over the table and show everyone you were off limits."

"But that's what I don't understand. He has his rules, I get that…" I trail off and glance away. What do I expect? That I'm special and he should break them for me?

"Veronica."

At the sound of my name I look back at her.

"Brandon *never* has to use willpower." She shakes her head. "*Ever.* He's had it so easy for so long he hates that you're a struggle. Hates that he can't control wanting you."

"Oh." And then I get it. For a man like him, who controls everything from his business dealings to the women he beds, giving in to me, to the attraction that burns like a wildfire between us, is like a failure to him. He thinks he should be able to control it because he says, then every time I move closer and he can't resist it's making him more nervous.

I'm making him nervous. Me.

I lick my lips. "What do you think I should do?"

She smiles and it's pure evil. "Make him sweat."

I nod. "I will."

I have no choice, for both our sakes.

I've ignored Brandon for the last two hours and it's been crazy busy so it hasn't been hard. I've seen him twice, and both times we shot each other dark, glaring looks and passed without a word. The good thing is I haven't had much time to think about it. To think about him and what I'm going to do about this thing that grows every time we get within ten feet of each other.

The night is crazy. Everyone decked out in elaborate outfits. Half-naked people. Completely naked people. I've seen more tonight than I have in my entire life. I've heard people scream and then explode into ecstasy. I've seen people having sex. I saw one woman spread over the bar. Another suspended from the ceiling. I saw a man being led around like a dog.

All things I'd process later when I wasn't running around like a maniac making sure everything was perfect. Making sure Brandon knew how competent I was, despite everything. Things finally settle down as people fall into the rhythm of the party and I stop by Brandon's group of friends to say hi.

Leo and Jillian are off somewhere, so that left Michael and

Layla and Chad and Ruby.

Layla is off the floor, sitting next to Michael in her pink dress, looking like an angel. He has his arm around her, but he smiles at me as I walked over to them.

"Are you guys having fun?" I ask, trying to pretend the last time they saw me didn't involve a scene with Brandon. "Do you need anything?"

Layla beams. "We're great."

Ruby pats the seat next to her. "Can you sit for a bit?"

I stare longingly at the booth. "I'd love to, but I'm afraid if I do I'll never get up again."

"Too bad," Ruby says. "But we understand."

"Veronica." Brandon's voice is cool behind me.

I snap ruler-straight and swing around. In an equally cool voice, I say, "Yes?"

His expression darkens. "Reggie needs you in the back."

"Fine." I turn back to his group of friends. "Duty calls."

Layla waves. "We'll be here."

I turn, narrow my eyes at Brandon, and a muscle in his jaw ticks. I have an irrational urge to slap him across the face, which surprises me as I'm not a violent person. "Anything else, *boss*?"

My sarcasm earns me another scowl.

If he thinks I'll shy away like one of those girls always cowering before him, he's got another think coming. Shoulders thrown back I hold his gaze.

He doesn't look away.

Neither do I.

The din of the crowd melts away.

And it's just him and me. Squaring off.

His brow rises. "Are you done?"

"Nope." The word is quick and flippant.

"Are you sure about that?"

This is stupid, I know that, but I can't give up now. "Absolutely."

We fall silent again. In the back of my mind, I realize we must appear crazy. I'm literally daring him into a pissing match, but he started it.

This isn't my most mature moment.

And you know what? I really don't give a fuck.

"How long do you think this is going to go on?" Layla asks.

"Could be all night," Michael answers, clearly amused.

But I still don't break.

"You're not going to win, Veronica." Brandon's voice is so low, so dangerous, I shiver.

I fling his words back at him. "Are you sure about that?"

"Absolutely." It's a promise. I can see it in the set of his body, the barely leashed aggression.

"Should we clear off the table?" Ruby asks.

Chad chuckles. "That might be wise."

Brandon steps toward me until he's towering over me, but I don't back away. "I have a lot more experience at this game than you do, Veronica."

"What I lack in experience I make up for in determination." I smirk. "Don't pretend you're not scared you're going to lose."

"Clear the table," Michael says.

"Not necessary." Brandon says, but there's still a flurry of activity. His expression flashes. "What are we talking about here? What exactly are you hoping for?"

It dawns on me. I want him to cave. I want him to snap and take care of all this tension and heat. I want him to take control. Of the situation. I gulp. Of me.

And then I know what to do. It's bold. Daring. Maybe even wrong. Or a mistake. But so what? Isn't that why I've blown up my whole life? Why my parents are barely talking to me? Why I went against all common sense and hounded him into hiring me in the first place? To live?

I know what I want. Smart or stupid, doesn't really matter. Because if I don't find out, it will be a regret, and I'm not willing to have regrets anymore. Even if that means heartbreak and disaster.

So I stop thinking, stop plotting, and act. I step forward, reach out, put my hand around his neck and pull. His expression flashes wide with surprise and I think he's going to resist me, but then I'm rising to my tiptoes, tilting my face.

And his mouth is blessedly on me.

He stiffens for a fraction of a second before his arm locks around my waist and he's hauling me close.

It's been too long and it's like I'm starving.

His tongue sweeps, touches mine, and I forget everything.

Our surroundings.

The audience sure to be gaping at us.

Everything but the press of this man's mouth on mine.

I plaster myself against his body. His arm tightens and his free hand slides around my neck, tangling in my hair.

The kiss goes hot. Untamed. Visceral and frantic. All the tension we've been fighting pours into the claiming of our mouths. Demanding and dirty. His head slants, and suddenly the contact's deeper, more intimate. Less about getting even and more about getting closer.

I want him. More than I've ever wanted anyone or anything. I'm practically vibrating with it.

"Christ. You need to break it up." The voice is loud and near.

We rip apart, and the surroundings come rushing back, blaring and noisy. The crowd and the music scraping along my over-sensitive nerves.

I'm shaking. Kissing Brandon was like being pulled into the eye of a storm.

I suck in a breath and see Leo and Jillian standing there, fingers intertwined.

Jillian is wearing a huge grin.

Leo cocks a brow. "We're all cool watching, but I figured you wouldn't want your employees getting a first-hand show."

Brandon's expression is the equivalent to a summer storm cloud.

I lick my lips. They still taste of him, are still swollen from the force of his possession.

"Umm…" I wave in the direction of the back. "I… Um… Reggie needs me."

Leo winks. "He's not the only one, honey."

Brandon stiffens next to me.

And I make the only choice I can at the moment and get the hell out of Dodge.

14.

Brandon

What in the fuck just happened?

I stare after Veronica, my mind dull as all the blood has rushed from my brain to my cock.

Leo shoots me a sideways glance. "Did I choose wrong?"

No, he hadn't. Because I swear to god I would have pounded into her right in front of everyone.

Not because of kink.

Not to exert my dominance.

Not to fulfill some exhibitionist fantasy.

But because I'd literally forgotten anyone was there. Where I was. Or the consequences of my actions. Once her mouth touched mine, I'd only had one driving thought, one driving need: *Claim her.*

Honestly, it's the only thought I have now.

I shake my head but it doesn't begin to clear.

I watch her walk through the room in the direction of the hallway that leads to the back. Where my office is. My eyes

156

narrow. Where my couch is.

My couch designed to fuck. To spread a girl out. To take.

I'm going after her. She's mine. I have to possess her.

I take a step in her direction and Leo's hand locks around my arm.

I jerk, somehow surprised to see him there. I bark, "What?"

Calm as shit, he increases his grip. "Take a second to think about what you're about to do."

I yank my arm away. It's like lust is pounding in my veins. Consuming me.

Leo looks me in the eye. "You're not thinking clearly. I know you want her, but do yourself a favor and give yourself a chance to think it through."

"He's right, Brandon," Michael adds, oh so goddamn helpfully.

"Fuck you," I say, then turn away from them.

She's mine. And nobody is going to stop me from claiming what belongs to me.

I race through the room in the direction she's headed. Several people attempt to get my attention but I brush past them, putting them off. My only coherent thought is Veronica.

Some part of my brain recognizes that I'm not thinking clearly but I don't care.

Through the crowd I see the flash of her white dress.

I weave around a waitress.

Take off down the hall.

She's about to go into the back where Reggie is waiting to talk to her.

Let her go.

Fuck that.

I sprint the rest of the way, and just as she's about to push through the door, I grab her wrist.

She spins around, her face going wide with shock. Her gaze dips to my mouth before her honey-brown eyes meet mine.

My need for her rushes through my blood like a drug.

I pull her away.

She doesn't say anything.

My fingers are tight around the fine bones of her hand. I tug her down a corridor, and the first door I stumble upon, open before pushing her inside a storage closet.

The door shuts, and I swing her around, slam her against the door.

She lets out a small oomph. Opens her mouth. But before she can say anything my lips cover hers.

And it's like a fucking bomb goes off.

Our mouths clash together. Our kiss is hard and brutal.

Her arms come around my neck and she's pulling me closer.

Pressing against me.

A desperateness I've never experienced with any other woman takes ahold of me and refuses to let go. I slant my head, deepening the contact, my mouth a searing brand as every cell in my body screams I take her.

Claim her.

Fuck her.

Own her.

Make her mine, absolutely and irrevocably.

I shove the hem of her dress up her thighs.

We shift.

Her legs come up.

I dip down.

My aching cock rocks against her cunt.

She gasps into my mouth, and I growl low in my throat as I thrust against her.

Frustration at the barriers between us have me lifting her up.

Her legs come around my hips.

I grip her ass in both hands, holding her in place and pound against her like I'm a fucking animal.

Our lips still fused together, she cries out, clutching my shoulders, her hips matching my rhythm.

My fingers dig into her.

All our heat. All our tension. It fills the room. Consumes me.

It's insanity.

It's not enough, but I can't gain sufficient control to stop.

Our panting breaths and fighting mouths and surging bodies are an unstoppable force.

Her legs tighten around me. If I don't stop, she's going to come.

If I don't stop, *I'm* going to come.

Completely clothed, dry fucking her like a teenager, I'm about to explode.

And I can't goddamn stop.

Her questing hips pick up speed and she starts to frantically rub her cunt against me. Harder and harder. I'm meeting her stroke for stroke.

Fuck.

Stop.

Fuck.

She tears away and her head bangs against the door.

Stop.

She moans, making crazed, mindless sounds, her eyes closed.

Her nails dig into my neck. "Brandon."

Stop.

Then her thighs clench around me, and she arches, her chest heaving, her lips parted in a desperate cry as an orgasm rips through her. She calls out my name in a husky moan, and as I watch the ecstasy race across her flushed cheeks and mindless expression, I do the unthinkable, and slip over the fucking edge.

Like a rutting beast, I come against her, unable to help myself.

I'm not inside her, I'm not even skin to skin, and it's an insane, intense rush of pleasure.

I hate her for it.

Veronica

As the last tremor of blinding pleasure sears through me, imprinting Brandon into my skin, our eyes meet.

We're bonded together in this hopeless, uncontrollable lust.

What can only be described as pure panic, followed by horror, rushes across his features. Then the spell breaks and it's like a bucket of ice water pours over us.

We stare at each other, unblinking.

My legs slowly fall from his waist.

His hands leave the curve of my ass.

I come to rest steady on the floor.

His palms run over my hips, pulling the hem of my dress down.

I rest against the door.

He steps back and rakes his hand through his hair.

"Brandon." His name is an uncertain stutter.

He shakes his head. "I'm sorry."

"Me too."

"You." He shakes his head again, and wipes his hand against his mouth like he's trying to rid himself of the taste of me. "That. Shouldn't have happened."

"I know." It shouldn't have, at least not like this.

What happened, there's something wrong about it. Something unbearably intimate and raw about being so desperate for each other that we couldn't pull away long enough even to rid ourselves of our clothes. I want to hide away from the fact that he'd made me so crazy I'd had to fight back the orgasm. Been unable to help myself from going over as his hard cock pounded ruthlessly over my clit.

A muscle worked in his jaw and he shoved his hands into his pants. He's not happy.

We'd broken. We'd been out of control. Unthinking. Mindless in a haze of relentless desire.

I know him well enough to know that Brandon doesn't like to be out of control. I've seen how he operates. He's cool, composed and refined about almost everything. Except when his mouth had been on mine. I could feel all his unleashed power spinning like an out-of-control top as he'd basically fucked me fully dressed against the door.

I think back to what Jillian said, about him never sweating. I'd made him sweat. I'd made him lose it on me.

And there were going to be consequences.

"Veronica." My name is already cold on his lips. His jaw hardens, and when he looks at me, his features are closed off and remote. "There can never be anything between us."

Every ounce of common sense I possess insists I accept this and leave. It would be so much easier that way. I want the words to come out of my mouth, but they don't. I tilt my head. "There's already something between us."

His shoulders straighten. "I'll concede we have an uncanny amount of chemistry—"

I hold up my hand. "Is that what you're calling it?"

His expression flashes. "It's enough, Veronica. It happened. It won't happen again."

I laugh, and wonder what kind of craziness has taken over me. "Stop saying things that you can't follow through on. It's a matter of time."

"We work together. And a work relationship is all we can ever have."

"That's an excuse, to remain distant, and you know it."

He shakes his head. "No."

I hate the cool politeness of his tone, so different from the man that had been burning me alive. I wave my hand. "So what's this? Just a minor annoyance?"

"Yes." He nods, as though affirming to himself.

I cross my hands over my chest. "I see. So it's common for you to want a woman so bad you can't pull away long enough to fuck her?"

Anger tightens his face, hardens his shoulders. "Maybe we got carried away."

"And when's the last time that happened?" I step forward and poke him in the chest. "You hate that I saw you like that. That I witnessed the great Brandon Townsend lose it." I poke his chest again. "You hate I have power over you."

At my next poke, he grabs my hand tight. "You need to watch it, little girl. You have no idea what you're messing with."

I throw my shoulders back. "What do you want to do? Tell me."

Aggression is practically vibrating off him. He steps closer. "I want to turn you around, put your hands up against the door and spank you." He moves closer. "Humiliate you." A little closer. "Control you." We're not a half an inch apart now. "I want to break you."

I instinctively take a step back.

He follows. "Ruin you."

My spine presses against the wood.

"Violate you."

He puts his hands on either side of my head. "Fuck you until the only person you ever want in your life is me."

I'm so hot, so mesmerized. "You need to control me?"

"Yes." His head dips down. "Like you're a fucking drug."

I have no idea what instincts are riding me. What's making me act this way. But it feels like something he needs and I don't question why. I lick my lips, duck down and shimmy so that I'm facing the door.

He's still bracing himself against the door and I put my hands next to him, peer over my shoulder and meet his eyes. "Do it."

He growls and a fierce need crosses over his face. "Veronica."

"Please. I want you to."

His hands fall away and he shifts back, gripping my hips.

I press my cheek against the wood and close my eyes. "I've thought about it. What it would feel like."

"And then what?" His voice is strangled.

"Then I fuck myself with my fingers and come."

He groans. "I can't do this." But he's already lifting my skirt.

"Please. I need it." I arch my back. "And so do you."

His hot palms sear over my satin-covered ass. "Why do you think that?"

My fingers flex on the door. "I don't know. I just do."

"We are playing with fire." He leans over me and presses against me. He's hard.

"I know." I can't help but press into it. "I don't want to stop."

"Why?" His fingers play over the edge of my panties, along the swell of my hips, and I shiver.

"You're the only thing that makes me feel alive."

He sucks in a breath and his grip on me tightens.

"I think I'm the only thing that makes you feel alive too. I think you hate it, but you need it."

"Veronica." My name is an urgent whisper now. He starts to drag my panties down.

And his phone goes off—the ringtone loud and alarming. He curses and immediately pulls my underwear back in place.

I jerk. "What's wrong?"

"There's a problem. I need to take care of it."

"All right." I straighten and adjust my dress over my hips. "I'll come to."

His gaze skims over me than he nods. "Let's go."

Brandon

It's three in the morning and I'm sitting alone on the couch in my office drinking hundred-year-old scotch straight from the bottle. After I'd dealt with the problem that had been the only thing that kept me from making another irrevocable mistake, I'd avoided Veronica for the rest of the night.

In fact, I've avoided everyone and I can't wait for the last of the crew to go home so I can leave and forget this night ever happened. I can't even think about the storage closet. Or how my palm twitches at the thought of smacking her perfect fucking ass.

I take a sip from the bottle, hissing a little as it slides down my throat.

What a fucking disaster. She's a disaster. Like a storm blowing into my life and fucking everything the hell up. I regret the day she stepped out onto that balcony. I should have sent her away the second she spoke, but I hadn't, and she's systematically destroying everything I have built my life around.

There's a knock on the door. "Come in."

The door opens, and while I'd been expecting Reggie, telling me they are finished, Michael walks in, and without a word, sits down on the chair and raises a brow.

I frown. "It's late, I thought you left."

"I did." He's wearing jeans now, and a black T-shirt. His six-five frame takes up all the space even in my oversized chair. He picks up a glass from the table and holds it out to me.

I sigh, lean forward and tip some of the amber liquor into the glass. In the low light it's the color of Veronica's eyes. It's like she's haunting me. I take another sip as he kicks back and stretches out his long legs, resting the glass on the arm of the chair, relaxed in his hand.

"Why aren't you home with your pretty fiancée?" I ask, even though I know why he's here.

"I thought you'd like some company." He takes a sip of his drink before looking at it. "I love this stuff."

"I'll make sure you get some as a wedding present."

He smiles. "Deal."

I scrub a hand over my jaw. "I don't want company."

"I know you don't want it. I thought maybe you needed it."

There's only one thing I feel like I need right now, and I sent her home hours ago. "I don't."

"You want to talk about it?"

"No." I scowl. "And what's with you guys always wanting to talk about shit now?"

He laughs. "I owe you."

"For what."

"That night I met Layla, you pushed me." His eyes narrow.

164

"Or don't you remember?"

I remember. Clearly, I'm an idiot for never expecting retribution. "Not that same thing."

His head tilts. "No?"

"No."

"You told me I'd watched her long enough and it was time to act."

"And I was right." I smirk. "You're welcome."

"I didn't want to act." He drains his glass and sits forward, putting the now empty glass on the table. I refill it, but he doesn't move to take it, instead he rests his elbows on his knees and laces his fingers. "I was scared shitless."

I don't ask the question—the why—he's looking to get from me, because I don't want to know the answer. But this is Michael, who's always been too intuitive for his own good.

He picks up his glass and reclines. "I knew what it would be like with her. How hard I'd have to fight for her. How she'd be a struggle and how it would never be easy with her. I wanted no part of it. Her, I wanted like she was my next fucking breath, but everything that came with it." He shakes his head. "I wanted it to be a deal breaker, and when I came to grips with the fact that it didn't matter, I kept trying to mentally prepare myself to handle her."

And I'd pushed him into it. Just like I pushed Leo into Jillian. But it wasn't the same thing.

When I don't say anything he cocks a grin at me. "Then you came along, cool as shit, and told me it was time, that you were tired of watching her punish herself, and every time I didn't act her chances of running into someone who'd damage her permanently would increase. And I went."

We'd known Layla far before she'd known us and while her story remained a mystery until much later; she'd walked through my underground club like a ghost, her eyes shadowed, on a quest for self-destruction.

"It's not the same." The response, the fact that I don't have to say Veronica's name, is all wrong. Revealing.

"Isn't it?" He scrubs a hand over his jaw. "There are some

things we can't control. Some things that take over and refuse to be tamed or fall into line."

"It's under control." A fucking lie.

"Brandon, I've known you a long time. I've seen you with a lot of women. She's shaking you." He narrows his eyes. "I've been there. I know how it is."

I shake my head and take three gulps of the bottle.

When I don't speak he asks, "Did you fuck her?"

"No." Worse. Much, much worse. What happened in that storage closet is one of the most embarrassing things that ever happened to me. I've had a warm, wet mouth on my cock and held off coming for hours. My control is legendary. I don't orgasm by rutting against someone, fully clothed, unable to help myself.

"But something happened."

I shrug. I will go to my grave before I admit that humiliation to anyone. It's bad enough Veronica knows.

"If you want to hear it, I'll tell you the problem. Because it's plain as day to everyone, but you're too close to recognize it."

The hair on the back of my neck pricks. I jerk my attention toward him. "What?"

"She's a submissive girl and she's daring you to take control."

My heart starts to pound a frantic rhythm in my chest. "No, she's curious. That's not the same thing."

He laughs. "Brandon she's begging you for it, and if it were anyone else, you'd see that."

I want to deny, it's my last hope I can resist her. "You're wrong."

"Think about it. If it was someone else, and you witnessed a girl acting like that, doing everything she can possibly think to incite a reaction, what would you say?"

I know exactly what I'd say. I grit my teeth. "You don't understand."

"What, because she works for you? So what?"

That excuse is flimsier and flimsier. I look away. "No, that's not it."

"Then what is it?"

I'm silent for a long, long time and he waits me out, probably because he knows what I'm going to tell him. And finally, the pressure becomes too much, and I do. "I can't control her."

He sighs. "That's because you're trying to control the wrong thing."

My gaze snaps to him.

He gives me a small smile. "Stop fighting how you feel about her, and things will get easier."

Is he right? I frown. I take a deep breath and ask him another question. "Is she still a struggle?"

He's quiet for a second then he nods. "Yeah, she is."

That's what I thought.

He shrugs. "She's still worth every single fucking second of it."

That's what I'm afraid of.

15.

Veronica

I'd taken the next day off because it's moving day. After what happened with Brandon last night, I can't decide if that's a good thing or a bad thing. He'd avoided me for the rest of the night, and I let him because it seemed prudent to give him space.

At least I'll be too busy to think too much about the ramifications.

I'm standing in the middle of the Gold Coast condo, decorated by my mother's interior designer, filled with lavish furniture that's supposed to belong to me, and I realize I don't want any of it. None of it feels like me.

I might not know who I am, or what I'm becoming, but I know it's not this life.

Living in a condo I didn't earn, sitting on furniture picked out by someone else, surrounded by people that don't know me.

I look out the floor-to-ceiling windows that cover one wall, providing a picture-perfect view of the city and I'm nothing but relieved.

I'm doing the right thing, moving to the small one-bedroom condo I can afford off my salary, it's my path to freedom. I'll miss the windows though, but it's well worth it.

My phone rings, and I run to get it from the end table. My heart about leaps into my throat as I see Brandon's name on the screen. Last night, when he'd told me to go home, I'd searched his expression, looking for any clue of what he wanted from me, but he'd been unreadable.

But here he is, calling me?

The excitement is like a rush through my system. *Be calm.* It's probably work, and only work. I press the call button and when I speak my voice is a bit too breathless. "Hello?"

There's a pause and even over the line tension crackles between us. "Good morning."

"Good morning." My tongue feels thick in my mouth. I search for something to say, and settle on. "How'd the rest of the night go?"

"Everything was good."

"I'm glad. It seemed like everyone had fun."

Awkward silence fills the line before he clears his throat. "You did a good job, Veronica. People respond to you, they like you and you're very charming. Everyone who spoke to me raved about you."

Pleasure beats in my chest, he's never commented on my performance since I started. "Thank you, I'm glad you're happy."

"I'm not sure if hiring you is the best or worst mistake I've ever made."

I sit down on the couch. "You haven't officially hired me yet, but you also haven't fired me either."

"No, I haven't. I'm not about to fire you because I can't keep my hands off you. That's hardly fair, is it?"

I'm so surprised he's brought up the attraction I can only suck in my breath.

His voice lowers. "Several men asked if you were available."

I bite my lower lip. "What did you say?"

"I said no."

His statement sits between us.

"Oh…" I trail off, unsure what to say.

"You're moving today."

The change in subject has me straightening. "Yes."

Another tension-filled second pulses the air. "Do you want help?"

I can't be processing this right. I say stupidly, "From whom?"

He laughs. "From me."

Slowly, I say, "You want to come help me move?"

"No, I don't. Moving is the last thing I want."

"What do you want?" The words shake, not from fear, but from lust. From hope.

When he speaks his voice is low and husky. "What I want right at this moment is to come over there, rip off whatever you're wearing, and without preamble, fuck you bare, with no condom."

"Oh." My whole body heats and I gasp at the bluntness of his words.

"And do you know why I want that?"

"No."

"Because I want to claim your cunt for my own. And after, with my come dripping down your thighs, I want to spank you, then push you to the floor and take you again. I want to use you. Exhaust you. Bruise you. Mark you. I want your body sore, your mind empty, and for you to still feel my cock inside you tomorrow."

Oh. My. God. I lean back on the couch and close my eyes, wanting nothing but the sound of his voice in my ear.

"Do you know the last time I wanted that from a woman, Veronica?"

"No." My voice is low and breathless, and even I can hear the plea in it.

"Never."

"Oh." I have no idea what to say and his confession has

reduced me to monosyllables.

"And you want that too."

It's not a question, but I still respond. "Yes."

"The tension between us is going to get worse if we keep fighting it, but I can't ignore the fact that we work together."

"I understand."

"Tell me, Veronica. What do you want?"

"I want it all." My answer immediate and absolute.

"And what's your definition of all?"

I take a deep breath and blow it out. "I want you and the job."

There's silence before he speaks, as though he's thinking. "Here's what I propose."

"I'm listening."

"Other than wanting to fuck like our lives depend on it, we really don't know each other that well. And right now the tension is clouding all our interactions, making it impossible to do anything but fight our attraction."

I smile, so relieved to hear him admit he's struggling. "I agree."

"I propose we get to know each other, spend time together."

My heart thrills. "I'd really like that."

"Good. But there's a catch." He pauses and clears his throat. "I think sex should be off the table until we're sure we have more in common than feeding our lust."

My mouth drops open and I sputter. "No sex?"

He laughs. "I do like that the prospect sounds horrible to you."

"But... How?"

He laughs again. "I figure we can fool around, and there will be orgasms, but as your boss, I don't want to tie you to me sexually until we know each other better, until we're more sure. I thought this could be a compromise."

"When's the last time you just fooled around with a woman?"

"Besides last night when we dry fucked like teenagers?"

Heat warms my belly. "Yes."

"I don't know, probably eighth grade."

My brow furrows. "What's changed? You seem more in control now."

"I am."

"Why?"

"I accepted that no matter what I do I'm going to want you. And I accepted that you scare me."

"I do?"

"Yes."

"Why?"

"I don't like not having control over my desires."

"I think there's more."

Three beats pass before he says, "Maybe. Someday, maybe I'll tell you, but today's not that day."

"That's fair." But I still want to know more. "If I don't want to pursue this? Then what?"

"Then we will go on working together and I will make sure the projects you work on don't put us in close proximity. Is that what you want?"

"No, it's not. I needed to hear what you'd say."

"Understandable. Anything else?"

I clear my throat. "What about…the other thing?"

"You mean my wanting to have control over you? Own you. Dominate you?"

I flush and I'm thankful he can't see me. "Yes, that."

"The truth is, I don't know yet. Is that something you want?"

I'm obsessed with thinking about it, imagining it, reading about it. "I…don't know."

"You have no experience with it."

"Right."

"And I have no experience without it."

I blink. "Really?"

"Really. It's always been there, even before I had a name for it."

"How do you mean?"

He chuckles. "You remember when you were a kid and you'd play cops and robbers, or princess in a tower where the hero prince comes to the rescue?"

"Yes."

"I always wanted to be the villain, holding the princess captive."

I swallow hard. "Oh."

"It's not something that's ever going to go away for me, and I'm not sure how easy it will be for me to keep in check, especially when you're being a brat."

A huge smile breaks across my lips. "I am *not* a brat."

"Veronica, you are the very definition of a brat." His voice drops. "I'm just dying for a chance to put you in your place."

I let out a little gasp. "Okay."

He laughs. "Back to the point. I'll try and keep it in check as we figure this thing out, but you should always be aware that for me, it's not icing, it's the cake. It's part of sex for me and I don't know how to turn it off. So if we end up fucking, that's going to be part of it."

"All right." I scrape my teeth over my bottom lip. "How will I know without experience?"

"Good point. We have two choices—and the decision is yours to make—we can either completely take it off the table while we're…" He pauses. "I have no idea what to call it."

"Dating?" My fingers tighten on my phone.

"God help me."

I laugh. "It's not that terrible. What's the other choice?"

"I can give you a taste of it while we're—" he sighs "—dating."

I cluck my tongue. "Poor baby, I know it's a real hardship."

"Veronica?"

"Yes?"

"Brat."

I smile. "Maybe a little."

"A lot."

Silence hangs in the air before he says, "What's your choice? Or do you need to think about it?"

I know what I want; it's not even a question. "I want the real you, not the watered-down version."

"I should warn you it will make our…dating much more intense."

"I don't care." I lick my lips. "I'm not looking for tame, I'm looking to live."

"Veronica?"

"Yes?"

"I'll be over in thirty minutes to help you move."

This is the last thing I expected today, and it's the happiest surprise I've had in a long time. Somehow, I have no idea how, but I'm dating Brandon Townsend III, and he's helping me move. Even though he doesn't want to. Even though it's against his better judgment, he's conceding.

I smile. "I'll see you soon."

Brandon

Veronica opens the door to her condo and we stand there, our gazes locked, unable to move. She's wearing worn cutoffs, a pink tank top, her hair in a ponytail and no makeup. She looks adorable and so fuckable I get hard just standing here.

She smiles and says breathlessly, "Hi."

"Hi." Somewhere in the wee hours of the morning, after catching a buzz with Michael, I gave up the fight and admitted I wanted her too much to stop. That I didn't want to stop. I'm not sure of my solution, but it seemed a reasonable course of action.

Her pink tongue flicks over her lower lip. "Thanks for helping me."

My gaze rakes over her. "You don't have anyone else helping?"

She laughs and it shoots straight through me. "Well, movers, of course. But do you actually think the people we know would help me move?"

"Good point." I shift my attention to the space behind her. "Are you going to let me in?"

"Oh, sorry." She stands back.

Maybe we talked. Maybe we made some decisions, but it's still awkward as hell. The air is filled with tension. It's a novel situation for me. I've been cool and collected for so long I'm ill equipped to handle raw, nervous sexual tension. I have no idea what to do about the fact that I itch to touch her and am uncertain of my ability to not lose control and rip her shorts off and impale her.

What worries me is it's not sex. It's the way I want the sex *from her*. I want to fuck her, not to relieve the ache in my cock, but as a brand. I want to come on her, in her, to mark her as my territory.

It's about possession. Not control.

This…need for her, clouding my judgment, is something I have no experience with and don't like, but the more I try and control it the harder it becomes. So I'm taking Michael's advice and seeing what happens.

She tucks a stray lock of hair behind her ear. "I'm not sure I like the way you're looking at me."

Her words snap me from my thoughts. I walk over the threshold and the door closes behind me. I turn to face her. "How am I looking at you?"

She takes a stuttery little breath. "Like you want to have me for lunch."

"I do." I meet her honey-brown eyes. "I don't trust myself with you."

"I don't trust myself with you either."

"I don't enjoy the feeling."

She flashes a smile. "I guess that's where we're different. I do."

I take three steps toward her and she presses herself against the wall.

That she subconsciously prepares herself to be taken by me is like a drug rushing through my system, feeding me, giving me strength and centering me. I stalk closer, cornering her, trapping her.

Her breath comes fast as her pupils dilate.

A primal satisfaction cuts through me like a knife. I put my hands on either side of her head. "Why's that?"

She tilts her chin up. "You're the first person I've ever really wanted."

I growl low in my throat, dip down and scrape my teeth against her jaw. I mean to say something cocky and arrogant, but instead whisper harshly into her ear, "Me too."

The tiny, needy gasp she gives me is my undoing.

My mouth covers hers. Hard and brutal.

I don't understand what she does to my brain, because kissing Veronica is like nothing on earth. With most women, I kiss for precision, to elicit a reaction from her, but this is nothing like that. It's like I can't take her mouth ruthlessly enough.

My tongue sweeps in as her hands slide around my neck. She moans against me. I grip her ponytail, holding her still while I treat her mouth like I'm going to treat her body.

Hard.

Relentless.

Possessive and claiming.

She responds by trying to climb up me, plastering her long, lean body against mine. Her leg comes up. I grip her bare thigh, bending and rocking my cock along her soft center. Her shoulders hit the wall, giving me leverage, and her legs lock around my hips. I thrust, and she meets me, stroke for stroke. It's like last night all over again, crazy and out of control, the lust pounding through me as our bodies strain and surge.

And she's right. I feel alive.

It's like craving something I hadn't known I was looking for. Hadn't known I needed and wanted, but now am hungry for. It steadies me. Makes me want more for her than me rutting against her like an animal.

I rip away, look behind me, spotting the couch.

Her legs loosen. Shaking my head, I grip her under the ass. "Don't move."

She bites her lip, nodding.

I swing her around, walk to the couch before sitting down with her on top of me. Her legs come from around my waist and settle next to me.

I grip her hips. "Stand up and take off your shorts."

Her expression flashes, and she starts to speak, but I cut her off. "Just do what you're told."

Her pupils dilate and I can see her questions.

I squeeze her hips. "Don't argue with me."

She sucks in a breath and slowly stands. With trembling fingers she unbuttons her shorts, and they drop to the floor.

Lust runs thick and hot in my blood, and my lids grow heavy. I flick my attention to her panties. "Those too."

She hooks her thumbs into her white cotton underwear and shimmies them down her long legs. I crook my finger, beckoning her to me and she looks at me hesitantly before straddling me.

I stare at her bare cunt, lick my lips before slipping my palms along her thighs. I shake my head. "So fucking gorgeous."

She flushes.

"Are you wet?"

She nods.

"Show me."

She dips between her legs and rubs her clit in a slow circle.

I grit my teeth as wetness glistens on her fingers. I take her hand, bring it to my mouth and suck her fingers clean. She gasps as my tongue laps at her skin, as I try and memorize the very taste of her. When I release her, I say in a low guttural voice, "Again."

She moans as her fingers once again slide between her legs.

I reach up, pull the band from her hair, and watch as it cascades wild around her flushed face.

Her head falls back as her fingers dance along her swollen pussy. Just as she starts to get lost, I grip her wrist and bring her to my lips where I suck and lick, and bite.

"Brandon." My name is a groan of pleasure.

"Again."

Over and over until she's mindless and needy, squirming on my lap, working herself closer and closer to orgasm.

"Again." I'm strung tight, my body demanding I take what's mine, but I'm not going to do that. I'm going to stick to my plan. Even if it kills me. At least this way I don't have to resist touching her. Tasting her.

She's making greedy little noises in the back of her throat, and it pushes me over the edge. Once more, I suck her fingers clean, then put her hand on her thigh and shove my fingers between her legs.

Christ. She's so wet she's practically dripping, and I glide across her skin with no effort at all. I rub her clit and she bucks into my hand, crying out.

"Ride my fingers. I want to watch you come." I grip her hip, and sink two fingers into her willing cunt. "Show me how much you want it."

At my words and the sweep of my thumb, she falls back, puts her hands on my knees and rocks her hips in wanton abandon. Almost immediately she starts coming, all over my hand, messy and dirty and erotic as her muscles clamp down on me. I work every last contraction from her body, relentlessly, until she flings herself forward and collapses on top of me in a heap, breathing hard and fast.

I tug her hair, forcing her to look at me. I brush my mouth over hers and stroke over her sensitive flesh, featherlight. "Good girl."

She moans.

I smile. "Soon I'm going to fuck you with my mouth and tongue."

"Oh god."

She pulses against me.

I laugh. "Don't we have work to do?"

"I don't think I can move."

"I haven't even done anything yet."

"I know, that's what scares me." She brushes her lips against my jaw. "Even while it thrills me."

178

I brush her hair off her cheek. "Veronica."

"Yes?"

"You need to move, because I'm about three seconds away from fucking you into the next century."

"Is that so bad?" She nuzzles my neck like a kitten.

"Take pity on me, I've broken every rule I have for you, at least let me keep this one plan."

She sighs, and burrows in deeper. "Oh, all right. But it's against my better judgment."

I grip her hair, fisting it in my hand and jerking her head up. I nip her earlobe. "You have no idea the slut I'm going to make you."

Her cunt grasps at my fingers still inside her. I mummer, "You like the sound of that, don't you?"

She nods. "Yes."

"I'm going to make you crave the most depraved things."

"Oh."

"You're going to beg me for them."

"Brandon?" My name is a needy little whisper.

"What?"

She licks at my pulse pounding in my neck. "I'm not above begging for you."

Jesus Christ. I am so fucked over this girl.

16.

"Veronica!" Brandon's standing in the middle of my new apartment living room holding a lamp looking grumpy, exasperated, and...well, kind of adorable. Although I'm pretty sure the image doesn't fit with his bad-guy persona and he wouldn't take it as a compliment.

I raise a brow. "Yes?"

"You need to get rid of half this stuff if you're going to live in this matchbook of a place."

I put my hands on my hips. "Oh my god, stop, it will all fit."

He rolls his eyes at me. "Where do you want this horror?"

I reach over and grab the lamp from him. "Hey! It's new."

He shakes his head. "Why?"

"I bought it at a thrift store with my own money. Be nice."

He stares at it like it's something foul. "You spent money on that?"

"Don't insult it." I hug it close, it's precious to me.

180

He points at it. "It's a fucking dolphin."

I smile. "I know. Isn't it cute?" It's hideous. I know that. I impulse bought it the other day because it seemed like the antithesis of my former life. I love it. When I'm ninety I will cherish it as a symbol of my freedom.

"It offends me just looking at it."

I laugh and pat him on the cheek. "Poor baby."

"Brat."

"You love it." It's been like this between us all day. Despite him giving me the best orgasm of my entire life on the couch back at my parents' condo, the tension between us is riding high and we've managed that tension by bickering. It's the most fun I've ever had.

To think, last night I'd gone home sure everything was hopeless.

I've always had to be so refined, so perfect, so well bred, I love this feeling of letting loose on him. Teasing. I've discovered there's nothing else I'd rather do than banter and fight with Brandon Townsend III.

We haven't touched much since the first time, both us sensing if we didn't stop we'd probably still be on that couch, all these hours later.

He narrows his eyes and shakes his head. "Please don't tell me you're going to put that…that…thing in the living room."

"Nope." I take off down the small hallway. "The bedroom."

"You will not."

"Will too," I call back over my shoulder.

"Veronica Westwood. I will not go down on you looking at that atrocity."

At the doorway I spin around and fix my attention on him before giving him my most charming smile. I shrug. "If you're going down on me, you won't be looking at it, so your problems are solved."

Then I slip into the bedroom, chuckling.

I'm bending over to plug it into a socket when he tackles me from behind, flings me onto the bare mattress and pins me down.

I scream and laugh as he covers me with his big body.

I suck in my breath at the impact.

"What am I going to do with you?" His tone is amused, his face relaxed in a softness I haven't seen on him before.

My thighs fall open, and as his hips settle between my legs, his eyes go dark. I lick my lips. "What are your ideas? Maybe I can help you choose."

His mouth quirks. "Are you this sassy with everyone?"

"No, only you." I arch, rocking myself against him, loving how he inhales sharply. Loving how he's already hard.

"I'm honored." His grip tightens.

"You should be." I can't help it; I grasp his hips with my thighs and circle because it just feels so damn good. "You're the only one that's ever seen the real me."

He rocks back, his expression turning dangerous. "We need to get up."

"I know." I arch, moaning when he hits the right spot. "God, right there."

He growls and slams his hips against me. "I want to fuck you."

"Yes." All the playfulness is gone.

"I won't, but I want to."

"Please." I roll my hips into his.

"No." He kisses me. His lips a savage press against mine. Everything between us turns immediately hot and desperate. Our mouths cling, clashing together. Almost fighting as we strain to get closer and closer and closer. His tongue moves against mine, matching the frantic movements of our bodies.

He lets go of my wrists and his fingers wrap around my throat. When he squeezes something lurking and dark jolts awake from deep inside me. I arch my neck, baring myself to him. I slip my hands around his waist, snaking under his T-shirt.

He rips away from my mouth and says against my lips, "You like this, don't you?" His fingers tighten, momentarily constricting my airflow.

My nails dig into his back. I nod.

"You're at my mercy." He bites my lower lip. "Helpless."

I cry out as an intense need takes hold of me. "Yes."

He whispers in my ear, "I need to take you. I want to fucking own you."

"Yes, that's all I want." I claw at his back. "Please, fuck me."

"Not yet."

"Why?"

His fingers tighten again, cutting off my air supply. "Because I plan on ruining you for all other men." He releases, lets me drag in a few breaths, and then squeezes again. "Once we take that step, I'll make sure you'll never fuck another man without thinking about me."

My lungs burn and he lets me breathe again. I suck in air. This should terrify me, but I can't explain it, it's making me dizzy with the darkest, deepest desire I've ever known and I don't want it to end.

He scrapes his teeth against my jaw. "You're going to have bruises on your neck. Every time you see them in the mirror it's going to remind you of my possession."

I bow my neck, asking for more. Needing more.

"You want more?"

"Yes."

"If you need to stop, pound your foot on the bed three times."

I nod.

His fingers stroke over my neck. A tease. "Pull your tank top and bra under your breasts."

I don't even hesitate; I just yank my top down and lift my breasts over my bra.

His grip doesn't constrict. Doesn't press, he merely hints at it as he takes one nipple in his mouth.

He sucks, and it creates the most exquisite sensation I feel everywhere. His leg slips between mine, pressing firm where I need him most. Again and again. Then he squeezes, blocking my air, pulling the hard bud with his teeth.

It's the most intoxicating sensation. His fingers on my throat. His lips on my skin. The hard tug of his teeth. It rushes hot and demanding through my entire body, sending explosions of tingles everywhere, from the top of my head to the tips of my toes.

The world takes on a hazy rhythm and I slowly grind away against his hard thigh in time with his mouth and hand. It's so good. Better than anything I've ever felt.

I want it to go on forever.

I grip his forearm, not to push him away but to feel the flex of his muscles as he controls me. If this is domination, I'll never be able to be without it for as long as I live.

He squeezes, sucking particularly hard on my breast.

I cry out. Dig my nails into his skin.

Then without warning, an intense orgasm rolls through me, stealing whatever breath I have left.

My entire body pulses and shakes as I ride his thigh. It goes on and on in endless waves. He lets go of my throat and I make the most inhuman sounds as the climax storms through me.

Panting for breath, I finally collapse onto the bed, practically sedated with bone-deep satisfaction.

He strokes over my skin, releasing my nipple as he props his head onto his palm and trails his fingers softly over my breasts.

My lids are heavy but I manage to blink up at him.

He smiles. "Feel better?"

I nod.

"Good."

We stay like that, catching our breaths, his hands tracing lazy paths over my skin.

Our eyes meet. He cups my jaw. "Veronica."

"Yes, Brandon." My voice is hoarse, scratchy.

He trails his thumb over my lip, still swollen from his kiss. "Don't *ever* let anyone else constrict your breathing like that, okay?"

"I don't want anyone else." I don't care what he thinks.

He's already ruined me.

"I know." He kisses me, long and deep. "I need to say it. It's not safe if you don't know what you're doing. So promise me, for my own peace of mind."

"I promise." I lick my lips. "I've never come like that before."

He nods. "It won't be the last time."

He rolls off me and sits up, dragging his hands through his hair before putting his elbows on his knees. He shakes his head a little and his back expands under his T-shirt as he sucks in a long breath before exhaling.

I realize he's fighting for control.

I've had two orgasms today. He's had none.

That's wrong. He's clearly not going to break down and take me, but there's something I can do for him. Something I want to do for him.

I sit up, stand, then turn to face him.

He gazes at me; his attention snagging on my naked breasts. A muscle in his jaw jumps. "Just give me a minute."

"I don't think so." I sink to my knees.

His expression darkens. "Veronica."

I put my hands on his thighs and move up. "I want to suck your cock."

When he speaks his voice is strained. "That's not a good idea."

"Why's that?"

He tangles his hand in my hair. "Because with the way I feel right now, I can't be gentle."

"I don't want gentle." I move to his zipper. "I want you."

He shakes his head. "You're used to blowjobs, which is different than what I need right now."

I pull open the button and unzip. Despite his protests, he doesn't stop me. I lick my lips and he groans. "What do you need?"

His fingers tighten, and the sting of pain prickles along my nape. "I need to fuck your throat. I need to use you."

I don't understand the difference, but I'm not about to

deny him anything. Right now, anything he wants, anything he needs, I'll give him. I run my palm over his erection. "Do it."

"Veronica."

I peer up at him. "Please?"

He growls, tightens his hand in my hair and pulls me in for a kiss that steals my breath all over again. Then he stands up, and I think he's going to reject me, but he pulls his heavy cock out of his jeans and twists my hair until I'm raised and kneeling.

He's long and thick and just gorgeous. I've never thought much about blowjobs before, I've done them because that's what good girlfriends do, but I never wanted a dick in my mouth the way I want Brandon's sliding over my tongue.

"Are you sure?" He fists his shaft and gives it a hard, firm stroke before rubbing it along the seam of my lips.

I meet his gaze and give him the truth. "I want to give you everything."

His jaw tightens. "And I'll take everything. Demand it."

"That's what I want."

"I hope you won't be sorry."

"Never."

He groans, and once again, strokes the head over my lips. I open my mouth to take him inside, but he shakes his head. "No. You sit there and let me take what I want."

I don't understand what we're playing with here, or what he wants from me, but I nod.

"I'm going to make you gag on my cock." He continues to rub the tip over my mouth. "All you need to remember is I want to watch you choking on it. Don't worry about trying to control your gag reflex. In fact, don't worry about controlling anything. Just take what I give you."

I nod my agreement again and the nerves flutter through my stomach.

He strokes my hair. "Good girl."

My breathing increases. I don't know what it is about those two little words that makes me want…something…but they do. I just don't have a name for it.

"Are you afraid?"

"Yes." I am, but in the most intoxicating way. Like the *click, click, click* up the steep hill of a roller coaster.

"Good." He presses the tip of his cock against my lips. "Open."

I do.

He fills me, slowly sliding over my tongue and stretching my lips. On instinct I raise my hand to grip him to control his movements but he slaps me away. "No hands."

I put them back on his thighs and he resumes.

Click, click, click.

His eyes lock on mine. "Don't look away."

I don't.

He fills me again.

Click, click, click. Up the roller coaster I go.

Shallow at first. A glance over my tongue before he pulls back out and rubs his cock over my lips. Features, feral and stark, highlighting the cast of his high cheekbones, he pushes back in. When he's partially in he stops, and his fingers tighten on my hair, holding me still. "Christ."

I hope the question I want to ask is in my eyes.

He smiles. "Never in my entire life has a girl looked so good on my cock. You're a fucking work of art."

Pleasure blooms in my chest. I could die making this man happy.

He pulls back out, then pushes back in. Again. And again. Color raises on his cheeks and his lids hood as he stares down at me. "That's right. Don't look away. Keep those pretty eyes on me."

He starts to move in earnest.

Thrilling me as I rush headlong down the steep hill and fling everything I have into pleasing him.

He pushes deeper.

And deeper.

And deeper still.

He thrusts hard, and hits my gag reflex.

When I choke, his expression turns fierce and I watch

transfixed as a cruel type of arrogance washes over his face. If I had any breath to give, it'd be gone, because he's beautiful to look at. Almost haunting and it mesmerizes me.

He thrusts again.

I gag, but instead of pulling out he pushes farther, closing off my airway for a fraction of a second before he pulls back out. That same dark intensity that overtook me on the bed washes over me.

"That's it." He moans, grips my hair, and shows me the exact difference between giving a blowjob and getting your throat fucked.

He is ruthless. Relentless. Unforgiving.

Mean.

It's messy and filthy.

I get caught up in looking pretty and appealing, and not like some depraved, crazy person with saliva running down her chin and onto her neck. I grip his thigh, digging my nails into his jeans, fighting the urge to raise my hand and control his movements.

He stops abruptly and shakes his head, pulling out.

I suck in air, attempting to catch my breath, but before I can orientate myself, he leans down and gives me the dirtiest, most savage kiss of my life. He pulls away and whispers against my lips, "Surrender, Veronica. Don't think. Don't try and improve on my behalf. Don't worry about how you look. This is exactly how I want you, your lips swollen, your chin and eyes streaked, looking like a hungry little cockslut. That's what I need from you, the surrender you've never given to anyone else."

Inexplicably, my eyes grow bright. I don't want to fail, but I don't understand what he wants. "Okay."

He kisses me one more time, and straightens.

He pushes between my lips. My instincts want to fight, to control, but he said to surrender, so I ignore the desire and relax my hand on his thigh and the hard clench of my jaw.

"Good girl. That's perfect." He strokes a finger over my cheek, the gentle touch at complete odds with his expression and the demanding rhythm of his cock on the back of my throat.

He pushes deep, but when I gag, I fight my body's natural response, relaxing more.

Satisfaction washes over his face, and he nods.

In a sudden flash, I get it. Crystal-clear clarity settles in the center of my chest and I know what he wants, what he needs. What only I can give him.

I surrender. I ease the tension in my jaw, release the tightness in my shoulders and neck and force all my muscles to melt for him.

For Brandon.

This man who I knew, from the second I saw him standing on that balcony that night, would change me.

He must see it in my eyes because all his hyper focus on me fades away and what is left behind is the most beautiful thing I've ever seen.

Pure, primal lust.

He goes faster, deeper, thrusting hard into my mouth, down my throat.

I'm choking, my eyes water and tears stream down my face, mixing with my saliva.

And I don't care.

All I care about is him. What he wants. Pleasing him.

The very air around us transforms, thickens with sex and desire.

He's breathing harsh now, panting, his lids heavy as he gazes down at me with utter possession.

It's surrender and it's power and something else I can't put a name to.

"Don't look away," he orders, his voice holding no hint of kindness or deference.

I might be surrendering to him, but in return he's revealing his true self to me. It's harsh, unrelenting and unleashed. It makes me greedy for everything he's been holding back from me.

I moan.

He curses. Thrusts harder. Bruising my lips and throat.

I let it all go. The thoughts empty, my mind goes fuzzy, and all I want in this world is to make him happy. To show him what I can give him, what I'll do for him. How he won't be sorry he chose me.

His grip tightens in my hair. "You're fucking mine."

Yes, yes, yes. Unable to speak, I vibrate the word.

"Fuck." His eyes never leave mine. "I'm going to own every inch of you."

I agree, with my eyes and my compliant mouth.

Holding tight, he pushes deep in my throat. "Don't look away."

I hold his gaze, our eyes locked, and something indescribable passes between us.

His grasp becomes painful, but I don't break contact, don't resist.

He growls, low and animalistic, before he thrusts hard and comes.

I swallow around his cock, and never looking away, he shoots hot and thick down my throat. I can't breathe, but I don't struggle as he moans and pulses one last time before he pulls back.

And still, we never look away, even though there's something unbearably intimate about what passed between us. His strokes become softer, gentle. He rubs a crooked finger over my cheek. "What am I going to do with you?"

I can't even speak. I don't know why, but my throat tightens like I'm going to cry.

He falls from my lips and crouches down. He brushes over my swollen mouth and I choke on the emotions storming through me, mixing with the most incredible, consuming desire.

He pulls me close, kisses my temple, before moving to sit on the floor and dragging me on top of him, settling me onto his lap. His arms close around me, and kissing my forehead, he holds me tight. "It's okay, it will pass."

"Touch me," I murmur into his neck. "Please touch me."

I can't explain what I need. How I feel.

He rubs my back, holding me close. "Tell me."

"I need something." I start to cry.

"It's okay. You're okay." He presses me into his chest. "Let it all out."

I take his hand, shift, and put it between my legs where I throb.

"Is this what you need?" He grinds his palm against me.

I nod. "I ache."

He kisses my temple again. "I'll take care of it, baby. Nice and easy."

With expert hands he unfastens my shorts and slips his fingers into my pants. He breathes into my ear. "So wet. So hot."

I lift my hips, but he holds me still. "Just let me do the work."

Eyes closed, I burrow close. "Please."

"I'll take care of you. I promise." His fingers circle my clit, over and over, sliding over slick flesh, making me gasp and shudder.

The crushing need surges and swells, and I clutch him tighter, burying deeper, my face pressed into his neck as I weep and wish I could crawl inside him.

"Sssshhh… I've got you." He circles faster, and I gasp and shiver.

Then the orgasm overtakes me and I tremble as the ecstasy sweeps me under and I melt into him. Hoping and praying that he'll never let me go. I'm his.

I only hope he'll keep me.

Brandon

Veronica finally relaxes in my arms, and I hold her close as she cries out what I've done to her. The tears don't surprise me. They're not uncommon. Submissive girls often experience a swell of unexplained emotion after they've experienced something intense.

It's everything else that surprises me. That shakes me.

Veronica becoming mindless and needy, surrendering herself over to my pleasure is expected. Me losing all sense of time and place, overcome by the driving needs of my body, are not.

She shivers in my arms, nestling closer, nestling her face into my neck.

I brush my lips over her forehead and keep rubbing her back in slow strokes.

I always care for a girl after I put her through the wringer. Always. Because it's the responsible thing to do, but in my darkest moments of self-reflection I recognized that even though I did it with care, I did it mechanically. It's what good dominants did. It's not like I minded, or resented it, because I didn't. But there was something detached when I held the girl in my arms.

With Veronica, detached is the last thing I feel. Instead, I feel impossibly conscious of her, impossibly soft. I want nothing more than to protect her, and take care of her until she feels like herself again.

Against my neck, she murmurs in a heavy voice, "Was that the…thing?"

I smile, pulling her closer. "Yes, that was the thing."

She tilts her face to me; her eyes fairly glow with the brightness of her tears. "Why do I feel like this?"

I run a path down her back. "It happens, you'll feel better soon. I promise."

"Okay." She turns back into me and puts her palm over my heart. "I liked it."

"Me too." Her mouth around my cock had blown my fucking mind. I'd lost it in the end, all my vicious desire to claim her riding to the surface and refusing to let go. And even though I'd violated her throat in the most filthy, possessive way possible, basically refusing to accept anything other than her complete surrender, it wasn't close to enough.

"I want more." Her words are thick, sleepy.

My chest squeezes. "What do you want?"

"Everything."

My throat is strained with foreign emotions I don't really understand. But I promise anyway. "I'll give it to you."

"Brandon?"

"What, baby?" I'm not even sure where the endearment comes from. I've never used it before.

"I want to be ruined."

Every single barrier I've erected over the last ten years is slowly and systematically being stripped away by her. I don't want it, but I don't know how to stop it either. So I tilt her chin, force her to look at me and say simply, "You will be."

17.

Brandon

We've been messing around for over a week.

Since we're not fucking, we seem to have channeled all pent-up sexual energy into fighting. I'm not sure why we have all this pent-up tension, because the truth is, I can't keep my goddamn hands off her. Our last argument ended with her straddled on my lap while she rode my fingers to orgasm. She'd braced herself on my knees and flung her hair back, giving me a show, her hips grinding and rocking in abandon. After, I pushed her to her knees and fucked her throat, my hands latched onto her neck to ensure the bruises I put there stay there. I like her marked.

That was about two hours ago.

And we're arguing again.

Her hands on her hips, her shoulders thrust back, her face tilted with defiance. She yells, "His numbers are wrong!"

It's gotten to the point that anytime she raises her voice in that sassy manner, it makes me hard. In a calm, reasonable tone, I say, "Cary's numbers are not wrong. He's been doing this for years, you've been here for two weeks."

She flings out a paper and it flutters to my desk. "I don't care if he's been here a century, his numbers don't add up."

I raise a brow. "I review those numbers every month. Are you saying I'm wrong?"

She rolls her eyes. "Of course I am. You're not above it."

I sit back in my chair and rake my gaze down her body. She's dressed in a black dress, all very conservative and businesslike. I want to rip it off her, but she's making serious accusations so I focus instead. "Explain."

"He's very good at it, but I think he's skimming."

She believes the head bartender at my underground club is stealing. This is the kind of thing I hired her for because I'm getting too big to keep an eye on these types of details. But I sincerely hope she's wrong, because Cary is one of my original employees, and I'd hate to think someone working for me for such a long time would do something like that.

She walks closer to the desk, opens the spreadsheet she's sent me, clicking on a cell to reveal an impossibly long equation. "Before you were doing inventory the simple way, ordering when your inventory got low, considering it profitable when you were in the black. There's nothing wrong with that, especially when you were smaller, but times have changed. I thought it would be more efficient to order for both bars, especially when you're thinking about opening a new place next year. I wanted a better way of tracking inventory, sales and maximizing our buying leverage. So I developed a simple algorithm designed to help correlate inventory and sales more tightly together." She runs her fingertip along the line of code. "I have accommodated for comps, variables, broken bottles, and of course there's always going to be some variance but his variance doesn't add up."

In the time I've worked with Veronica I've discovered she's some sort of math whiz. Her definition of a simple algorithm makes zero sense to me and might as well be written in a foreign language. I frown at the numbers. "How does that mean he's skimming?"

She tilts her head toward the computer. "Pull up his monthly reports and I'll show you."

I pull up the latest report, opening up the spreadsheet, while her intoxicating scent wafts over me. Serious discussion or not, I can't resist the urge to touch her. With my free hand I wrap my arm around her waist and tug her down on my lap.

She doesn't protest.

At the beginning of the week, after I'd believed I'd at least taken the edge off my hunger, I'd determined I'd keep things strictly professional at work. That lasted about thirty seconds after my Monday morning meeting and I've given up the fight ever since.

I'm not sure how I feel about admitting defeat, but the rewards seem infinitely worth it.

She shifts on my leg, leans forward to point at the rows at the bottom of the screen. "It's not that his numbers are wrong, or don't total, it's that his numbers don't make sense based on the formula I developed."

I put my hand on her thigh, and work her hem up so I can touch her skin while I study what she says the numbers should be based on what Cary reported. "You're right."

She shoots me a sly smile. "Does this surprise you?"

I pinch her. "Brat."

She shifts her hips toward me before leaning over my desk and running her finger over the computer screen. "See this is the inventory numbers from the month before."

I grit my teeth as her ass nestles against my cock. "Go on."

She squirms again.

God help me.

"When you plug those numbers into the formula and sales trends, the variance is too high." She presses back against me. She's doing it on purpose. Enticing me. "It's not a ton, maybe a thousand dollars over the month, but it's still a lot when you consider the place is only open three nights a week."

This math I can do in my head, even with her squirming away on me. "About two percent."

"Right."

"Let's call him in and talk to him to see what he has to say."

"Done." She slides farther up my lap. "I asked him to come in tomorrow, it's on your calendar."

"Aren't you a good girl?" I grip her hips. "Are you rubbing against my cock on purpose?"

"Of course." She straddles my legs, leaning against my chest before turning her face toward me.

"What do you want?"

Her lips skim along my jaw. "Isn't that obvious?"

Veronica is not like other women I've been with. She's forward. She doesn't wait to see my next move, instead she instigates. This isn't a trait I believed I liked, but I'm wrong. It forces me to plot on the spot, and before her I hadn't realized how long it's been since I've been spontaneous. How long it's been since I've had to think, instead of going through the motions of some scene I orchestrated in advance.

With her, I'm entirely in the moment.

I've been taking it very easy on her and she's getting cocky in her power, of which I've allowed. I like lulling her into a false sense of security, only to watch her eyes get wide when I pull the rug out from under her.

Which is what I'm about to do now. I run my hands over her stomach. "No, tell me."

"You know." She smiles against my skin before sinking her teeth into my jaw.

It shoots straight to my balls. I grip her hair and twist, yanking her head back. "I want to hear the words, explicit and dirty, from your mouth."

The pulse in her neck flutters and quickens. "I want you."

"Not good enough." I dip my head and lick across her throbbing jugular. "Tell me what, how and why."

"Brandon." My name is a needy sigh. She swivels her hips, trying to entice me into giving in to her.

"Here's how this is going to work. This is your last chance to tell me, if you don't, I'm going to work your needy little cunt up until all you can think about is coming, and then I'm going to send you on your way. Next time I see you, I'm going to ask again. If you don't tell me, we'll start the process all over. During this time you will not sneak off and have an orgasm on your own, no matter how desperate."

She gasps and her knuckles whiten on the arm of the chair.

Power threatens the very confines of my civility. It's why she's such a risk, and so fucking addictive, I keep the beast that lives inside me carefully under wraps. An almost impossible feat with Veronica because I'm like a pacing caged tiger waiting for someone to open the door.

I give her an open-mouth kiss on her exposed throat. She shivers. Her neck is her weak spot, which makes me hard. It's so open and vulnerable, available to me at all times, in all circumstances. I raise my head. "In fact, from now on, I control all your orgasms."

She arches, her breath turning fast. "What do you mean?"

I normally start small, safe and easy, but fuck that. I can't do that with Veronica. Don't want to. With her I'm greedy and demanding. "I mean you can't come without my permission under any circumstance. If I'm not there and you want to touch yourself, you'll call or text me first and tell me how and why you want to come. If I say yes, after you'll tell me about it and thank me like a good girl. If I say no, you'll suffer until I'm in a more giving mood."

"That's insane." Even as she says the words she grinds her hips against my cock. Her lips are parted and her chest is a rapid rise and fall.

"It is. But you're going to give me what I want." I work four buttons of her blouse, then pull her breasts up to spill over her demi bra. I stroke my thumbs over her nipples and bite her throat, right where it curves into her shoulder.

She groans and bows to meet my hands.

I tease her, pinching and pulling and twisting until she's writhing on my lap. She can come like this, and sometime very soon I'm going to show her, but that's not for right now. Instead I lighten my touch, and drop one hand to her thigh before hiking up her skirt and cupping her silk-covered mound.

I grip her, hard enough she gasps. "Oh god."

Grasping tight, I growl into her ear, "Your pussy belongs to me now. I own it. It's mine and I control who touches my property." Lust and a dizzying primal possession runs fast in my blood. "That includes you. So if you want to touch, you'll ask. Do you understand me, Veronica?"

"This is crazy." Her objection is expected, but everything about her body is on board.

I release my hold and slip my fingers into her panties where she's soaking. I glide my fingers over her slick folds. "I can tell how much you hate the idea." I slide into her, pulling out and pushing back in, letting her wetness ring through the air. "If this is so crazy, why are you so wet, girl?"

"I don't know." She rocks into my hand, seeking the pleasure I'm keeping out of her reach.

"Take a guess." I hold her jugular in my teeth and lick my tongue across her captive flesh. "Tell me why you're dripping into my palm."

Her fingers are tight on the chair, and I set a dirty rhythm, pulling her nipples with one hand and grinding against her clit with the other. "I'm waiting, Veronica."

She moans. "My brain tells me…oh god…" She jerks into my touch.

I lighten my pressure so she doesn't go over and ruin my point. I tsk in her ear. "I don't remember you asking me to come, so for your sake, you'd better not. Now tell me."

"I crave your possession." She leans back and whispers in my ear, "Anytime you talk about me being yours it drives me crazy."

This I already know, it was established the first time I claimed her, but I'm looking for new information. "What else?"

She squeezes her eyes shut. "I want you to control me."

I follow my instincts. I press down on the heel of my hand and grind it over her pelvic bone. She cries out and grips my wrist. "Oh god, right there."

I laugh, evil and cruel. "I can keep doing this and make it so you never go over."

Her cunt contracts hard around my fingers and I have my answer. I understand submissive girls, and Veronica is very new and probably doesn't have the words or experience to articulate what's driving her so crazy, but I know. I whisper in her ear, "Ah, now I see. You like the thought of being denied."

She shakes her head, even while she's rocking mindlessly into my hand. "No."

"Are you sure about that?" I grip her hair and turn her face up to mine. I kiss her and tension is like a bomb detonating. I've fallen into that zone now, riding instinct and desire and power. I pull away and say, "It doesn't make you wet to think about me saying no to you? You begging me? Being desperate for an orgasm I won't give you?"

"No." The word is a breathless, meaningless pant. Between her legs grows impossibly wetter, more swollen, hotter.

Christ. "Are you sure about that?" I pick up the pace.

"Yes."

"Do you want to come, Veronica?"

"Yes." She turns toward me and clutches my shirt.

I pump my fingers into her cunt. "No."

She gasps and moans.

"When's the last time you came by yourself?"

Her head falls back. "Last night."

I bite her bottom lip. "After I gave you all those orgasms you still needed to come again?"

"Yes."

I pull out and make a V with my fingers, sliding them around her clit. I drag her panties down her legs, stopping at her knees so the elastic bites into her skin. "I hope you enjoyed it, because it's the last one you get for free. From this second on, you don't even touch your cunt without my say so."

She bucks against my hand.

"Do you want to come?"

"Yes."

"Beg me."

Her head falls back. "Please, Brandon, please."

"No."

She groans. "Please."

"No." I slide into her and she's so wet it echoes through the room. I whisper into her ear, "You don't think I feel how fucking hot it makes you every time I say no? You don't think I feel your cunt get wetter every time I talk about denying you?" I raise my fingers and paint her lips so they glisten and then I take her hand and bring it between her legs. Her slim fingers run over her flesh, zeroing in on her clit. "Have you ever been this wet?"

She shakes her head.

Into her ear I say, "Do you want to come?"

"Yes."

"No."

She moans and keens.

I laugh, gripping her wrist and pulling her away. I cover her with my palm. "This is my pussy and I like the thought of you walking around dripping and desperate, so we'll save that orgasm for another time."

My phone beeps and I look down at my desk, and when I read the message I chuckle. "Excellent."

She pants at me, questions in her big honey eyes.

"Leo's on his way, he'll be here in two minutes." I give her my most evil smile. "Let's get you situated."

Veronica

I'm on fire. I'm not sure I have any working brain cells left.

Brandon squeezes my hip. "Up you go."

I stand on wobbly legs, attempting to wrap my brain around what just happened. And why. I don't understand how him saying no to me is such a turn on. It was like it flipped some switch in my brain. Every time he said no I just got hotter and hotter, like I would do anything just to come.

I don't understand it, but it's not the time to question. Leo will be here any second and I have to pull myself together. I shake my head to clear it. It doesn't work, but I think I can manage a simple sentence.

I turn to Brandon, who gives me that smug, evil smile I'm becoming familiar with. I smooth my hair and clear my throat. "I'll…um… See you later."

He raises a brow. "Where do you think you're going?"

I start to raise my panties, trying not to think about my slippery thighs. "To my office."

He shakes his head. "No, you'll stay here."

Oh no. My cheeks flush, I can argue once I'm together. I continue pulling up my underwear, but he holds up his hand. "Stop."

I freeze, almost on instinct. As though my body listens to him more than me. I chew my bottom lip. Is that part of the *thing*? My gaze flies to his.

He tilts his head and studies me. Like a cat he prowls over, fastens one button on my top before nodding.

I blink down at my blouse. It's indecently low and my breasts are spilling out from my bra, making my nipples clearly visible under the silk. To my horror, this knowledge makes them pucker up tighter.

He laughs. Wraps his hand around my nape and tugs me close, kissing me hard and unrelenting, not stopping until I'm breathless. When he pulls away he palms between my legs. "Who does this belong to?"

I gulp as my body responds like a shot of heroin. "You."

"Exactly." He falls to his knees, and then his mouth is on me, his tongue licking over my clit.

I cry out, holding onto his desk for dear life so I don't topple over. I don't know how he does it, but he goes down on me like it's a dirty make-out session, and every time my eyes practically roll into the back of my head. I hook my leg over his shoulder and start rocking to meet his mouth, to increase the pressure, just when my body quickens, he pulls away.

He grins up at me, and even from his position on the floor

he looks powerful.

I shake my head. "You're wicked."

"Baby, I'm just getting started."

That's what I'm afraid of. Hope for.

He pulls my panties up my legs, but instead of putting them back in place, he positions them right under the curve of my ass before tugging my skirt down where it belongs, and getting up off the floor.

I stare at him in horror. "I can't walk around like this."

"Since you won't be walking, it's not a concern." Then he sits on the chair and puts me on his knee.

I try and scramble away. "What are you doing? Leo."

"I'm experimenting." He squeezes my hip. "Be still."

"But—"

There's a knock on the door.

Brandon calls. "Come on in."

I try and get up, but his arm is like a vise.

Leo opens the door, and walks in. The second he sees us, his brows rise up his forehead. He looks at me, then at Brandon, then back at me. With a chuckle, he shuts the door.

I try again to squirm off Brandon's lap.

"Be still." His words are like the lash of a whip.

I go instantly quiet even while I want to die of humiliation. Which, somehow morphs in my brain and sends blood rushing between my legs.

Casual as can be, Leo strolls over, like it's not at all unusual for me to be on top of my boss, and sinks down into the chair. He grins, winks at me before turning to Brandon. "She's spirited but I knew at the end of the day she'd be good at following instructions."

Brandon's hand covers my hip and it feels hot and territorial against my skin. "She's a good girl, aren't you, Veronica?"

I want to crawl into a hole. And I want to come like it's my next breath.

The warring emotions confuse me and I frown. I point to the door. "I should go."

Leo laughs, then his gaze rakes over my body, pausing on my chest. "You might be a distraction."

My nipples pull even tighter.

Brandon's palm moves up to my waist. "Indeed."

I'm unable to help myself and I hiss, "I'm mortified."

"And wet." Brandon's grasp squeezes.

I gasp. "Brandon!"

Leo shrugs. "He's not telling me anything I don't already know, girl. You look and smell like sex."

I scream and cover my face with my hands. "This is perverse!"

Leo laughs. "There must be something we can do with her and Jillian."

I have never been more humiliated in my life, or as turned on, it's insane.

Brandon studies me, looking me up and down. "I think that can be arranged."

I don't even want to know what that entails. Or do I?

"She's pretty primed by the look of her."

"She certainly is." Brandon raises a brow. "What do we owe the pleasure?"

"Jillian's dad had some clients that were supposed to be in town cancel and he has eight tickets to the Cubs game Friday he's throwing our way. First row, in the sun on the first base line."

How are they just sitting here? Talking like nothing is going on? When I'm in this state? How can they even focus?

Leo continues as if this is the most normal thing in the world. "If you both can take off, it will be the eight of us."

"We'll be there." Brandon doesn't consult me.

"We'll meet at Murphy's before the game."

"Sounds good."

Leo juts his chin toward the door. "You interested in a quick lunch? Or are you too preoccupied?"

Sweat blooms across the base of my spine.

"Sure." Brandon pats me on the ass. "Can I trust you to entertain yourself?"

I've gone crazy because my immediate thought is running to my office and rubbing my clit. At the vision, I flush with horror. What has he done to me?

He narrows his eyes. "So no?"

I straighten as properly as I can. "Of course. I have work to do."

I hold my breath, terrified he'll say something humiliating in front of Leo again, but he nods. "Good. Up you go."

A strange sense of mild disappointment settles in my chest. I stand.

I look down; almost surprised I can remain upright. My naked breasts and peaked nipples press against the silk of my blouse. The elastic of my panties cut into my skin, right below my ass. My state of dress has me hyperaware of my body's every reaction.

Leo and Brandon stand too, watching me.

I smile. "Have a nice lunch."

The corners of Leo's lips tilt.

"Veronica?" Brandon's gaze rakes over my body, sending a fresh wave of heat through me.

With as much dignity as I can muster, I tilt my chin. "Yes?"

"Do you have any meetings while I'm gone?"

I shake my head.

"Good. I expect you to look exactly as I left you when I return."

Unable to help myself, I glance at Leo.

He chuckles. "God help anyone that walks into your office."

I might die, of lust or humiliation. It's a toss-up.

"Do we understand each other?" Brandon steps toward me, wrapping his hand around my neck.

My breath is shallow when I speak. "Yes."

"Excellent." Then his mouth covers mine.

His tongue strokes against mine.

And I'm lost in him.

I never want to let him go.

I melt into him. Wrapping my arms around his back and

pressing close. His fingers tighten. His hand comes up to the curve of my hip.

I rise to my tiptoes, molding myself into the spaces I fit best.

Our heads slant. The contact deepens. Our mouths—

"Do I need to give you a minute?"

Leo's voice breaks the spell and our lips part but Brandon doesn't let go.

His gaze meets mine, and his blue eyes burn like cold fire. "No."

"You sure?" Leo asks, and his tone is amused, although I can't pull my gaze away from Brandon to see his face.

"Yes." Brandon leans down and whispers in my ear, "No touching while I'm gone."

I nod, and release a long breath, overwhelmed and wanting. Needing him. I skim my mouth over his jaw and he tightens his hold. I whisper the truth, low enough for only him to hear. "I don't know what you think you're waiting for, I'm already ruined."

He raises his head, and his expression steals the air from my lungs, it's dark and possessive. He grips my chin. "Tonight."

I don't know where the word comes from, but I utter it anyway. "Please."

He kisses me with a wicked promise, and then he's gone.

18.

Leo waits until after we've ordered drinks to start interrogating me. "So…"

"Don't start." I clench my jaw. That kiss. I'd meant it to be dirty and fun, to humiliate her a little in front of Leo because she so clearly gets off on it, but instead it backfired, and morphed into something powerful and revealing.

Something I'm damn well sure Leo didn't miss because I know he recognizes it. I've seen him kiss Jillian that way. I'd never understood the difference until today. The difference in the way you kiss a girl that's crawling inside you.

He grins, cocks his head to the side. "It sucks at first, I'll give you that."

I pretend to study the menu like I was at a five-star restaurant, and not the pub down the block from the club where I've eaten a hundred times. "I don't know what you mean."

Leo laughs. "Sure you don't."

"It's just sex." I shrug as though it's no big deal, when it's a very big deal. It's so much more than sex. But I can't help wanting to maintain the façade, because I need to hold on to it. For my own sanity.

At some point, I don't even remember when, I'd shut off my emotions. I hadn't been uncaring, but I'd been detached. So cool and remote nobody really touched me. I had relationships; I'd had women submit to me. I'd cared for them, orchestrated their fantasies, but I never committed. I've always told women I wasn't cut out for monogamy, which I never found odd, as it's quite common in our circles. I believed it too. While I admired the dedication Michael, Leo and Chad have for their women, admire their unwavering devotion; it's not for me.

My friends are the closest I've ever come to attaching to anyone, and even with them, I'm a touch removed.

I believed this was the way I was made.

Believed I didn't want any of what they had.

But Veronica is systematically flipping every switch I'd always believed was shut off.

I haven't even looked at another woman since that night on the balcony. And when she'd whispered I'd already ruined her, that I was waiting for nothing, I'd been smacked over the head with the truth.

With all the women I've taken to bed without a thought, I'm scared to sleep with Veronica.

I can control sex. But I can't control how I feel about her.

I hate it.

I'm addicted to it.

Sex with Veronica is going to ruin me as much as it will ruin her. I'm afraid of it, because it will mean for the first time in my thirty-four years, I will be vulnerable to another person. Weak. Powerless. She has the ability to cut me off at the knees.

I have no idea how to handle it. Handle her.

I glance up to find Leo studying me with that cop's expression.

I open my mouth to say something dismissive but instead ask, "How do you do it?"

Leo scrubs a hand over his jaw. "Do what, exactly?"

I don't want to have this conversation. I want to ignore it. But I'm not sure that's an option anymore. I also know Leo will understand. We're alike that way. Or at least we were, until Jillian came along.

I clear my throat. Shake my head a little. I don't quite have the words to articulate my question.

He tilts his head. "How do I control Jillian when she so clearly controls me? When she can crush me so completely?"

Yes. That's exactly it. I nod.

He leans forward and puts his elbows on the table. "By

understanding they aren't mutually exclusive. I think, with guys like us, yes it's our nature, but it's a convenient way to detach."

I nod again. It is. It's so easy to shut off that way, to place a boundary between me and the girl sitting at my feet. Especially when I attract women into cruel, casual dismissal.

"With Jillian that wasn't possible. She forced me to attach. It's why I resisted her for so long. My instincts warned me and they were right." He meets my gaze and his expression is deadly serious. "Here's the truth, even though it's hard to see until you make it to the other side. It makes it impossibly better. Which seems counterintuitive, but is true. Jillian makes me better. That she can break me, but chooses surrender instead, just makes the power I hold over her that much greater. That much sweeter."

I look away, over his shoulder to the packed lunchtime crowd. "She's messing with my head."

"I'm sure she is." He laughs. "It's not like I didn't do some pretty stupid things with Jillian."

I return my attention to him, and nod. "True."

He shrugs. "You'll probably do something to sabotage it, but try not to, okay?"

"I'll try." Already knowing I'll fail. Every day my panic over Veronica grows.

"I'll tell you something that should help. If you're interested."

"What's that?"

He cocks a grin. "It's not one-sided."

I furrow my brow. "What do you mean?"

"What you're feeling, you're not alone. Veronica is as consumed by you as you are by her." He chuckles. "Women are just better equipped to handle the turmoil."

He's managed to touch on something lurking deep under my skin, something I can barely admit to myself. Something that makes me uncomfortable. The words are out of my mouth before I can filter them. "You don't know that."

"Yeah, I do. I have eyes. You guys are fucked. Just let yourself drown and it gets easier."

I take a deep breath. "Michael said the same."

"Michael should know. The only way he was able to get Layla to stay was to commit and never waver." Leo laughs. "But he had the advantage of a stable past to keep him grounded."

This is true. Michael comes from a good, close-knit family. Leo does too, except his twin brother was murdered when they were only nineteen and it fucked him up.

And then there's me.

I nod. "Thanks."

"Anytime."

An image of that kiss, her lips clinging to mine, fills my head.

And I admit it—at least to myself—I'm starting to need her. I don't know how or why and I guess it doesn't matter. She's starting to feel like a part of me.

My vicious desire to claim her, to possess her fills my chest, but instead of repressing it, of trying to lock it away, I let it consume me.

I surrender. To it. Her. And whatever disaster awaits.

Veronica

I'm sitting at my desk, trying to focus, but my thighs are slippery, and a pulse has grown between my legs.

I don't know why I did what Brandon asked. My panties are where he put them, and my breasts are still bare under the silk of my top. I keep telling myself to put everything right, to look respectable, in case someone walks in, but I can't seem to make my fingers cooperate.

Every time they stall.

I don't want to disobey him.

I don't know why. Well, that's not entirely true, but I'm embarrassed to admit how I'm fast becoming addicted to being on edge like this.

I want to ask someone, Jillian maybe, if this crazy, desperate, consuming lust is normal. What am I suppose to do? Call her up and ask?

I suck in a breath and my nipples abrade against my blouse. I want to touch.

I have never wanted to touch more.

I blink. I've been staring at the same spreadsheet for thirty minutes, not doing anything.

I have to work.

I have to concentrate.

My door slams open and I jerk back with a start.

Brandon's standing in the threshold, he crooks a finger. "Let's go."

All the air leaves my lungs "Go?"

"My house. Now."

I stand, my legs wobbly. Finally. Thank god.

I start to walk, and I flush with heat because he has to see I didn't put myself back together. I force myself to continue until I'm standing in front of him.

His expression grows feral as he looks down at me. "Your nipples are hard."

"Yes." I won't be ashamed, he did this to me, and he should see the consequences.

"Did you keep your panties where I put them?"

"Yes."

"Are you wet?"

I suck in a breath. "So wet. You're all I could think about."

He grips my throat and forces my chin at a higher angle. "Do you have any idea how much it pleases me that you kept yourself exactly as I left you?"

I shake my head and offer a stuttery, "No."

"It does. More than I can articulate." His fingers squeeze. "I have never wanted to fuck anyone as much as I want to fuck you. But more than that, you are the only woman I have ever wanted to own. To keep for myself."

I melt into him. "Yes."

His gaze dips to my lips. "I can't touch you right now

because once I start I'm not going to be able to stop. This is not going to be pretty, but I'm at least going to lay you out on my bed."

I grip his wrist where he's captured my throat. "Please."

"I want you to understand something."

I lick my lips and nod.

"You are the only woman that has ever been in my bed."

My brow creases because I don't understand.

He meets my gaze. "Women have been to my house, but never to my private bedroom. You'll be the first."

I bite my lip and when the words come I don't hold them back. "And the last."

He releases his hold on me. "Get whatever you need and come with me."

I smile. "Your wish is my command."

He leans down and delivers a hard kiss before pulling back. "You're fucking right it is."

19.

Veronica

There's dead silence as we stand at the foot of his bed.

I can barely breathe. Barely think for wanting him.

I'm scared, and nervous and excited. It feels like I've wanted him forever. Like it's always been him, even when I didn't know it. Now I'm finally going to have him.

He places his hands on my shoulders before running his palms down my arms. He dips his head to brush his lips against the curve of my neck. "This is your last chance to back out."

I lean against his chest. "Why would I want to back out?"

His arm goes around my waist, his hand flattening on my stomach. "Because this will change us, and there's no getting around that. Once I slide my cock inside you, you'll be mine. I will own you, and you think you know what that means, but you don't. You won't until you're in the thick of it. The first time we talked, you'd said you wanted something different, that you wanted to be free to become your own person. I don't want to take that away from you."

I peer at him over my shoulder, and his expression is serious, creased with concern. I turn to face him, rise to my tiptoes and brush my mouth over his. "From the second I saw you on that balcony I knew my life was going to change because of you. You're all I want, you're the only thing I've ever wanted."

His fingers trace a path up my arm to curl around my nape. "Are you sure?"

"Yes."

He bends down and our lips meet. And it's like an explosion.

Everything we've been playing at, everything we've been skirting around and avoiding, evaporates and there's nothing but raw, consuming need.

His head slants, his tongue claims, and his mouth is hungry.

Burning me up, making me dizzy.

He growls.

I moan.

The kiss grows hotter, deeper, more intoxicating.

He grips my shirt and rips. Buttons fly as my blouse is shredded from my body. The tattered scrap of silk falls to the floor and his mouth is on my breast, covering my nipple.

I clutch at his head, threading my fingers through his hair as he sucks deep and long, sending a bolt of pleasure straight through me. I cry out, digging my nails deeper.

His other hand covers my exposed nipple and he rubs his thumb in a slow circle, matching the rhythm of his wicked tongue.

"Brandon." His name is a moan.

In answer he bows me back, his teeth scraping over the distended bud as he plucks.

I'm so on edge. So worked up. And his mouth is just too damn good. Pleasure pulses through me, swelling inside me. My knees buckle and we fall in a heap on the floor.

His mouth covers me again.

I arch.

He bites me.

I try and rock against him, but my skirt doesn't allow it. I grow frustrated, needing more, wanting something. "Please."

My nails rake down his back, he's still covered in a blue shirt that matches his eyes, and I frantically start to unbutton him, but without ever removing his mouth from my breast, he grips my wrists and holds me down.

I jerk up.

He lifts his head and meets my eyes. "All I can do right now is fuck you. Everything else is off the table. But I'm at least going to make you a needy mess first."

"I'm already a needy mess." I tilt my hips. "Touch me and you'll see."

His long fingers ensnare my wrists in one hand, and he works his way down my body and under my skirt.

When he touches my wet thighs, he curses.

When he glides across slippery flesh, he groans.

He slides his fingers over my clit and I bite my lower lip, and shake my head helplessly. "If you don't stop, I'm going to come."

A muscle jumps in his jaw. He plunges inside and I moan, my head falling back against the carpet. In harsh words he utters, "I'm fucking addicted to you."

I tilt my hips into his hands. "Then take me."

He kisses me, harsh and brutal, his mouth bruising me as his grip marks my wrists.

I have no doubt I'll have marks tomorrow. And I'm glad. I want everyone who sees me to know what he's done to me. That I belong to him.

I want his possession. Claiming.

I'd wear a goddamn sign if he wanted.

I just need to be his.

I think he needs this too.

Suddenly, he rears back, and strips his shirt over his head.

I go to touch him but he slaps me away. "Not yet."

I don't question him. Because I know he's on the very edge. That whatever control he still has is frayed and tattered, and almost in pieces.

I want it stripped away.

I want him primal and out of control when he finally thrusts inside me.

He leans on his haunches and rips my skirt off, taking my panties with him, until I'm naked except for my heels. Lids hooding, he undoes his pants, and takes his heavy cock into his hand, stroking up and down before meeting my gaze.

His expression is stark, beautiful, and so mesmerizing I can't look away. His cheekbones are a hard slash of bone over flesh. He's the most gorgeous man I've ever laid eyes on and he's mine.

Like I'm his.

He knows it and I know it.

The only difference between us is I've accepted the inevitable, and he hasn't. He's still trying to figure out how to control the madness between us, but all I care about is surrendering.

To it and to him.

Jaw clenching, he speaks, "I want to fuck you without a condom."

I raise my hips, and offer him everything. "You can fuck me however and whenever you want."

He shakes his head. "That is a dangerous promise to make to a man like me."

I smile. "I know."

He pulls me so my thighs are splayed wide around his knees and positions the tip of his cock along my slit.

We both hiss at the contact.

He drags his erection between my folds, teasing me, taunting me. I thrill, my nipples pulling impossibly tighter. He grips my hips and continues his slow glide. "I don't even care if I get you pregnant."

"Me either." I gasp as the tip of him rubs against my clit. "You won't, but I wish you could."

There's something twisted about this, and I like it. He wants to keep me. I want him to keep me. Right here, wild and unguarded, is the only time he can admit it.

His fingers tighten on my hips. "Would you like that? My come spilling inside you?"

"Yes."

"I'm not going to let you wash it away." His hold on me is like a vise and his pace picks up, thrusting dirty and mean against my pussy, but not entering me. Driving me crazy. "In fact, I'm not going to be satisfied unless you're constantly dripping."

Oh my god, this is the hottest I've been. I start pumping my hips greedily against him. "Yes. I want that."

"Tomorrow, at the office, first thing I'm going to rip your panties off, fuck you and make you give that presentation with my cum dripping down your thighs."

I moan, and grip the carpet, wanting more leverage. "Yes."

"I'm going to write my name on your skin."

"Oh god." My body is climbing and there's no stopping it.

It's like in this moment we can say all of the things we've been secretly thinking. Like there are no barriers between us.

"I'm going to turn you into a greedy little slut. All you're going to be able to think about is the next time I give you my cock."

I grind my clit against his erection. "Now, Brandon. I'm begging you."

On the next pass he slams into me and it takes my breath away. I slide back along the floor but he grips me and yanks me back to him.

He covers me, kisses me, and impales me.

I have never in my life been fucked like this.

He's hard. Demanding. Relentless.

It consumes me.

He pounds into me, thrusting harder and harder, until our mouths break apart, no longer able to maintain contact.

He grips me around the neck and whispers in a harsh breath, "Look at me."

My lids snap open.

He hammers into me, hitting a spot so good I cry out, but

don't lose eye contact.

He squeezes my throat. "Mine."

"Yours."

"Your cunt. Your mouth. Your body." He presses his fingers deeper into my skin, cutting off my air. "Your very breath belongs to me."

He releases and I drag air into my burning lungs.

The orgasm is barreling down on me, fast and furious, is an unstoppable force. In the back of my head I remember him saying he wanted me to ask, and as I meet a particularly brutal thrust, I cry out, "Can I come?"

He growls, low and feral and shifts his angle, taking away the immediate threat. "No. Not yet."

"Please." I rake my nails down his back, digging into his skin. "Please."

"That's right, beg me like a good girl." He picks up velocity, his expression turning cruel and demanding. "Beg me."

"I want to come, please let me come."

"No." He pummels me, but he somehow manages to make it so the orgasm threatens, but doesn't tumble over. "Beg me harder."

My mind is a fuzzy haze, barely able to string together a coherent sentence, but I do my best. "I need you."

He squeezes my throat again. "Who do you belong to?"

"You, Brandon."

"That's right."

"Yes."

He makes a low guttural sound. "Christ, I need to fuck you harder."

I don't know where the words come from, but they well inside me, and I slow, raising my hand to his face and stroking his cheek.

His eyes lock on mine.

"Do you want to hurt me?"

He nods. "I need you marked."

I crane my neck, let my hands and legs fall to my sides, and offer up my body. "Do it."

"I-I—" He shakes his head. "I don't have control right now."

"Do it," I whisper, and let my body go limp. Not understanding how I know to do this, but knowing it's true.

The first blow is across my breasts and I scream from the fiery sting of his hand directly across my nipple.

It explodes against my skin, radiating out and racing along my nerves before shattering in my pussy. I don't understand, but it's so fucking good I lose my mind. I cry out, "I'm going to come."

"Come." He hits me again, and again, leans down and bites my neck, so hard I see stars and then the orgasm is rushing over me, hot and fierce, like it's breaking me in two.

It goes on and on, blinding waves of ecstasy crashing over me. I call out his name, and he goes faster and faster and faster.

Fucking me harder.

Deeper.

And then he growls, and comes inside me, setting off another crescendo of crashing sensations.

I'm in love with him.

I need him.

He shudders and groans and collapses on top of me.

I stroke his hair, loving the feel of him heavy against my body. I close my eyes and melt into him.

I'm never going to let him go.

Brandon

It's the dead of night and I'm lying in bed with Veronica, the moonlight streaming through the large windows. She's asleep, after I've exhausted her, and now I'm watching her.

I've never watched a girl sleep before.

The sheet is a tangle around her waist, and my palm rests on her bare stomach. Her breasts are pale in the white glow, her nipples puckered and pink. There's a mark I sucked into her skin at some point on the swell of her breast. One that will be visible above her bra, one that I'll just be able to make out tomorrow, depending on what she's wearing. The base of her neck, the curve of her shoulders are also bruised and marked.

In sleep, the slope of her throat looks so delicate it's impossible to believe she could take such rough handling. But she had. My gaze roams up to her face. Her lips are full and swollen from my kissing and biting. Her eyes closed her face tilted away from me as her hair spills out over my pillow.

I'd taken her over and over again. Despite all the women I've slept with, she's still the best sex I've ever had. There was something elemental about it, as though being inside her was what had been missing in my life.

I don't understand the urges she invokes in me. The stark, primal demand I take her, the almost violent shudder of my possession. I've never experienced anything even close to it, and I have no idea how to deal with it.

At one point, my hands hard on her hips, driving my cock deep inside her, I'd look down at her and thought, she was destined to belong to me. There had to be some way to meld her to me, make her part of me. I'd started gripping the base of her jaw and growling that she belonged to me, that she was mine, that I'd fuck her until I'd marked her, until I'd ruined her. The more I said, the hotter and out of control everything became. It only increased the need, until I ruthlessly possessed her body, until we'd both come in shaking, mind-numbing passion.

The type of women I enjoy get off on being told they're property, that they belong to you. It's part of their nature. I've always fed into that nature because that's what I was supposed to do.

This is different.

There was something dirty and intense about it. The way it got us off.

I don't even know how to articulate it.

She stirs, her legs shift against mine and she rolls into me, throwing her arm around my waist and nuzzling into my neck.

I pull her closer. When I kiss her temple, she makes a contented kitten sound that makes my cock hard. I've never had a woman in my bed before, and Veronica feels like she belongs here.

She presses closer, puts her thigh on my hip and angles so my erection brushes her slickness. I put a hand on her waist and tease her clit with the head of my cock. She purrs against me and I smile, dipping down to her ear, I whisper, "You have a greedy cunt."

She works her hips, sliding along my shaft. "I can't explain it."

"Try." I lean down and suck on the curve of her neck.

"It's like a need." She gasps as I enter her, soft, slow and shallow, nothing but a tease. "I just want you inside me."

Keeping my strokes light, I bend down to whisper in her ear, "Mine."

She melts.

And I stop thinking for the rest of the night.

20.

Veronica

"Veronica, this is your mother." Her refined voice fills the line, and I pause fiddling with my hair and straighten.

"Hi, Mom." I haven't spoken to her since our last argument, and it appears she's finally broken. "How have you been?"

"Let me cut right to the chase." Her tone is the one she used when I was a teenager and wasn't happy. It used to work back then, but I find it has no effect on me now.

"Yes, let's." I walk out of the bathroom where I'm getting ready to go to the Cubs game with Brandon and his friends. A day I've been looking forward to, and I hope she doesn't manage to ruin for me.

"Your father is quite unhappy with you."

"I'm well aware of that." It's not like I can ignore the obvious. I'm not sure how long he'll continue not speaking to me, but he's stubborn and doesn't like to be defied, so I'm not expecting much.

"Why didn't you tell me you were working for *that man*?" She utters the words like they are something foul. "Imagine my embarrassment when I learned about your employment during lunch at the club. I had to pretend I knew all about it, and it put me in an awkward position."

I straighten my shoulders. No matter how old I get, no matter how many choices I make, my parents still have the power to make me feel like a child. "Daddy and you aren't speaking to me, why would I have told you?"

"Because you're our daughter."

I sigh. "Then act like it, instead of ostracizing me. I'm not going to back down, I'm not going to stop what I'm doing, you'll either accept it, or not talk to me. But that's your choice, not mine." I don't want to deal with it today. All I want is to have fun with Brandon and his friends.

There's a silence over the line and I can practically hear her thinking. "Veronica, why, out of all the places to use your talents, would you take a job from Brandon Townsend. You know what people say about him."

The buzzer for my door rings and I walk over and let the man in question in. We've been inseparable since our night together, and despite all the sex we've had, my heart quickens at the thought of him. Into the phone, I say, "There's only one reason, because I wanted to, isn't that enough?"

"But his reputation." She hisses the words.

"Nobody minds his reputation when they want to make money off him." It's the truth. He might not be a part of us anymore, but they are all salivating for a piece of him anyway, if they admit it or not. I point out something my mother can't deny. "His family is one of the most prestigious in all of Chicago. You should be happy I've been offered a job."

There's a knock on the door and I open it, allowing him in. I put my fingers on my lips and mouth. "Mother."

He nods, and his gaze sweeps over me. I'm wearing a white sleeveless romper with a red woven belt around my waist and matching shoes. He's in jeans and a Cubs shirt and looks absolutely mouthwatering.

"That job is beneath you. Is that what you're doing with your education? You went to Harvard, Veronica." But I'm already distracted away from my mother's words.

He steps close and wraps an arm around my waist, pulling me into his embrace to brush his lips across mine. I hook my fingers into the waistband of his jeans to keep him near and meet his eyes. "I'm exactly where I want to be."

His gaze darkens.

My mom says, "You know you're ruining your father's deal. You need to make amends with Winston."

Brandon's expression flashes, and he grips me tighter, leaning down to whisper in my ear, "Over my dead, fucking body."

A smile flirts over my lips. I don't know if it's wrong or not, but I love his possession. His claim over me. It does something to my insides, making me want to melt and fuck simultaneously. I lean into him and speak into the phone. "I'm sorry, but if Daddy's deal hinges on me marrying Winston, maybe it's not a great deal to begin with." I close my eyes as Brandon hugs me tight, and I forget myself. "In fact, someone needs to tell Winston to stop harassing me."

Brandon jerks back and studies my expression, frowning.

"He just wants to talk to you, Veronica, you owe him that."

Shit. I shouldn't have said that. I've made no mention to anyone about my problems with Winston. I don't want Brandon to know. He'll worry, and I can deal with it on my own. It's my problem, not his. My brain spins, as I search for a way to answer my mom, but not alarm Brandon.

But he takes the decision away from me by plucking the phone out of my fingers and saying to my mother. "This is Brandon Townsend, and no, she does not owe him."

I twist, attempting to get the phone away from him, but he locks his arms around mine, trapping me.

I hear my mother's voice. "Put my daughter back on the phone."

"I will, in a moment. This isn't the way I would have chosen to introduce myself, but we don't always get an option.

It's a pleasure to meet you, Mrs. Westwood, I know you don't know me, but you can trust I have Veronica's best interest at heart. So understand this, Winston Bishop is not to come near her again. Please make it clear to everyone involved his presence in her life is no longer welcome."

My mom sputters. "This is none of your concern."

"That's where you're wrong. Veronica, and everything that involves her, is precisely my concern."

I still.

The line goes silent.

Brandon runs his mouth over my neck, releases me, and then hands the phone back. I take it and my voice is a bit breathless when I speak. "Everything's good, Mom."

"Veronica, what is your relationship with that man? Whatever it is, will not be tolerated."

It doesn't surprise me, but it still stings. I take a deep breath. "I have to go, I'm running out the door."

"When your father finds out about this he will not be happy."

"He's already not happy," I point out the obvious.

"Veronica, he is counting on you to make things right with Winston."

"That's not going to happen." There's no point in asking why my family seems unconcerned with my happiness. Happiness is not an aspiration in my social circle, business and advancement and standing are all that matters. "Goodbye, Mom."

I hang up before she can continue. I shake my head and beam at Brandon. "Sorry about that, are you ready to go?"

Please let it go. It's not something I want to talk about. It's a gorgeous day and I don't want anything to ruin it. Maybe if I pretend it's not a big deal Brandon will not mention it.

I turn away to grab my purse, but he grips my arm and swings me back around. "Not so fast, girl."

I flutter my lashes, hoping to pass for light and breezy. Because I can handle the Winston thing on my own. "We're going to be late."

"I don't care." He narrows his eyes on me. "What exactly did you mean about Winston harassing you?"

Okay, he's not going to let it slide. While I hoped, I'm not surprised. All I can do is downplay it. I wave my hand. "It's nothing, I promise. He's just been a little insistent we talk is all. I've been thinking I should agree to meet him and get it over with."

"Explain." His jaw firms into a hard line. "What does a little insistent mean?"

I shrug, as though it's not a big deal. "It's nothing, he keeps calling and texting wanting to talk."

"How many times has he called?"

I tilt my head. "You mean today?"

A low growl emanates from his throat. "For starters."

"I don't know, a few, I can handle it." I scrape my teeth over my bottom lip. "Can't we go enjoy the game?"

"After you tell me how many fucking times, and I'm not going to take vagueness as an answer."

I shake my head. "It's nothing. It's not your concern."

His expression turns into a storm cloud. "I thought we were clear, but apparently we are not. I'm going to tell you the same thing I told your mother. Everything—and I do mean *everything*—about you is my concern. So if I ask you a question, I expect an answer. A truthful answer, not evasion. I'm the boss here, not you. Do we understand each other?"

We stare at each other, gazes locked together. I grit my teeth. "This has nothing to do with sex."

Like lightning his hand strikes out, and he circles my neck, pushing me back until I hit a wall and I'm held captive. "This is not a selective arrangement, Veronica. I explained that. You do not get to pick and choose when I exert my control. Your wellbeing is my responsibility, so you either tell me, or I will find out myself. And if I have to find out myself, you can trust you will not like the consequences of forcing me to spend time doing something you could have told me in thirty seconds."

I can't help it, the strength of his power, his hand on my neck, that look in his eyes, it's distracting me. Making me want him. I already feel that special kind of liquid heat pooling in my belly and warming me all over. I lick my lips. "What will you do?"

He lowers his face so it's mere inches from mine and whispers, "I promise it will not be pleasant for you."

I'm almost positive this isn't supposed to set me on fire, but it does.

His gaze flicks across my features and he shakes his head. "I can see your wheels spinning. Your excitement in what I might do. But trust me, this is not the time to test me and find out. Tell me what I want to know, make me happy. Please me and I'll make the lust you feel right now child's play. And when you come, it will be so hard it will hurt." He shrugs. "Or don't, and who knows the next time you'll get an orgasm."

A variety of emotions storm through me, warring and waging an inner battle I don't really understand. But I'm going to give him what he wants, and that's all that's important right now. I open my mouth, but before I can speak, he squeezes my neck and says, "Do not sugar coat it, girl. The truth."

I nod and his grip loosens. I take a breath and tell him what he wants to know, hoping for the best when I do. "Today he's called me five times."

His blue eyes grow flat and cold. "It's not even noon."

"I know." I blow out a breath. "I've got it under control."

"How often has he been contacting you, on average?"

"It depends."

"On what?"

I shrug. "On how much he's had to drink."

"Give me a rough estimate."

I don't want to, but I'm stuck now. He won't let it go, and he is best friends with cops, who knows what he'll be able to find out with their help. I swallow hard. "I'm not sure, between text and calls he's probably contacting me twenty or so times a day."

He releases my neck, sliding his fingers over my jaw, the softness of his touch belying the hardness of his face. "He's stalking you."

I shake my head. "No, it's not that, he just has never heard the word no before."

"Wrong." He studies me. "Why didn't you say anything?"

"Because it's not your problem."

"Wrong again." A muscle works in his jaw and he drops his hold on me and begins to prowl across the room, agitation in his step. When he stops, he says, "You and I are going to make an appearance at the Baldwin gala this weekend. Every single person in that circle is going to know you're mine." One brow rises. "Do you have a problem with that?"

"No, Brandon." Not only do I not have a problem with it, a public pronouncement from him sends a thrill right through me.

"Good girl." He prowls back over, grabs me by the upper arms and claims my mouth with his.

His lips are hungry. His tongue sweeping. It's possession. In every way.

His right hand snakes down my side, curling over my hip, before sliding up the hem of my shorts. The fabric is loose and flowy and it doesn't take him more than a second to slip his fingers into my panties and circle my clit.

The sensation pulses through me as his fingers relentlessly play, working me up as he takes my mouth. I've never been kissed like Brandon kisses me, like sex and sin and the best kind of wickedness.

He lifts his head, moves to my ear. "I'm going to touch you all day. And I'm going to deny you all day."

I whimper. I have no idea why it makes me so hot, I wish it didn't but, god, it's the best. I shake my head because already the orgasm is pounding at the door demanding entrance. "No, please."

His thumb strokes as he slides two fingers inside. "When you're wet enough, then we'll see, but you're not nearly aroused enough for my tastes."

I gasp. I'm so slippery and he knows it. My head falls back against the wall and I arch to meet his hand. "How much more can I be?"

He nips at my neck. "We'll find out, now won't we?"

As I start to quicken, he pulls away. It makes me so frustrated I scream and punch him on the arm.

His lips quirk and his brows rise. "Did you just hit me, Veronica?"

I instantly come to my senses and I snap to attention. "It was your fault, you made me."

"Did I?" He steps back and shrugs. "You've got to pay now."

I shake my head. "I—forgot myself."

"Oh, I don't mind." He smiles, and it's pure evil as he reaches for my belt and starts to undo it. "I've been looking for a reason to spank that ass of yours, and here it didn't take you long for you to hand me one."

"Brandon, the game."

"We have plenty of time." The belt falls to the floor and he reaches for the thin straps of my romper, and pulls them down my body. He pauses at my breasts, rubbing his knuckles over the hard nipples through my bra.

Goose bumps break out over my skin, and he continues down his path, stripping me from my nude panties that fall to the floor. He slides his fingers between my legs. "Your cunt is addictive." He smirks. "And wet, but not wet enough."

He tilts his chin. "Get down on your hands and knees."

Tension kicks up inside me. "Here?"

"What's wrong with here?" His voice is so smooth, so controlled. It should cool me, but it doesn't, if anything it increases my hunger, especially at the way his blue eyes burn. He puts a hand on my shoulder and presses. "Down you go."

My lashes flutter as I contemplate my options, but between the expression on his face and the insistent pressure on my shoulder, I find myself sinking to my knees. I hit the hardwood and satisfaction flashes across his features.

He nods. "Elbows on the floor, ass up, legs spread."

Nerves light across my skin because he's going to spank me, and I've never been spanked before. I lick my dry lips, swallowing hard.

He strokes a finger over my jaw. "Trust me."

I do. More than anyone else he's the person I trust. With a deep breath I lower to the position he indicated.

He walks to stand so I can stare down at his shoes. For endless moments he's still, saying nothing, and as I imagine him watching my prone, stretched-out body, my desire mixes with my unease and transforms into heat. He touches my hair before skimming down the length of my spine, over the curve of my ass. He squeezes, not hard, but enough to make me hyperaware of my position.

He slides a finger over the seam of my ass, dipping inside to graze along sensitive flesh, he pauses circling over puckered flesh. "Someday, very soon, I'm going to fuck your ass."

Involuntarily, I clench. I don't know why, but the words inflame me, making me ache. Before I can process enough to speak, he moves away, tapping my inner thigh. "Wider."

I adjust my legs, and cool air brushes over skin normally hidden. I moan, closing my eyes as he slips his fingers over my slickness. "Very nice, Veronica, but still not wet enough."

"Brandon." His name strangled from my lips.

He plays over my clit, working me up as I start pushing back to increase the friction. Just when I'm about to tumble over the edge, he moves away.

I pound my fist against the hardwood, and he laughs, low and wicked.

He waits for me to cool down before starting again. Over and over. Relentlessly. Until I'm gasping and cursing and begging him. But he doesn't deliver.

Slippery wetness slides down my inner thighs, and just when I've completely forgotten about anything but him touching me, he pulls back and strikes me, hard and full across my ass.

Fiery pain bursts along my skin, making my eyes water, before an indescribable pleasure quickly follows. Before I can process what I'm experiencing, he slaps me again.

I groan, dropping my head down low as his hands weave a tapestry over my flesh.

It hurts.

It feels good.

I hate it.

I love it.

I want it to end.

I never want it to stop.

It's just an endless sea of contradictory emotions.

My breath comes fast, matching the rhythm of his blows. I reach out and clutch at the floor as he increases his pace, the strength and power of his hand.

He stops and I gasp out a breath. He reaches between my legs and ruthlessly thrusts two fingers inside me. Almost instantly the orgasm swells and he pulls away, and spanks me again.

How long it goes on like this, I have no idea, but I'm mindless in a haze of pleasure and pain, overloading my senses, making me ache in ways I didn't know I was capable of aching.

Suddenly, without warning, he grips my hair and yanks me up, pulling me to my knees. I gaze up at him, blinking to orientate myself. His expression is cruel and unrelenting. With an evil smile he unbuckles his belt and slowly slides his zipper down, freeing his cock.

I'm hardly able to breathe. My skin is on fire, radiating from where he'd struck me.

He runs his cock along the seam of my lips. "Open wide, girl."

I open and he slides inside my mouth, filling me completely, not stopping when he meets resistance, just pushing past all that. I gag, and he fills my throat. When I swallow, he curses, his hold at the nape of my neck tightening. His features sharpen, harden, and I've never seen him look so beautiful.

I'm so on edge, so needy, as he works his length into my throat, my fingers slide over my clit of their own volition.

I need an orgasm. I need it. I have to find release.

As I start to quicken, his hand strikes out and slaps my fingers away. He growls. "None of that." Then he releases my hair, grabs both my wrists, and I lose my balance as he shifts me to the wall.

I right myself, but he's so fast I'm now pressed up against the wall, my wrists imprisoned by his hard grip. He's ruthless now, as I've learned he gets when he's full of the dominance that's such a part of him. Immobilized, I can only sit there as he pumps his hips, filling my mouth with his thick cock.

"That's right, just let it happen." He moves harder. Faster. With no regard to me, but instead of cooling me, it only makes me hotter, wilder. More desperate. He fucks my throat like he has every right to do so.

My hands clench into fists as tears stream down my face.

I want to touch.

He looks down at me, and our eyes meet, and god, what passes between us something is feral and untamed. He shakes his head. "You were made for this."

Yes, that's exactly right. For him. I want to speak the words, but that's impossible.

Thankfully, he fills them in for me. "Yes. Mine."

Helpless, my lashes flutter.

Then he comes down my throat in a jolt, spilling so much cum it slips from my lips and slides down the length of my throat, and into the valley of my breasts.

He yanks away, releasing me as I slide to the floor. Then he's on me, his fingers on my clit. He was right. I can be much wetter. I cry out as the orgasm almost crashes down on me, but he stops, moving to my inner thighs where he strokes over their slickness.

He grips my chin and forces me to look at him. His blue eyes burn. "I think you can do better."

I shake my head.

"Yes." He brings me close to orgasm over and over again, until I'm slumped against the wall, my mind completely blank, except for one thing. I must come.

Only, he won't let me.

"Please." My voice is reed thin, and filled with desperation. "Please, Brandon. I'm begging you."

He circles my clit. "No."

"I'll do anything." I promise, meaning every word.

"No."

The orgasm threatens. I'm shaking all over. His spanking only managed to create an exquisite heat, a fullness that makes every touch more keen and biting.

I clutch at his arm. "What can I do?"

He pulls away, and whispers, "Suffer."

"I am."

"Good."

"I hate you," I yell as he denies yet another orgasm.

"I know." He moves, straightening to stand upright. "Up you go."

Still using the wall to support me, I blink at him. "I need it."

He nods. "You're not going to get it."

"Why are you doing this to me?"

He crouches down, cups my jaw and kisses me, so sweetly it's hard to believe he's being such a bastard. When he pulls away he says, "Because you love it so much, and suffer so beautifully."

Unable to speak, I shake my head.

"I'll make you a deal."

Hope springs up, filling my chest. I gaze at him.

He smiles. "I'll let you have an orgasm under one condition."

Deep in the recesses of my mind, where I'm still capable of rational thought, I sense a trap, but I'm not able to stop myself from stepping into it. "Anything."

"Look me in the eye and tell me this isn't the most alive you've ever felt, and I'll let you come."

I open my mouth, close it, then sag against the wall. I can't. It would be a lie. Never in my life have I felt this alive, so aware of my breath, the brush of air along my skin, the heavy pounding of need. The longing, the lust, the awareness of everything, it's like every cell I possess is engaged in him, in life.

He pushes back my hair from my damp neck. "I'm giving you exactly what you crave. What you need. Remember that."

My throat tightens and I say in a shaky voice, "I still hate you."

He smiles. "I'd expect nothing less.

Brandon

It's in the middle of the game when I'm finally alone with the Leo, Michael and Chad. The girls all went to the bathroom together, and I suspect they'll be gone for a bit as they recap to each other their own custom-designed torture. Submissive girls get disgruntled when they aren't messed with on a regular basis, but they still need to bounce their indignation at our gall off each other.

As soon as they disappear down the stairs leading to the concession area, I turn to Leo and Michael. "I may have a problem."

They both raise their brows at me and Michael says, "What's up?"

Ever since I found out about Winston Bishop I've had to restrain my temper. My first instinct was to go right to the guy's house and fucking kill him, but a cooler head has prevailed. I understand Veronica now, understand her need to build her life and exert her independence. I have no desire to take that away from her. But I can't sit idly by and do nothing while Winston makes things difficult for her.

The trick is to help her deal with the problem of her ex-boyfriend on her own, but still support her. I'm hoping that announcing my presence in her life, and our appearance at the gala will solve the issue, but it never hurts to be prepared. And this is the benefit of having cop friends.

I scrub a hand over my jaw, still able to catch her essence that's seeped into my skin. Like she's becoming a part of me. Although, it's not causing the panic I'd have expected. No, I want her too much for that. She's like a drug that has no signs of a half-life.

I glance back to where the girls disappeared before returning my attention to my friends. "Veronica's ex-boyfriend is stalking her."

All three of them frown, their shoulders tightening. We protect what's ours, and because Veronica belongs to me now, that includes her.

Leo's head tilts. "What exactly is he doing?"

"I found out by default, but apparently he's been calling her and texting her twenty or so times a day. I'm guessing that's a conservative estimate." Anger flows through my blood at the thought. Not only at his persistence, but that she didn't tell me about it. That all this time she's been suffering and failed to mention it.

"Has he escalated?" Leo asks.

"What would that look like?" Because I don't know what a cop's definition is.

Michael interjects. "Has he attempted to make contact? In person?"

My brow furrows. "Not that I'm aware of. According to her he just calls and texts wanting to see her, to talk about their relationship." The word tastes like dirt going down.

I think of this morning, pumping my cock into her wet, hot mouth. The primal possession swelling inside me as I used her while denying her. Veronica has no idea how hard it was for me not to let her slip over the edge. The only thing that stopped me is her utter greediness and the knowledge that she loved it so fucking much. She's been slippery wet every time I've touched her since. I've worked her needy cunt periodically through the day, and when she looks at me with defiance and lust, it kills me.

She's starting to feel made for me. Her secret kinks aligning too perfectly with mine.

I tighten my hand into a fist. That asshole doesn't understand she belongs to me. But I'll rectify it soon enough.

"Has he threatened her?" Michael asks.

"No, not that I'm aware of." I scrub my hand over my jaw. "I'm going to make my presence in her life known and see if that stops him."

"Good idea," Chad says. "That'd be my first step too."

Leo crosses his arms. "She can file a report, but it might not be useful at this point. He's operating in a bit of a gray area. Emotional distress is a component of stalking but harder to prove."

"What do you suggest?" When the crowd cheers, I turn my head to see a runner flying around second base.

"See if he stops when he knows you're with her," Michael says, his voice hard. "If it doesn't, maybe we can pay him an unofficial visit."

I nod. "We'll have to be careful, his family is powerful, and I don't want to cause trouble with you on the force."

"Understood." Leo nods. "Keep a close eye on it, detail records, screen shot all text messages and email communications. Records of his calls. That will help build a case if he doesn't back off."

Michael's eyes narrow. "Whatever you do, don't try and take care of it yourself."

I scoff, air huffing out in a bite. "Do you expect me to idly stand by and do nothing?"

Michael glances at Leo and Chad before returning his attention to me. "Yeah, make it clear she's yours, but do not fucking engage and end up the one in jail."

"All I intend to do is talk to him."

Again my three best friends look at each other as if they know something I don't.

Chad is the one that speaks for them. He shrugs. "Easier said than done when you feel like the girl you love is being threatened."

I jerk back at the word. I'm not in love. I don't do love. I'm incapable of it.

Granted, I'm infatuated with Veronica, there's no question about that, but that's not the same as love. It's chemistry. The protest fights for purchase and I let it free. "It's not love. It's not like that between us."

Leo raises a brow. "Sure as shit looks like love from here."

I shake my head. That panic I hadn't been feeling begins a slow simmer. Love means weakness, and I'm not good with weakness. Weakness makes me stupid and impulsive. I roll my eyes, dismissing them. "Don't be ridiculous."

Michael sighs. "Just do not engage. Understand?"

I nod. "Understood."

I can see the logic in his point and decide to let it go for the time being. I'll play my hand and figure out my next move if it doesn't resolve the problem.

Over my shoulder I see a flash of white. I turn my head and watch as Veronica steps out of the dark corridor and into the sun. The wind blows her hair, and she's smiling. My chest gives a hard thump at the sight of her.

Christ I want her.

Want her as much as I want my next breath.

However, there's no way I am in love with her. I don't even know what that feels like, but this can't be it.

She catches me watching her and her entire face brightens as she meets my eyes.

She doesn't look like any other woman here.

She looks like mine.

But it's not love. It's lust and chemistry.

That's all.

21.

Veronica

The limo pulls to a stop in front of the Navy Pier Gala Ballroom, and Brandon squeezes my thigh, left bare by the slit of my black dress. "You ready?"

It's my first public event since the night I met Brandon, which now feels like a lifetime ago. So much of my life has changed since then, including the man beside me. The man that's opened me up to new experiences and helped me discover who I am.

The man I'm desperately in love with, although I've kept that to myself.

Despite my nerves—and I am nervous—I'm ready. It's like I'm presenting the new me to these people that I've known my entire life. As both part of, and removed from, this world that until a short time ago was all I'd ever known.

I peer at Brandon, devastating in his tux. They'll all talk, we'll be the highlight of gossip behind whispered fingers, but secretly there won't be a woman there that isn't jealous of me because of him.

I smile. "I'm ready."

Instead of getting out of the car, he leans over and brushes my mouth with his. "You look beautiful."

"Thank you, so do you."

He laughs, those dimples of his flashing and making my heart melt. "If he approaches us, let me do the talking."

At the suggestion I frown.

Brandon shakes his head. "Not a discussion. Let me do this."

"But…why?" I brush my hair back over one bare shoulder. "I am perfectly capable of handling it on my own."

He sits back and stares at me for what feels like endless moments before he speaks. "You are fully capable. It's one of my favorite things about you. All that fierce independence mixed with such a little slut."

I gasp, my mind instantly returning to this afternoon where he'd spread me over his desk and been so wicked until I'd been a hot, needy mess. Between my legs is still wet and swollen, a fact impossible for me to ignore, considering my lack of undergarments. By his command, I'm naked under my slinky dress, which is floor length, but skims over my body like it's been painted on. Earlier, I'd mentioned that I feel practically naked, to which he responded was precisely the point.

I bite my lower lip. "So why?"

He trails one finger over the skin of my thigh, making distracting little circles. "Honestly, my reasons are purely territorial. I want there to be no doubt in his mind that you fucking belong to me."

"That's honest." Still looking at him, my head drops back along the seat as his hand travels higher.

He pauses when he reaches dampened flesh. "You like the idea."

"I do." He has no idea how much.

"Me too."

"Is it true?" I want it to be true.

His expression turns fierce, a direct contrast to the softness of his stroking touch down the curve of my neck. "Yes. You're mine."

I want to tell him I love him, but I hold the words back. I don't think he's ready and I can't risk scaring him. Instead, I nod. "Yes."

His thumb brushes my clit. "Let me have this, Veronica."

When he talks like that, in that voice, I can't deny him. "Okay."

"Good girl." He kisses me hard before pulling back. "Let's go."

I nod, and his hands slip away, leaving me cold, as he knocks on the window and the driver that's been waiting patiently for us opens the door. He steps out first, and I see the flash of bulbs go off as the society rag photogs catch their first glimpse of him.

He holds out his hand to me, and I grasp it, stepping out to face the public. Brandon, who's always ignored the press, slides a hand around my waist and pauses, letting them photograph us.

I glance up at him. He's making sure we make the papers, which is a surprise. So...when he meant public claiming he *really* meant public claiming.

He squeezes my waist, and we walk up the red carpet always laid out for events like this. I hold my breath as we walk into the room. The massive domed room is decked out, dripping with a sparkling but understated extravagance. Twinkle lights, huge white floral bouquets, and linens are everywhere, like Cinderella's ball.

We stand at the threshold and it only takes fifteen seconds for our presence to register and ripple throughout the room. For those who care about that sort of thing to notice. Once it occurs, Brandon takes my hand and leads me through the crowd, stopping every few seconds to greet people, shaking hands like a politician. If you didn't know his true feelings, one would think he was in his element. But I know the truth, he's doing this for me, and me alone.

My heart swells with pride.

We reach his parents first, and his mother glances between us. Both his parents are well kept and elegant as is expected of old Chicago money. His father, a distinguished, handsome man in his sixties, nods. "Brandon, Ms. Westwood, this is a surprise."

We shake hands and I give him my most brilliant smile. "It's a pleasure to meet you, Mr. Townsend, please it's Veronica."

His mom, who actually kind of resembles Helen Miren, takes a sip of her Champagne before saying, "You said you weren't coming."

Brandon shrugs, curving a proprietary hand over my hip. "I changed my mind."

She turns her attention to me. "I presume you had something to do with this, Veronica?"

I laugh. "Hardly, as you know, Brandon doesn't tend to do anything he doesn't want to."

"Indeed," she says, a ghost of a smile spreading over her lips. "I'm pleased to see you, Brandon."

"I'm sure you are," he says, before addressing his father. "Dad, do you think you could arrange a round of golf at the club between us and the Westwoods?"

This shocks me, and surprise flashes across Brandon's parents' features in time with my own.

His dad tilts his head. "Are you entering back into the fold?"

"Don't get excited, I'm just dabbling."

His dad's jaw tightens. "With your talent for making money, I have no idea why you continue to waste it."

Brandon flashes a smile. "My talent for making money is what allows me to do so."

His mom clears her throat. "I'm sure we'll be happy to arrange something." She glances discretely at me. "I'm not sure how you two even know each other."

"You can thank last month's benefit you forced me into for that." Brandon rubs the curve of my waist. "Veronica cornered me and harassed me into a position."

"I see." The older woman looks at me. "Well done, dear."

A waiter passes and I swoop a flute from the tray, handing one to Brandon before taking one for myself. "It was nothing. It only took constant badgering to wear him down."

"How interesting." Her chin tilts. "Would you join us for brunch tomorrow morning?"

"No," Brandon says.

At the same time I say, "Yes, we'd be happy to."

He frowns down at me. "We're otherwise engaged."

Brandon's parents might be wealthy and reserved, but I sense no hostility toward him. If anything, the slight wistfulness in his mom's eyes makes me believe she'd like a better relationship with her son. Brandon doesn't talk about them much, only telling me that they were fine, didn't talk to him for a while when he abandoned their life, and that he has negotiated to attend events for them.

Their quick offer to see him tells me they'd like to change that. I flash a smile at him. "I don't believe so."

He grasps me tighter. "Yes."

I shake my head. "No, I think brunch with your parents would be quite lovely, especially if you expect me to play eighteen holes of golf." I appeal to his mom. "That sounds like a fair trade, don't you think?"

"That I do."

All three of us turn to look at Brandon.

He sighs. "Fine."

His acquiescence, only to please me, makes me fall for him even more, even though I didn't think that was possible. I beam up at him. "Thank you."

Brandon's mother wastes no time. "How's ten thirty at the club?"

Another place where we will be seen. I nod. "That works beautifully."

Out of the corner of my eye, I spot my parents watching us. My father is frowning, my mom's brows are furrowed. I tilt my head at Brandon. "My parents."

He smiles at his mother and father. "That's settled then,

and don't forget about golf."

His dad nods. "Consider it done."

Brandon's ensuring that our families appear intertwined to everyone who matters, but most important, sending a message to Winston and his family that they are no longer in the fold. It's amazing what can be accomplished without words in this world.

We take our leave, and Brandon guides me with a hand on the small of my back to where my parents stand.

I smile. "Hi, Daddy."

"Veronica." His voice is hard, showing no sign he's willing to forgive me for my transgressions. He shifts his attention to Brandon. "I see you've taken my daughter under your wing."

Brandon's arm slides around my waist. "It's a pleasure to meet you, Mr. and Mrs. Westwood. Veronica has been quite an asset to me."

My dad's shoulders square. "That doesn't surprise me, Veronica has always been a resourceful girl. Although I'm not sure her talents aren't wasted in her current position."

I peer at Brandon, whose grip tightens on my hip before he shrugs. "I'm sure you're right."

"Are you going to rectify that?" my dad asks bluntly.

I shake my head. "Daddy, stop it. I'm exactly where I want to be."

The expression on my mom's face tightens. "We only want what's best for you, Veronica."

"As do I." Brandon smiles pleasantly. "Her role will expand if she decides to continue to work for me. If that's what she wants."

This is new information. We have not discussed I'm currently under his employ only as a contractor. I am enjoying the work, but I'm always up for more of a challenge.

My father's eyes narrow. "What are your intentions toward my daughter?"

Brandon takes the question in stride. "I can assure you I only want what's best for her."

"And you think you're it?" My dad's face reddens.

My mom's lips purse as she studies my father. "Herald, your blood pressure."

"Yes, I do," Brandon answers, his voice strong and sure.

I sigh. "It's my decision. And I choose Brandon."

"Even if we don't approve?" my father asks.

"Even if you don't approve." I meet his eyes, and don't waver. In this I have no doubts.

Brandon rubs along my waist. "I don't think it will come to that."

"And why do you think that?" My dad's expression is hard and implacable.

"Because, despite what you may feel about me, my family is powerful and influential," Brandon continues smoothly. "My father will be contacting you to join us next week at the club."

He lets that hang in the air, letting it sink in. Because it will matter to my parents. Brandon might be a black sheep, but he's still part of a family that should not be fucked with.

"How lovely," my mom says, nodding graciously. "We'll be looking forward to it."

"As will we." Brandon shifts his attention to my father. "So there's no room for misunderstanding, Veronica is not an option for Winston Bishop. Whatever business you have with the family will have to be concluded without her help."

My father and Brandon stare at each other, and something unknown to me passes between them for several tense, awkward moments, before my dad nods. "Fine."

"Good, I'm glad we understand each other," Brandon says, then shifts toward me. "Would you like to dance?"

A waltz is playing and I'm desperate to get away from this situation. I smile. "That would be lovely."

"It's been a pleasure to meet you, I look forward to seeing you next week." And with that, Brandon turns me toward the dance floor.

We walk, the crowd parting a bit, and I can feel the whispers at my back as Brandon swings me into his arms.

He glides me perfectly across the floor, maneuvering me until we are front and center. If Winston is in attendance, there's no way he can miss our presence. I position one hand on his shoulder. "Well, that went as well as can be expected."

Brandon strokes down my back. "Do you see what I do for you?"

For perhaps the first time, his words and his actions really sink in. He's shunned all of this for years, but he's putting himself right in the middle of it, for me. Because I matter to him. I'm important. This isn't about our chemistry, or sex, or desire. In that moment, the full weight of what he's doing for me resonates deep inside, and I feel like his. Not just my body, but all of me.

I beam up at him, going to my tiptoes I brush my mouth against his. "Thank you, Brandon."

His hand skims up my back and curls around my neck, and he stares deep into my eyes. "What am I going to do with you?"

"Do you need ideas?"

He shakes his head, dips down and kisses me. "Come with me."

"Anywhere." And I mean it.

Brandon

Walking away wasn't easy. But it needed to be done.

I tug Veronica into an alcove, far enough away from the party that we won't be interrupted, and press her against the wall. I cover her body with my own, placing my hands on either side of her head and gazing down at her.

In the darkened shadows her face is lit by the iridescent glow of the lights. She's so fucking beautiful my heart squeezes. It seems I cannot get enough of looking at her. I meet her honeyed eyes, my gaze dipping to her mouth, and then back up again. I shake my head.

She licks her lips. "What?"

Something unnamed thickens in my blood and I confess. "I

adore everything about you."

Her expression fills with happiness. "I adore everything about you too, Brandon."

I lean down and whisper in her ear, "You drive me crazy."

"But in a good way." It's not a question.

"Yes." I skim my lips over the soft skin at the curve of her neck. "I'm glad I couldn't say no to you."

Her breath hitches. "You have no problem saying no to me now."

I smile against her. "But only because you like it so much and beg so sweetly."

"Well, what do we have here?" A snide male voice comes from behind me.

That didn't take long. Slowly I straighten, lazily turning to face Winston Bishop.

He's wearing a tux, a drink in one hand, and his eyes are hard on Veronica, my fingers fall to her hips and I find her tense, her muscles tight.

I nod, shifting and sliding my hand more firmly around her waist. "Bishop."

"Townsend." My name clipped, he raises a brow at Veronica. "Is this why you haven't been answering my calls?"

She goes to open her mouth but I interject before she can speak. "Yes, and it's in your best interest if you cease, she's not interested."

He scoffs. "She can speak for herself."

I smirk, knowing it will drive him crazy. "From my understanding she has been, but you haven't been getting the message."

His gaze turns, narrowing on me. "This isn't your concern."

I run my hand slowly, proprietarily over Veronica's hip. "But it is. Veronica is very much my concern."

Rage flashes over his features, stark and barely contained, before his expression smooths over. "Veronica, we need to talk."

This time I keep quiet, letting her take over.

She takes a deep breath, glancing at me before returning her attention to Winston and shaking her head. "There's nothing to talk about. It's over."

He jabs a finger in my direction. "Because of *him*?"

Her shoulders straighten. "Because of me."

I smile a little.

Winston's face shudders with anger again before he conceals it, and it sends a whisper of a chill through me. I know that expression. I used to wear it myself when I was an entitled little prick that thought the world owed me something and I was above paying a price.

Veronica's chin tilts. "Please leave me alone. You need to stop calling me, stop texting me. It's over, and it's time to move on."

Winston stares at her for a long, tension-filled moment, before he nods. "Fine, Veronica." His face shifts into a sneer. "Bitsy is a much better lay than you anyway."

Veronica tenses fractionally before smiling. "You two are welcome to each other, it has nothing to do with me."

Winston slugs down the rest of his highball. "Good luck, Townsend, she's cold as fuck in bed, but the connections are good."

Veronica has told me about her abysmal relationship with Winston Bishop, so I know all about their lackluster sex life. He's attempting to bait me, and even though I want to rise to the occasion, I don't. Because it's what he wants and not getting the satisfaction will eat at him far more than any response I'd give. "You can go now."

Veronica just smiles. "Take care, Winston."

He looks first at me and then at her before saying, "This is a mistake."

"Mine to make," Veronica says.

He gives me one more sneer before spinning and walking away.

Veronica turns to me, sucking in a breath before blowing it out. "I suppose that went better than I thought it would."

I nod. "Hopefully that will be the end of it."

"I hope so." She shakes her head. "I don't understand why

he's so insistent. It's not like he was in love with me or anything."

"He's not used to hearing the word no." I glance back at the party in the main room before returning my attention to her. "But you'll tell me if he approaches you again."

"I will." Her expression brightens and she rises to her tiptoes and brushes her mouth across mine. "For now let's enjoy the night."

I curl my hand around her waist. "I can do that."

Right now I feel like I'd do anything for her. She's seeped into my blood and there's nothing I'm able to do to stop her. She has power over me.

Power I can't control.

I'm not even sure I want to. Not with her standing there in her black dress, hair curving around her shoulders, those honeyed eyes staring up at me, sucking me in.

Breaking me.

Veronica

I'm in the bathroom, washing my hands when Bitsy walks in. The woman I'd considered one of my closest friends.

Her gaze flickers over me before she lifts one perfectly arched brow. "Brandon Townsend the third, well, congratulations. That's quite an accomplishment."

I straighten. It seems this is the night for confrontation. "He's not a prize."

"Isn't he though?" She gives me a smile that doesn't even come close to meeting her eyes. "I called him that night, but you couldn't help yourself, could you?"

I don't address this because there's really no point. She can't comprehend that she'd never get Brandon, with or without me in the picture, because to her he's a trophy, not a person. All she sees now is a perceived competition between us and that I won. "Is that why you're sleeping with Winston?"

She smirks. "Oh, little Veronica, I've been sleeping with Winston for ages."

It doesn't surprise me, nor does it have any effect on me. I nod. "Well, you're welcome to him. As a friend, I should tell you that I walked in on him with a blonde that definitely wasn't you, so be careful. Take care, Bitsy."

I step around her and walk out the door. In that moment, I've never been so sure that walking away from this life was the best decision I could have ever made. Because eventually, I would have been sucked in, and lost all my humanity and sense of purpose.

I exit the restrooms, making my way toward where I left Brandon, ready to get the hell out of here. We did what we came here to do; now all I want to do is leave. Maybe we can meet up with Brandon's friends, the friends that are starting to be my friends as well, and I can be reminded of what decency looks like.

Gaze trained on Brandon, leaning casually against the wall, hands shoved in his pockets and my chest squeezes. I can't believe he's mine. I think of all the things he's done to me, the things he's promised to do to me, and shiver. Somehow, someway, he fits me.

He feels like a home I'd believed I'd never have.

I walk past an alcove, and suddenly a hand grips my upper arm, hard and tight. I flinch, attempting to jerk away, but my high heels work against me, and I'm tipped off balance.

I fall into Winston's arms.

He wraps around me like a snake and my heart starts to gallop in my chest when I see the look on his face. I've only seen that look in his eyes once before, and it terrifies me now, the same way it terrified me back then.

I push at his chest. "Winston, let me go."

"No." He grips me tighter, pulling me farther into the recesses of what I now see is a hallway. "You're going to listen to me."

I shove harder. I need to get away from him. I can't let him separate me from the party. Panic fills the back of my throat.

"Winston, stop. What is wrong with you?"

I use my feet as weight to fight against him, to slow him down, but it doesn't deter him. He picks me up, dragging me into a darkened room and locking me inside.

The room is pitch-black, and beads of cold sweat break out over my skin, as I flail around in my blindness. "Stop. Let me go. Why are you doing this?"

He slams me against the door, body checking me to hold me prisoner, as he fumbles around in the dark, before flicking on a light switch and filling the closet with a dim yellowed glow.

I scream. It pierces the air for a split second before he covers my mouth with his hand, and gives my head a sharp, vicious shake.

I bite him.

He yelps in pain, straightens and backhands me across the face.

My eyes tear as pain explodes along my cheek and I understand the expression seeing stars. I touch my sure-to-be-bruised skin, and meet Winston's stunned gaze.

Gone is the out-of-control rage, and left in its place is panic.

Which somehow scares me even more.

Because it's desperate.

He reaches out and gently cups my shoulders. "Veronica, I'm so sorry. I didn't mean it, sweetheart."

I flinch before I start shaking. "Don't touch me."

"It will never happen again. I promise." His voice is filled with remorse.

I place my palm against my hot cheek. "Why are you even doing this? You don't love me, Winston."

He strokes my upper arms and my skin crawls, but I'm not sure how to get away. Everything is eerily silent, like that strange, still calm before the storm. Like one wrong move will send him over the edge.

He smiles then, soft and reassuring. "Everything will go back to the way it was, okay."

"No. Are you crazy?"

His face shudders, revealing the monster that lives beneath the surface. "I'm not crazy. I just need you back."

"But, why?" I don't understand any of this.

He laughs. "I'm not getting cut off because of you, Veronica. And that's final."

"What are you talking about?" Fear lodges in my chest, and I look down at the door handle. If I can open the door, we'll tumble out into the hall and I'll be free. I have a better shot if I keep him talking, keep him thinking that I'll consider this insanity.

He presses his body against mine, full and flush. "You, your family, the deal between our fathers, it needs to happen."

"Winston," I say, my voice calm and steady, betraying none of the panic bouncing around inside me. "If the deal makes enough money, our fathers will go through with it, with or without us."

He shakes his head, and starts squeezing my upper arms, until I gasp in pain. "You don't understand, this is my last chance. He's going to cut me off if I don't marry you like I'm supposed to."

"You're hurting me." I clench my teeth against the pain. "Please, stop, you're hurting me."

He squeezes tighter. "You have to listen. Just do this for me, and we'll be even."

I have no idea what he's talking about and my baser, survival instincts shift into high gear, blocking out strategy and logic, and replacing it with an uncontrollable desire to fight my way out of this.

I kick him in the shins.

He stands back and punches me in the stomach. Pain explodes, and all the air leaves my body.

"Listen to me, you little bitch. I'm not losing everything because of you." He smacks me across the face again.

I can't process how this is happening. All I can do is think about the pain.

The door is suddenly thrust open and I tumble out into the

hallway, falling to a heap on the floor. I blink, and see Brandon's face for a split second, before he lunges at Winston.

I try and speak, but Winston has split my lip and the words are nothing but a muffled cry as madness breaks out.

Brandon tackles Winston to the floor and starts pummeling his face with flying fists. I struggle to sit up, wincing at the pain in my stomach before I manage to right myself.

I yell, "Brandon! Please stop."

But he's beyond hearing. He smashes his fist into Winston's nose and the crack of bone crunches through the air. "Don't ever fucking touch her again, do you hear me?"

Another smashing blow to Winston's jaw.

I begin to cry. I scream, "Brandon!"

Suddenly, he's lifted off Winston, his arms still flying through the air as he attempts to release himself from the hold.

I stumble to my feet and step in front of his vision. His gaze snaps onto mine and twists with rage. He snarls, "He hit you."

I swallow through my tears. "I'm okay, I'm fine. I promise."

He jerks his attention back to Winston, who's been pulled from the floor. Brandon growls, low in his throat. "You're a fucking dead man."

"Brandon, please," I whisper.

Uniformed security rushes in, and then everything is a mess of chaos and yelling and activity that blurs my vision, until the cuffs snap over Brandon's wrists.

I pull at the officer. "Wait, no, he was protecting me. Winston grabbed me and hit me."

The officer nods. "You can come down to the station and give your statement, but we have to bring them both in."

"But he did nothing wrong." I'm pleading now.

Brandon's jaw is tight and he nods. "Veronica, it's okay. Call Michael and Leo and they'll take care of it."

"Okay." My mom comes up behind me and wraps a silky shawl around my shoulders and hugs me tight. I turn to her. "Please don't let them take him."

"We'll get it taken care of," my mom says, her expression more worried than I'd ever seen it.

Brandon's eyes lock on mine. "Don't worry, this will be over before you know it."

The officers turn him from me, and he's taken away.

The crowd parts, and all I can see is his broad shoulders. Ones I've cried on and have held me. And in that moment I know.

Know he's it for me.

Know exactly what our life is supposed to look like together.

"I love him," I say out loud.

My mom squeezes me. "I know."

The entire world shifts into crystal-clear focus. "I've got to make calls, I've got to take care of him."

My father appears before me. "Veronica, your face. We should take you to the hospital."

I shake my head. "No, I need to get to Brandon. He's the only one that matters."

But they whisk me away, separating me from the man I love. The man that needs me now more than anything.

22.

Brandon

I rub my weary eyes with my thumb and forefinger as I sit on the cold hard bench that lines the holding cell I've been stuck in for over an hour. My mind flashes back to the blinding rage I'd experienced at the sight of Veronica's beautiful face, bruised by Winston's hand.

My stomach rolls, thinking of the marks I'd made on her, and they mix together in my head, tangling until they mesh and I feel as much a monster as Winston.

He'd hurt her.

He'd laid his hands on her and marred her skin.

I'd gone crazy. In that moment, when my head had been nothing but a buzz of white noise and I could think of nothing but killing him for daring to touch her, I'd learned two things about myself.

The boy I'd been—impulsive, destructive and out of control—capable of violence, he still lived inside me. Hidden and lurking, just waiting for the right circumstances to rear his ugly head.

And I was in love with Veronica.

Somehow, someway, I'd fallen so completely, so irrevocably, I didn't have the first clue how to fight my way out. She'd taken ahold of me, holding me tight in her grip, refusing to let go.

There was the click of the door, the metallic unlocking.

Elbows on my knees, I look up to see Michael and Leo standing there. They both are wearing jeans and black shirts, badges hanging around their necks, arms crossed, that fucking cop expression on their faces.

They look more than partners, with their matching grim-lined mouths and hard eyes, although I suppose they are now. They're family. Brothers in every way but blood.

Michael shakes his head. "You couldn't fucking listen, could you?"

There's a loud noise, and then the bars slide open.

Leo sighs. "We warned you."

From my seat, I glare at them and hold out my hands. "Did you see what he did to her face?"

They nod, their jaws hardening.

Michael says, "Yeah. She gave a complete statement."

I shake with rage. "He hurt her. I couldn't let him hurt her."

To my horror, my throat tightens and my eyes fill with an unfamiliar burn.

My two best friends come and sit down on either side of me.

Leo pats me on the back. "Yeah, I know."

Michael shrugs one big shoulder. "Love can make you crazy."

I don't even deny it. I can't.

Leo clears his throat. "Bishop's in the hospital, you broke his nose and jaw."

"He's already talking about suing you," Michael says.

"I don't give a fuck. It was worth it." My hands clench, and I can feel the blood thirst running fast in my veins, wishing I'd had time to do more. A legal battle will be inconvenient, but I have more money than god and I'll win in the end. Of course, only the lawyers will get rich, but fuck 'em.

Leo nudges me. "As cops, we have to say you should know better, but as your friend, good job."

"Can I go home? I need to find Veronica."

"We're getting you released on your own recognizance." Michael nods. "We're just waiting on the paperwork."

"Everyone is waiting outside for you," Leo says.

Veronica, is all I can think about. I need to make sure she's all right, that she's not suffering. "Where is Veronica? We need to protect her."

Michael frowns. "Her parents took her to the hospital to have her checked over, and then she'll be here."

This panic, it's clawing at me. "What if Bishop gets to her? What if he takes her and I can't find her again?"

"He's in the hospital and under guard." Leo's voice is like steel. "He's not getting to her."

The events of the night rush over me, making me break out in a sweat. How I'd felt uneasy when she hadn't returned in a normal time, how the unease turned into desperation when I'd been unable to locate her. The dread crawling over my skin as I'd searched.

But most of all, how I'd felt powerless.

I was in love with Veronica.

All these years, I'd been right to stay away from emotional entanglements. It made me as weak and helpless as I'd always feared.

My teeth ache from clenching them too tight, from repressing emotions that want to spill over and seep across the path in front of me. I shake my head and, fingers laced hard enough my knuckles hurt, I croak out, "I can't do this."

There's silence from these two men who know me better than anyone.

My shoulders bunch, waiting for a response, not sure what I'm hoping they'll say.

Leo speaks first. "Yeah you can."

"I can't. It's awful."

"You just don't like feeling helpless, we get it." Leo's tone is so calm, so steady, and it makes me want to punch him.

I think back to the turmoil of his relationship with Jillian, how cool I'd been. How foolish and naïve. "She makes me weak."

Michael laughs. "You're looking at it all wrong."

"You don't understand." My voice rises and even I can hear the strained panic, matching the stutter of my beating heart. I remember the last time my heart beat like this. I'd been coked up for thirty-six hours, staring out the window knowing my life had to change.

"We do," Leo says.

"She'll make you stronger if you let her." Michael states this like it's easy, and for him it is. That's the kind of man he is, strong and unwavering. He'd stood down all Layla's demons and hadn't even blinked.

I shake my head again. I can't articulate my turmoil. How I felt when I looked down at her, crumpled at my feet, face bruised because I'd been stupid enough to let her out of my sight. I'd failed her. My first true test, and I'd failed.

"Don't do it, Brandon." Leo punches me hard in the biceps. "I can see where you're going, and trust me, you'll regret it."

"He's right," Michael says softly. "You don't have to take this route. You can choose to go another way."

I don't know how to be like them. I was raised with privilege. Everything in my entire life has been handed to me on a silver platter. I've never had to work for anything. Even this small empire I've been quietly building for all these years, it's only afforded to me because of my station in life. Because of my trust fund, my name, my connections.

It has nothing to do with me.

I'm not like Michael and Leo, who'd both been raised by self-made men and women. They'd grown up being taught the value of work, of perseverance, and morality.

I run my hands through my hair. "When are we going to

get out of here?"

Leo and Michael silently look at each other, an entire conversation passing between them without words. Finally, Michael nods and gets up. "I'll go check."

When he's gone, Leo sighs. "I warned you, remember. I told you that you were going to panic."

"I remember."

"You're in the thick of it now. But you have a choice, don't be stupid, don't risk her because you don't always get another chance."

I scrub my hand over my jaw. "She deserves better than me."

Leo laughs. "So what?"

I frown. "Isn't that what love is, letting someone go to find someone better for them? Being selfless?"

"Fuck no."

I glance at him and he grins at me. "Don't be an idiot, we're all selfish pricks when it comes to love. Because the truth is, we never really know. There are no guarantees. Jillian could have married some rich investment banker that lavished her with all the things she deserves. She could live in a penthouse overlooking the lake, and her husband could give her the connections to make her art career thrive."

His jaw ticks a bit, probably at the idea of Jillian with another man, but then he gets back on track. "If I were selfless, I would have let her go that night she confronted me at Michael's birthday, but I wasn't. Now she's married to me, a cop. With the way things are going, she'll out earn me within the next year or two. I wanted her and I took her because I didn't want anyone else to have her. Big fucking deal. I work my ass off to keep her happy and entertained. I work to make sure she never regrets the things she's given up for me. That's all I can do, because in the end, I'm selfish and I'm not giving her up."

What he's saying makes an odd sort of sense, but it doesn't appease me. Doesn't quell the panic rushing through my veins at warp speed the way I know he's hoping.

He crosses his arms and continues. "You think Michael isn't selfish too? Because he sure as fuck is. You think he doesn't know that every time he leaves the house Layla worries at least once if he's going to come back home. You don't think he knows what he does for a living is Layla's worst nightmare?"

I swallow, I hadn't thought of it that way.

"If he were selfless, he'd quit for her, right? But he can't and it kills him a little bit that he can't do it for her. Every day they face each other knowing he might put her into a situation where she's forced to live that nightmare all over again. She loves him anyway because safe doesn't necessarily mean happiness. Not for women like Jillian and Layla, not for women like Veronica."

I nod. I'm done with the lecture. I have nothing to say but my mind tumbles with chaotic, destructive thoughts I can't control.

Leo falls silent, seeming to understand his words fall on deaf ears, but he doesn't make any move to leave.

Instead we sit like that, for how long I have no idea, but finally the door buzzes and Michael walks in with a uniformed officer.

He glances at Leo before looking at me. "You're good to go."

I stand up, grab my tux jacket, and nod. Even though I'm walking to freedom the click of the doors make me feel like I'm being led to a death sentence.

With Leo, Michael and the uniform in front of me, I walk down a hall and through a door. As we walk into the station, bustling with activity, I see them all there.

Jillian, Layla, Ruby and Chad. I blink. My parents are there, my dad looking gruff and disgruntled, my mom looking worried.

The crowd parts and there stands Veronica. Flanked by her parents, that barely register at the sight of her.

She's still long and lean in her black dress. Still beautiful and heartbreaking.

259

Our eyes lock.

Her hair is a mess, and when I take in her split lip and bruised jaw I want to kill Winston Bishop all over again. I walk over to her, and gently slip my hand around her neck. I rub my thumb over her lip, careful not to hurt her. "Are you okay?"

She clutches at my forearm. "I'm just bruised, I'll be fine, I promise."

I nod, not quite able to believe it. "The doctors?"

"They wouldn't have let me leave the hospital if I wasn't okay."

I don't feel relief. I feel nothing but raging, impotent panic. I slide my hand down her arm and circle her wrist. "Come with me."

"Where are we going?"

I look into her honeyed gaze and shake my head. "I have no idea."

She blinks up at me. "Are you okay?"

"No, I'm not."

She licks her lower lip, and when she winces, the anger beats at my chest, calmed only when she nods. "I'll follow you anywhere, Brandon."

I take her hand, and turn, walking out of the station without a word to my friends or family. I don't know where I'm going, or what I'm doing, or exactly what's happening to me.

All I know is I have to get out of here, and she has to go with me.

I'll figure it out as I go.

Veronica

We're flying at thirty-five thousand feet, in a private plane, on our way to the Swiss Alps. Why? I have no idea. I'd asked Brandon, but he'd just shrugged and continued to watch me with a worried, watchful gaze.

I rubbed my teeth over my sore, swollen bottom lip, and wince. His eyes darken and anger storms through his expression. He stands, holds out his hand. "Come with me. I need to take care of you."

My brow furrows, but I take his outstretched palm, and let him lead me to the bedroom in the back of the plane. When we get there, he puts his fingers on my shoulders and presses until I'm sitting on the edge. Then he kneels down, and begins to remove my strappy sandals, his touch soft, as though he might break me.

I stare down at his bent golden head, and in that moment he looks like an angel. I touch his temple, stroking over his hair. "I'm okay, Brandon."

He nods and continues his work. Removing the first shoe before following with the second. When he's done, he rises and works the straps of my dress down my arms, pulling me up so that it falls to my feet and I'm left standing there naked.

I think back to getting ready for this evening, my excitement. My anticipation. The shiver of desire racing down my spine as I slipped on my dress and thought about him taking it off later.

It feels like a million years ago. Another lifetime, belonging to another woman.

Never would I have thought I'd end up like this. Bruised and confused.

All I want is for us to be okay, but he's so silent. Almost still. His expression guarded and remote, with only the brief hints of the storm lurking inside him.

He walks to the bed and pulls down the covers, motioning for me to get inside. I do what he wants because as much as I want to press him, instinct tells me I shouldn't.

He tucks me in, then goes into the bathroom, returning with a washcloth. He sits down and presses it to my lip.

"You're bleeding again." His voice cracks.

I try and smile. "I'll be good as new before you know it."

He shakes his head. "It doesn't make me feel better."

I touch my fingertip to his palm. "It's over."

"I shouldn't have let him get to you, I should have been there."

I grip his wrist. "You're not responsible."

He finishes washing off my lip and throws the cloth on the small table next to the bed. He shifts, putting his elbows on his knees and bending his head. "Over the years, I've watched men care for their women. I've watched them hold them tight, crooning in their ear and kissing their temple as they push sweaty hair from their cheeks. I've listened to them talk about their responsibility, protecting what's theirs, love."

He pauses and I don't speak, waiting for him to continue. He swallows hard as he clasps his hands tightly between his splayed knees. "I've always done my best to mimic that behavior, knowing that's what was right, what I was supposed to, but I never felt it. I went through the motions, detached and emotionally unavailable."

He glances at me, his blue eyes stark and afraid. "I liked it that way. I don't like feeling vulnerable. I don't like feeling out of control. And I sure as fuck don't like feeling powerless."

It's his armor. The wall he's built around himself as protection. To change and become the man he wanted to be. It's a shield, to stay removed from the world. And it's crumbling because of me.

I shift on the bed to rest on the headboard and whisper the words I've been wanting to say. "I love you."

He jerks his head up, and his hands clench. "I love you too, Veronica." He runs his fingers through his hair, aggressive. "I hate this."

Not what a woman wants to hear the first time the man she's devoted to says he loves her, but I nod. "I know."

"I feel like I failed you."

"You didn't."

He puts his hand on his chest. "But it sits there, burning inside me."

I tilt my head. "We can do this, I know we can."

His gaze sweeps over my body. "You should rest."

He goes to move, but I take his hand and hold it steadfast. "Stay with me."

He nods, kicks off his shoes and climbs onto the bed next to me. His strong arms curl around my waist. He kisses my temple. "Sleep."

I close my eyes and let myself drift off. Somehow I'll make him believe.

Brandon

I don't know why I wanted to come here, but it was a compulsion and I didn't resist. Maybe it's because it's where I came last time I felt my life spiraling out of control and I didn't know where else to go.

As we've made the trek up the Swiss Alps to the resort nestled in the side of the mountains, we've been mostly silent. We'd stopped, gotten clothes and supplies, and the whole time Veronica watches me with patient, wary eyes, but not questioning my actions.

It's part of what I love about her. That she doesn't fill the space.

When we finally make it to our location and settle into our room, I turn to her. "Can we go for a walk?"

"Yes." That one simple word sends a shiver of lust down my spine, tightening in my belly. I haven't touched her because I am afraid I might hurt her, but I want her like I want my next breath. I want to climb inside her, forceful in my possession and need to claim her, but I refrain. I don't have gentleness in me right now.

I take her hand and we walk outside, up the path to the scenic vista point overlooking a lake that looks like glass, with the mountains in the distance. I study the scene before me, in all its majestic glory, waiting for peace to wash over me.

It doesn't come.

"It's beautiful," Veronica says, shading her eyes from the sun. "I've never been here."

I nod, willing that calmness and surety to seep into my bones, but it continues to elude me. I clear my throat. "I came here that summer I took off for parts unknown to find myself. I did some of my best thinking in these mountains."

Out the corner of her eye, she glances at me. "Is that why we're here?"

I look down at this woman who's somehow become integral to my life. "I suppose that's as good a reason as any."

She takes my hand. "It can make you strong if you let it."

I grip her fingers. God, this needy feeling sitting in my chest is relentless. I can't stand it. "What can?"

She smiles, but it's marred by the split on her lip and the dark yellowish bruises that have formed along her jaw. "Loving me."

I frown. "How do you know?"

I shrug a shoulder. "Because loving you has made me strong."

The statement gives me pause and I contemplate her. "How has it done that?"

She looks out over the vista, exhaling deeply. "Can't you see how you've changed my whole life?"

I release her hand and wrap my arm around her waist, pulling her close. "You did that all on your own, Veronica. Everything you've done, everything you've accomplished, you've done despite me, not because of me."

She laughs, tilting her chin and pressing a kiss to my jaw. "Don't be dumb. You don't know anything about it, Brandon."

I cock a brow. "Name one thing that doesn't involve orgasms."

She rolls her eyes at me. "Do you honestly think that's all you give me? Because that's ridiculous."

It strikes me then that orgasms are all I've ever given a woman. All I've ever wanted to give. And now that I'm in love I can't figure out what comes next.

Veronica pulls out of my embrace and faces me, her expression hard and serious.

I can't help getting distracted by her appearance. People will probably think I abuse her. The thought sends a shudder through me. I don't know if I'll ever be able to lay a stern hand on her again. And what really jars me, what turns my stomach, is that I experience a sense of deep loss at the prospect.

What kind of person am I? To feel upset that I can't hurt her?

I've always looked at my dominance as an extension of my control. Not only over the girl, but over myself. Yes, I made her suffer, but it wasn't out of anger, or rage, or any emotion at all.

The complete opposite of how Veronica makes me feel.

I can't risk being out of control with her because I cannot

bear to hurt her any more than she has been. But I can't begin to translate my chaotic emotions into all that measured action. It's an endless loop that has no solution.

I hate myself for needing it right now. Wanting it. Especially when she needs care, not ruthlessness.

She sighs, and cups my jaw, pulling my chin to force me to look at her. "You and I, don't you see? Don't you understand? We're different sides of the same coin. It's what we recognized in each other that night out on the balcony. We fit. We complement each other. We make each other stronger. You push me and I push you, and we end up in a better place because of it."

"I don't see how I've helped you." I'm being stubborn, but I can't seem to help myself. This empty pit in the bottom of my stomach won't let me go.

She rises to her tiptoes and brushes her mouth against mine. I want nothing more than to sweep in and lay claim to her. Because, fuck, it's like a live tangible thing inside me, but I restrain my baser emotions. She brushes my cheek with her fingertips. "You made my world Technicolor."

The words don't bring me any sort of peace. Instead, they irritate me, because I'm putting her in a position where she has to soothe me. *She's* taking care of me. It should be the other way around. It needs to stop.

I need to take care of her. She's the one that's hurt. She's the one that suffered. I'm responsible and I didn't protect her. Maybe, if I take care of her now, properly, this turmoil will ease.

I take her hand and press a kiss to her palm before lifting my head. I tug her back toward the resort. "Come on, you need to rest."

"I'm fine, Brandon," she says in a tone that would normally incite some sort of correction from me.

But I ignore it. Tamp down the desire to reel her in. I smile back at her, and keep walking up the hill. "I need to get ice on your face. I'll take care of you, Veronica. Trust me."

She sighs, long and heavy. "I do."

Veronica

Not going to lie, I've been appeasing Brandon, and after a week of him taking care of me I'm beginning to go a bit crazy. Currently, we're sitting in the resort restaurant, eating lunch, and I'm acting like a petulant child. I cross my arms over my chest and puff out my now mostly healed lip. "I want to be on the conference call."

"You should rest," he says in a calm, gentle tone. "I'll take care of it."

"I don't want to rest. I'm tired of resting. I'm fine."

"You still have bruises."

Argh! This is all wrong. I cannot stand him treating me like I am a fragile flower that might break at any second. At first, I indulged his need to protect me, assuming it would fade right along with the marks on my skin, but I see now that was a huge mistake. I should have stopped it the first day.

I need him to twist me in that way he has. I need him to call me out on my defiance. I need him to take me in hand. But no matter how much I goad him, he doesn't respond. I roll my eyes. "Barely! It doesn't even hurt anymore."

"It's better to be safe than sorry. And I don't see how the rest can hurt you. It's a vacation you should be relaxing, not taking work calls."

"You're taking work calls," I point out, in hopes he'll see reason.

"That's different."

"Why?" I throw up my hands in exasperation.

"I'm the boss."

I raise a brow and snap. "Are you sure about that?"

It's a bratty thing to say and his jaw tightens in response. For a split second hope surges that he's going to stop being careful and call me out, but it's dashed when his expression turns mild.

With his fork, he gestures to my plate. "Finish eating and we'll take a short walk before we get you into bed."

Not too long ago, Brandon saying he was going to get me into bed would have induced heart palpations as I imagined all the wicked, evil things he might do to me. That's no longer the case because now getting me into bed means *sleep*. Rest.

I know this because Brandon will not touch me, at least not in the way I crave.

No matter what I do.

Or how I try and seduce him.

His only physical response is soft kisses, and tucking me against him to hold me close. I'm going mad. Last night I thought I got him. Lying in bed, I'd pressed my ass against his cock. He'd been hard. I'd rubbed, and tension flared. He'd gripped my hip and thrust against me only to instantly still. Then the bastard turned to his back, nestled me against his chest, and told me to go to sleep.

So. Much. Sleeping.

It's so, so…frustrating.

I want to scream.

I can't stand it one more second. I won't. I slam my hand on the table, making people jump and glance in our direction. "I don't want to sleep."

All pleasant like, he smiles, but it doesn't reach his dimples or his eyes. And there's certainly no menace. It's…paternal. "The fresh air will tire you out."

I stare at him, and shake my head. "Brandon, you have to stop this."

"Stop what?"

"Stop mothering me. Stop making me nap. Stop pestering me." I drag my hand through my hair. "You're driving me crazy."

"I'm taking care of you."

"You're acting like a robot, I can't stand it."

His forehead creases, and something I can't decipher flashes over his features for a split second before he says, "Let's walk and you'll feel better after."

"What's wrong with me will not be cured with a walk." I hiss the words.

His brow furrows. "Do you need to see the doctor?"

I let out a screech. "No! I need..." I'm a loss for the words. "You!"

"I haven't left your side."

"No! Not like this." I lean across the table, gesturing wildly. "Don't you want to take control of me? Don't you want to fuck me? Torture me? Twist the knife?"

His jaw hardens. "We'll talk when you're better."

"I am better. I'm *fine*."

He nods. "Maybe we can head farther up the path today then."

I blink at him, and can't stand it one more second. I need to get away. Tossing my napkin to the table, I stand up. "I'm going out."

He moves to follow.

I hold up my palm. "Alone, Brandon."

"I don't think that's a good idea."

I put my hands on my hips. "I don't give a shit what you think. I'm leaving." I turn on my heel and say over my shoulder, "Don't follow me."

Despite the beauty surrounding me, I need to escape.

I stomp my way to the concierge. "How can I arrange transport into the village? Immediately?"

The elderly gentlemen, decked out in his starched suit, smiles graciously. "We have a car that can take you."

Excellent. "Can they leave now?"

"I'll have the driver pull around and meet you out front, Mrs. Townsend."

I blink at the name. My heart skips a beat at the man's assumption. The sound of Brandon's name being mine causes an ache deep in the pit of my stomach. Some of my righteous anger fades away and is replaced by sadness. I nod. "Thank you."

Ten minutes later, after I'd grabbed my purse and phone, I'm in the car taking me to the village. My shoulders slump and defeat washes over me. He didn't follow. My Brandon would have followed. My Brandon would have chased me down, tossed me over his shoulder, and taught me a proper lesson.

This Brandon lets me go.

And I don't know if I can return.

24.

Brandon

Okay, maybe I took the protective thing a little too far. But I was just trying to take care of her. To show her how much she means to me. Isn't that how men prove they love a woman? By cherishing her?

After Veronica stormed off in a huff, I'd searched the hotel for her, only to be told by the concierge that Mrs. Townsend had taken the hotel car into the village and hadn't returned yet.

At first I'd been confused as to why he was talking about my mother, only for it to dawn on me he referred to Veronica. My heart skipped a beat at the thought of her being my wife. I'd never once thought about marriage. I'd always assumed I'd never get married.

Since the man said it, I haven't been able to get it out of my mind.

I'll worry about that later. Right now, I contemplate if I should go after Veronica.

There was a van taking tourists into the village in an hour, but what if I miss her coming back up the mountain as she's already been gone a couple of hours. I weigh my options, and in the end I decided to give her space.

Because, maybe, we both need it.

What I'm doing isn't working, she's clearly unhappy. I'm not happy either, but I'm not sure what to do about it.

I know what she wants, what I want, but I can't seem to take the steps to make it happen. I don't know why. When the urge rears up in me, I coil tight to strike, but then I hit a wall.

It's as frustrating to me as it is to her.

With a sigh, I walk into the bar and over to the counter. The bartender, a pretty Asian girl with long sleek hair and dark, mysterious eyes, smiles at me. "What can I get you, sir?"

"I'll take your best bottle of whiskey."

She nods, and grabs a glass. "Neat or on the rocks?"

I shake my head. "No. I want the whole bottle. Charge it to my room."

She furrows her brow. "I'll have to ask my manager."

"Fine."

I wait the few minutes necessary for her to discuss this with the person in charge, and when she comes back, she hands me an unopened bottle. I don't even look at the label, just sign the tab and take it.

Back in my empty room, shades drawn, I sit on the winged-back chair, overlooking an unlit fireplace, and twist off the cap. I don't bother with a glass. I drink straight from the bottle. An hour passes with no sign from Veronica and I start to worry in my alcohol-dulled state. I'm not drunk yet, but I'm well on my way.

I need at least to check in on her.

I call her, but it goes straight to voicemail.

I text her, and I'm not surprised there's no response.

She's angry and suffocated. I can't even blame her.

To think, in my circles I'm known for having a gift with women. I scoff into my drink before taking another sip. What a joke.

After stewing for an indeterminate amount of time, I glance

at the clock and with a sigh, call the only person I can think of that might help.

Michael picks up the phone. "It's after midnight, so I'm assuming this is important."

"Nice hello." My voice is thick and bitter sounding.

Michael sighs. "Hang on, let me go to the other room."

There's shifting and background noise, and a murmured—go back to sleep—to Layla, before he comes back on the line. "What's up?"

I clench my teeth. "I'm losing Veronica."

There's a beat of silence before he says, "Explain."

And I do, I tell him about the trip, how I thought it would somehow bring me the same clarity it had the first time around, but that I'm more confused than ever. I explain that, somewhere along the way, I've lost my sense of dominance over her, to the point I question if it was ever there to begin with.

"She wants it, she walked off in a storm because I won't give it to her, but…" Throat tight, I manage to croak out, "I don't know. Whenever I think of trying, all I see is her crumpled up on the floor, bruised and clutching her stomach. So, instead, I end up insisting she rest. Which is driving her crazy."

I finally take a breath and still, unsure what he's going to say or if he'll say anything at all. I brace myself for something scathing, although I don't know why, because this is Michael.

Finally he speaks. "You're wondering if I can relate, because of Layla."

It's not a question, but I answer it as if it is. "Yes."

"You do realize it's not the same, don't you?"

"It feels the same."

"I can understand that, but trust me, it's not." Michael's tone is soft with none of the censure I'd been prepared for. "Veronica was hurt, and scared, but she's not traumatized."

"How do you know?"

"Does she flinch when you touch her?"

"No." I shake my head.

"Does she cry? Or stare off into space with blank, empty eyes?"

"No."

"Does she have panic attacks?"

"No." I'm beginning to feel silly.

"Does she avoid talking about it?"

"No." She doesn't, she's brought it up, and I'd told her we didn't have to talk about it.

"Does she exhibit any signs that raise the hair on the back of your neck?"

"Not really." Unless I count the burning in my gut to claim her like it's the last thing I'll ever do on this earth.

"So, basically, she's pissed because you're treating her like a fragile victim."

I frown. Have I been? Yes, yes I have. I clear my throat. "I guess that's right."

"Well stop. It's not good for her, or you."

"But—"

"Let me finish." He cuts me off. "Even at the beginning, when Layla flinched at an unexpected touch. Or had a panic attack out of the blue, I never treated her like a victim. I was careful. I made fucking sure I knew her triggers before I slept with her, but I didn't coddle her. I pushed her. Called her on her shit. Didn't give her choices. And didn't let her get away with even the slightest challenge. Because, at the end of the day, I never forgot what she is or what I am. What she needed from me was not to treat her like every other person in her life. What she needed was someone to push against that would not budge. Does that make sense?"

It did. Or at least it was starting to untangle the knots in my head. "It's just—" I blow out a deep breath and say the words. "I don't know how to love her and not feel out of control."

"Who says you need to feel in control?"

I frown. "I've watched you with Layla for a long time now. You never seem out of control with her."

"I control my dominance, and her submission, not how I love her."

I try and let that sink in, as it's something all my friends have said to me over the course of my relationship with Veronica, but it's a struggle. Like they all understand a nuance lost on me. "I'm trying."

"Stop trying. Stop waiting for it to make sense, for you to feel like you did with every other woman you've been with, because it's never going to happen. You love Veronica. It's not going to be the same. And right now, denying yourself, and her, part of what makes you unique together is going to ruin you."

I pinch the bridge of my nose with my thumb and forefinger. "I'm doing the best I can."

"I understand you're confused, but at bare minimum stop treating her like a porcelain doll, that's never going to work." He chuckles. "She's spirited, and with a spirited girl, being submissive makes her feel powerful. So in essence, right now, you're depriving her of that power."

The notion niggles at me, but it won't form into a tangible thought, but I'm done talking. Right now, I need air. "Thanks."

"You're welcome. Call if you need anything."

I laugh, shaking my head. "What the fuck is happening to us?"

He chuckles. "I don't know, I guess we're adults or something."

"It sucks."

"Yeah, it does, but it has its advantages too."

"That's the rumor." But I'm not entirely sure it's true.

We hang up and I put the bottle down, stumbling around the room, searching for my shoes before going downstairs. I step out of the resort and turn right, walking up the mountain path, stopping at the first vista point to stare over the water, awash in the grayness of dusk. I think back to the first time I was here, drying myself out, trying to figure out how to become a human being.

Every day I trek up this path, stare at the nature, and wait for that same clarity I experienced back then, but it doesn't happen.

And it doesn't happen now.

A sliver of fear weaves a path down my spine. Maybe I'll never figure it out and I'll lose her because of it. Because I don't know how to let go, or give in, or whatever the hell they all keep talking about. I'm missing something elemental.

It will be my demise as much as it was my savior way back when.

I stare, and I stare. First at the mountains, then at the water, and when nothing happens, I turn my attention to the faint lights of the village below.

The village Veronica disappeared into to escape me. She's down there, wandering the streets. She has to come back, right?

My jaw clenches and I turn, walking farther up the path to another scenic spot.

I wait. But that mysterious thing doesn't come; no matter how much I try and force it.

It's hopeless. It's not going to happen.

With a sigh I turn back toward the resort, returning to my room once again to pick up the bottle. Since nature isn't working, might as well go for blinding drunk. At least my brain will shut off. I glance at my phone, but there's still nothing from Veronica.

I'm not going to press because I can't give her what she needs right now.

Everything is too convoluted and messy.

I can barely think, let alone plot.

Maybe it's for the best. I'm clearly not cut out for this relationship stuff. Yes, I love her, but I don't know how to translate that into anything meaningful and lasting.

I imagine watching her walk away. Letting her go to find someone who can give her what she deserves. Maybe that's what love is, letting them find someone better.

Maybe that's my only option.

There's a noise at the door and my head jerks up just in time to watch it fly open.

Silhouetted by the hallway Veronica stands in the doorway,

hands on her hips. I can't see her face, but her stance is formidable, and I prepare myself for the worst. She stalks into the room and slams the door behind her.

"We need to talk." The words are hurled into the darkness. She walks over to the drapes and yanks them open, casting a pale muted light over the room.

"All right." My voice is calm, too calm, refined and distant, revealing none of my inner chaos.

She stalks over to me, leans down and cracks me across the face.

It...stuns me. I blink at her as the sound rolls over the room.

She slaps me again.

My temper flares, bright and hot, but I manage to say calmly, "Veronica."

She frowns. "No! Stop it!" She strikes again.

I want to rise to the bait. She's pushing me and I want to push back. The desire to haul her up, throw her to the floor, and fuck this aggression right out of her burns in my stomach. But I resist. I can't come at her in anger. It's irresponsible. I raise a brow. "Are you done?"

She screams, and moves to hit me again, but this time I grab her wrist, deflecting the blow. Her eyes flash and her breath hitches.

She's looking for a fight. She's wild with it.

Despite my hold on her wrist she climbs onto my lap, straddling me.

I put my hand on her hip to steady her but she leans forward and nips my lower lip. I flinch, and my grip on her wrist tightens. "What has gotten into you?"

"Not you." Her free hand draws back to strike, but I spot it a mile away.

I lash out, clasping it, jerking both to rest behind her back. Restraining her sends a jolt of hunger through me. It's been so long, and I want her so bad. I grip her tighter and spit out, "Behave yourself."

"Make me." She squeezes me with her thighs, thrusting her

cunt against me.

I'm hard.

She's violent and out of control.

And it's making me so hard I ache.

"You want me." She rocks again. She scrapes her teeth against my jaw. "Take me."

"We need—"

"We need you to take me." She begins fighting the confines of her bound wrists.

Our breathing kicks up.

Our gazes clash.

My control threatens its already frayed tethers.

She bites my lower lip, hard enough to draw blood.

I yelp, and my control bursts into a million shards, shattering across my vision. I growl. Clasp her wrists in one hand and grab her by the throat. "You're going to pay for that."

In answer, she moans and begins to fight me. Squirming on my lap, trying to break free, twisting and arching.

I rear up, standing as I take her with me.

Her legs go around my waist.

Desire, so long controlled, runs hot and thick in my blood, blocking out all rational thought. I take three steps and toss her onto the bed.

She starts to speak.

I clasp my hand over her mouth to silence her as I rip off my belt in one smooth movement. With a deftness born of years of practice, I put the leather into her mouth before flipping her over and tying it around the back of her head, gagging her.

The buckle thuds against her spine and satisfaction shivers over my skin.

Determined to fight me, she struggles, writhing on the bed before me.

Finally, at long last, dominance seeps across my skin, calming me. I cover her body with my own to whisper menacingly into her ear, "I think it's best you shut up now,

Veronica."

Of course she doesn't, making all sorts of noises as she bucks under me.

I stand, and yank her jeans and panties down her thighs. I don't warm up, I don't even think, all I can do is act. I smack her ass, so hard she screams around the belt in her mouth as my handprint blooms bright red on her pale skin.

Yes. This is what I need.

The power flows through me, filling me up.

I spank her again.

And again.

I show no mercy.

When she attempts to fight I shift my position and put my knee on the small of her back to halt her movements. I continue my work until my breathing is coming in shallow pants and her skin is bright red.

I shove my hands between her legs.

She's soaking wet.

Laughing, I stroke over her clit.

She rocks into my hand.

Almost immediately she begins to quicken, and when I pull away she rests her head on the bed and gives me a muffled groan.

I shift my attention to her face. Her hair is a mess, damp at the temples. Her cheeks are pink and tear streaked, her eyes closed, her lips parted.

But it's her expression that stills me.

Blissful. That's the word that comes to mind. I lean down and say, "You're going to do whatever I want."

Eyes still closed, she nods.

"And right now, I want to fuck you. Use you for my own pleasure."

She nods again.

"I don't care if you get off." I brush my lips over her cheek. "I want you to suffer."

Her lashes flutter open and her honeyed gaze meets mine. What I see there stuns me. Her eyes practically glow with life.

In their depths I see all the answers I've been searching for.

Hope.

Longing.

Understanding.

Desire.

Peace.

And most of all love.

All the chaos and panic and fear that's been beating away at me since that night at the banquet settles. Is washed away by her.

I get it. What they'd all been trying to tell me. It makes sense. My love for her might rage and consume me, but it doesn't make me less, doesn't steal anything away from me. Loving her is my power. She'll make me a better, stronger man, not a weaker one.

She can break me, but she won't because she has no reason to hurt me.

Everything that's been rioting inside me settles. I touch her hair. Later there will be time for ruthlessness, but right now, I need her to understand. "I love you, Veronica."

She nods and I see her love shining in her eyes even though she can't speak the words.

I see everything I've been doing clearly and I tell her the truth. I lay myself bare. Let myself be vulnerable. Show her my weakness. "I'm sorry. I've been using you being hurt as an excuse to distance myself. To push you away. Somehow, I thought if I surrendered to you, to how I feel about you, that I'd lose everything I'd built for myself. But I see now that's ridiculous. I understand."

Tears slip down her cheeks and I brush them away. "You scare the shit out of me."

A single nod.

"I thought you'd make me weak. But I see now, you'll make me a better man." I untie the belt and let it slip from her mouth. I brush hair out of her face. "I love you more than I've ever loved anyone or anything in my entire life."

She licks her lower lip. "I love you too, Brandon."

I flip her over and kiss her.

I kiss her long, slow and deep, until passion and desire has us hot and straining. My tongue tangles with hers, melding together, as we turn frantic.

In a hurried rush we shed our clothes and the second we're naked, I settle between her splayed thighs and sink into her. This, right here in this moment, is about emotional bonds, not physical ones. It's about connection.

I grit my teeth as she envelops me, slick and tight.

She gasps, clasps me around the waist and arches into me.

I grip her throat, tightening my fingers around the slender cords as she shudders under me.

I thrust into her.

Her gaze meets mine.

Intimate and raw, we come together. Joined. Melded together by both our hearts and bodies.

Slowness gives way to intensity as urgency and passion consume us.

I move harder and faster.

She digs her nails into my forearm.

When I feel her tighten around my cock, I tighten my hold around her neck, her most vulnerable spot.

She comes, the contractions rippling down the length of me, driving me insane.

I release her throat and she gasps for air, moaning as her body shakes.

I lose myself in her, stroking in and out until the orgasm rips up my spine and bursts across my eyes, so hard my vision blurs and I go blessedly mindless.

After, I collapse on top of her, panting for air. When my heartbeat finally begins to slow I rise to stare down at her.

Her lashes flutter open and she beams up at me. "Hi."

I chuckle. "Hi."

She bites her lower lip. "I'm glad you're back."

"Me too." I kiss her, and brush a lock of hair from her face. "I want to marry you."

Surprise flashes across her features and she blinks at me.

"You do?"

"Yes, I do. As soon as possible."

"What if I want a big fancy wedding?" Her eyes flirt up at me.

"Then that's what you'll get."

"Are you asking?"

I shake my head. "No, not yet."

"Okay." She hugs me tight. "I'm probably a sure thing."

I kiss her neck. "The surest thing I'll ever do in this life."

She laughs and it's happy and light and full of love. "Aren't you glad I coerced you into hiring me?"

"You have no idea." I gaze down at this woman that came into my life and somehow made me a man. "We have things to discuss."

"Oh yeah?"

I nod. "You came without permission, and now you're going to have to pay."

She pretends to consider this before nodding. "I'm prepared for a life sentence."

Good. Because that's exactly what I'm going to give her. "All right, but I'm warning you there will be no opportunity for parole."

EPILOGUE

Veronica

Michael and Layla's wedding day is picture perfect. Like the gods smiled upon them, the day so clear and mild for this time of year, the owners of the establishment opened up the outdoor space and we had the whole place to ourselves.

The happy couple looks as gorgeous and as otherworldly as the day I met them, which now seems like a lifetime ago. It's been a long hard road for them, Layla in particular, considering her past, but it has culminated into this perfect day. The night a couple weeks before the wedding, that marked the same length of time when her first engagement ended in murder, we'd all hunkered down in their new townhouse and played games until the wee hours of the morning to distract her. And she made it. Now she radiated happiness as she beams up at her new husband, who hasn't left her side.

I'm talking to Jillian and Ruby, both in champagne-colored bridesmaid dresses, while Brandon is off with the groomsmen taking pictures. I glance down at my left hand, adorned with my engagement ring, and I can't help the smile that spreads across my lips. I love it so much. Not as much as the man that's attached to it, but I can't deny its perfection.

In typical Brandon fashion, he'd surprised me by taking me to Paris for the weekend and proposing on the private balcony of the historic apartment he'd bought overlooking the city, as my engagement present.

It's ridiculous, I know. He can't help himself. And I can't complain about a man that loves me so much he wants me to give me a home in Paris because I said it was one of my favorite places on earth. Would you?

The apartment matches the grandeur of my ring. A three and a half carat, emerald-cut antique with a platinum band. A Townsend family heirloom that made Brandon's mother cry the first time she saw it on my finger. She'd said she believed Brandon would never get married and the family treasure would go to some distant cousin since Brandon is the last in his bloodline.

Yeah, yeah, talk about your first-world problems, but I can't deny my future mother-in-law her happiness.

The whole time Brandon had sat there, shaking his head and rolling his eyes, but I knew he was happy she was happy.

With me around, I'd been forcing him to spend more time with his parents. It turned out the Townsends all secretly wanted the same thing, unity and connection, but they were all too stubborn to admit it.

Since I didn't want to be a hypocrite, I've made peace with my own parents, who, as I predicted, welcomed Brandon with open arms. Almost as though he'd been their idea all along. I let them have their pride because Brandon and I know the truth, and that's all that matters.

With me pressing the issue, we're all starting to resemble— gasp—an actual family.

Everything is falling into place.

Winston was out of the picture after a reporter dug up stories of him abusing young women. And since I pressed assault charges against him, he's currently awaiting trial, and too busy working on his defense to worry about suing

Brandon.

The other night our families had dinner together and preparations for the wedding began. Brandon tried to contain our mothers, threatening to elope if they didn't rein it in, but they didn't listen. By the time the night ended they had a list of five hundred people to invite.

Later, as we lay in bed, sweaty and exhausted, I promised him I'd take care of it. I'm still formulating a plan to give everyone what they want. My current idea is an intimate wedding just for us, and a reception for our families. It doesn't seem like a bad compromise.

"Where is your mind off to?" Jillian asks, startling me from my thoughts.

I smile at her, shrugging. "I was contemplating how I was going to satisfy Brandon and our families on this wedding business."

Ruby laughs. "Good luck with that."

"It will work out." I grin. "By the way, I made joint appointments for us at Belle Vie Bridal Couture the Saturday after Layla gets back from her honeymoon."

Ruby wrinkles her nose. "At that expensive place?"

"Uh-huh." I tilt my head as I see Brandon, Leo and Chad coming in our direction. "I told them to pull dresses with an edge for you, and I promise you won't be sorry."

Chad slides up to Ruby and puts his arm around her. "Won't be sorry about what?"

I wave a hand. "I'm going to find Ruby her wedding dress, and it's going to be spectacular."

"Oh no," Ruby says, sighing but laughing at the same time.

As Leo settles in next to Jillian, Brandon wraps his hand around my waist, slowly curving down to my hip encased in silk. He'd insisted on picking my dress for the wedding, and I think I'd been fucked in every changing room in Chicago during our shopping excursion. He'd finally settled on a body-hugging, pale yellow silk slip of a dress that managed to be both wedding appropriate and sexy.

His fingers brush over my hipbone, calling my lack of

panties to attention. "And will you be finding a dress for yourself?"

"Of course." I smile up at him. "It will be nice to pick out my own clothes for once."

It's an exaggeration, but they all laugh, as I knew they would.

He leans in close and smiles against my skin before kissing the curve of my jaw right next to my ear. "How's my gorgeous girl?"

"I'm fabulous. How about you? Are you surviving?"

He squeezes me tight. "As long as you're around, I'm more than surviving."

"So does that mean you're happy you've officially hired me?"

He laughs, brushing his lips across mine. "Best decision I ever made."

"Good." I pull back and clap my hands. "I have a surprise for you."

"Oh really?" Brandon's eyes gleam with happiness and it makes him so devastatingly handsome my heart skips a beat. "Do tell."

"I think I found you and Chad a building. It's not for sale yet and I promised the agent a bonus if we made an offer, if she showed it to us before it went live. I made an appointment for us Tuesday after work." I turn to Chad. "Can you make it?"

"Yeah, that should work." He pulls his fiancée close. "Ruby will come too and we'll go to dinner after."

She taps him in the stomach. "Hey, don't I get a say?"

"Of course not." He kisses her temple.

Layla and Michael come over, hand in hand, smiling.

Leo clasps Michael on the back. "It's official now, we're forever entwined."

He laughs. "We were already the second you married my sister."

"Nope. Now Layla can't escape either." He winks at his new sister-in-law. "You're trapped, girl. And we all know how you hate that."

There's more laughter and when a waiter comes by we all grab fresh flutes of Champagne.

Michael holds out his glass and we all rise up in a circle to meet him.

When we're all joined he says, "To us."

My throat grows a little tight as I look at this group of people who have all come to mean so much to me. I glance sideways and my gaze meets Brandon's. I can't believe I wondered if love was possible for us. How silly. I don't think my heart could be any more full.

Glass still raised, eyes never leaving mine, he says, "To happily ever after."

Yes, I believe it will be.

Get a taste of book 1 in the series—CRAVE

Eleven P.M.

Two months. Five days. Twenty-one hours.

It's my new record, although I have no sense of accomplishment. No, I'm resigned as I walk down the dark, deserted alley. The heels of my knee-high, black patent boots click against the cracked concrete in echo of my defeat. The distant sounds of the bass thuds in my ears in time to the heavy beat of my heart.

My own personal staccato of failure.

I'm not sure why it's always a surprise. Maybe because, at first, my conviction is so strong. By now my pattern is long and established—I vow, I crave, I give in.

Rinse. Repeat.

But, like any good addict, I always swear this time is the last.

Of course, I try. My therapist has given me "management tools" to get me through the hard times, and like a good patient, I follow her instructions to a tee—I meditate, do yoga, and write all my crappy feelings in the journal she insists I keep.

Only, it's backfired and become part of the ritual. When the cycle starts, it's a matter of time before I end up here.

I'm sure when John brought me to this underground club the first time, he'd never envisioned I'd be back on my own, wandering through the crowds, looking for my next fix. The club reminds me of him, and I wish I could go somewhere else so I wouldn't be confronted with my betrayal, but I don't have a choice. There aren't ads for places like this. Or maybe there are, and I don't know where to look.

Swift and sudden, anger clogs my throat, and for a split second I hate him for changing me so irrevocably, and leaving me so permanently. Fast on the heels of anger, the guilt wells, so powerful it brings a sting of tears to my eyes. In the pockets of my black trench coat, my nails dig crescents into my palms.

I push away the emotions. Exhaling harshly, my breath fogs the air as I spot a hint of the red door that signals both my refuge and my hell. I hear the muffled hum of music that will crescendo once I'm inside to pump through me like a heartbeat.

My pace quickens along with my pulse.

As much as I hate giving in, I can't deny my relief. Once I step through that door, I don't have to pretend. I don't have to be normal.

The tension, riding me all day, distracting me in meetings, making me wander off in the middle of conversations, ebbs. A twisted excitement slicks my thighs as the bare skin under my skirt tingles.

I haven't bothered with panties. It makes things easier, quicker. Less about getting off and more about taking care of business.

I have on my usual club fare: short, black pleated skirt that leaves a stretch of thigh before my stockings start. A sheer, white silk blouse unbuttoned low enough to show the lace of my red demi-bra. My lips are slicked with crimson and my dark chestnut hair is a tumble of shiny waves down my back.

My outfit is carefully orchestrated. I leave as little to chance as possible.

No leather or latex. I'm not into bondage. Chains and rope do nothing but leave me cold. Once upon a time I loved to be restrained by fingers wrapped tight around my wrists, digging into my skin, but now I can't handle even a hint of being bound.

I reveal plenty of smooth ivory skin, my clue to guys into body modification or knife play to stay away. I like fear, but not that kind. I want my bruises and scars hidden away, not worn like a badge of honor for the world to see.

My wrists and neck are free of jewelry so the Masters don't confuse me with a slave girl. I tried that scene once, thinking all their hard play and intense scenes would focus my restless energy and make me forget, but there is no longer anything submissive about me.

2.

The scream leaves my throat, echoing on the walls of my bedroom, as I start awake. I jerk to a sitting position, sucking in great lungfuls of air. Drenched in sweat, I press my palm to my pounding heart, the beat so rapid it feels as though it might burst from my chest.

I had the dream again. Not *a dream*—dreams are good and full of hope—no, a nightmare. The same nightmare I've had over and over for the last eighteen months. An endless, gut-wrenching loop that fills my sleep and leaves my days unsettled.

I miss good dreams. Miss waking up rejuvenated. But most of all, I miss feeling safe. I'd taken those things for granted and paid the price.

Lesson learned. Too late to change my fate, but learned none the less.

On shaky legs I climb out of bed and pad down the hallway of my one bedroom, Lakeview condo and into the kitchen, my mind still filled with violent images and blood trickling like a lazy river down a concrete crack in the pavement.

I go through my morning ritual, pulling a filter and coffee from the cabinets. Carefully measuring scoops of ground espresso into the basket as tears fill my eyes.

I blink rapidly, hoping to clear the blur, but it doesn't work, and wet tracks slide down my cheeks. But even through my fear, my ever-present grief and guilt, I can feel it. It sits heavy in my bones, familiar and undeniable.

The want.

The need.

The craving that grows stronger each and every day I resist. That the dream does nothing to abate the desire sickens me.

I know what Dr. Sorenson would say: I need to disassociate. That the events of the past and my emotions aren't connected, but she can't possibly understand. Throat clogged, I brush away the tears, and angrily stab the button to start the automatic drip.

My phone rings a short, electronic burst of sound, signaling an incoming text. I'm so grateful for the distraction from my turbulent thoughts I snatch up the device, clutching it tight as though it might run away from me.

I open the text. It's from my boss, Frank Moretti. *CFO is leaving to "pursue other opportunities". Need to meet 1st thing this AM to discuss.*

I sigh in relief. As the communications manager at one of Chicago's boutique software companies, this ensures a crazy day I desperately need. Frank will have me running around like a mad woman. I take a deep breath and wipe away the last of the tears on my face.

Salvation. I won't have time to think. Won't have time to ponder what I'm going to do tonight. I type out my agreement and hit send, hoping against hope I'll be too exhausted this evening to do anything but fall into bed, dreamless.

Too tired to give in to my drug of choice.

ABOUT THE AUTHOR

Jennifer Dawson grew up in the suburbs of Chicago and graduated from DePaul University with a degree in psychology. She met her husband at the public library while they were studying. To this day she still maintains she was NOT checking him out. Now, over twenty years later they're married living in a suburb right outside of Chicago with two awesome kids and a crazy dog.

Despite going through a light FM, poem writing phase in high school, Jennifer never grew up wanting to be a writer (she had more practical aspirations of being an international super spy). Then one day, suffering from boredom and disgruntled with a book she'd been reading, she decided to put pen to paper. The rest, as they say, is history.

These days Jennifer can be found sitting behind her computer writing her next novel, chasing after her kids, keeping an ever watchful eye on her ever growing to-do list, and NOT checking out her husband.

Printed in Great Britain
by Amazon